I0612381

THE CORNISH CRIME SERIES

SAVAGE TRUTH

JULIE EVANS

ѵіncі
BOOKS

Vinci Books

vinci-books.com

Published by Vinci Books Ltd in 2026

1

Copyright © Julie Evans 2025

A CIP catalogue record for this book is available from the British Library.

Paperback ISBN: 9781036710705

By Julie Evans

The Cornish Crime Series

Prologue

1984

BYRDIE WILLIS REMEMBERED the date the angel spoke to her: 23rd October 1984. She remembered it because it was exactly one month after her sixth birthday and the night her mum disappeared.

She'd gone downstairs for a glass of water. The telly was playing to itself. She'd guessed Dad must be home from work, and Mum had taken him up a cup of tea while he got changed out of his overalls and took a shower but then remembered he was on nights all week at the dockyard.

She'd drank the water in the kitchen, then wandered into the sitting room as the man on the news was talking about children starving because of a war in Africa. She'd gone back to bed worried, knowing she'd have to add the children to her list of people she prayed for every night. The trouble was her list kept getting longer.

It had started short enough. Mum and Dad, Gran and Grandad and their canary Joey, but then she'd begun thinking about all the people she'd left out and what would happen if she didn't pray for them too. Uncle Ron and Auntie Jean. Her cousins Ruby and Michael. Her teacher, Miss Hunter, and Mrs Tippett, who owned the sweet shop and whose ankles spilt over her shoes because she stood all day behind the counter. Mr Jenkins, the lollipop man, who had to go out in all weathers to keep them safe. Her best friend Katie and her baby brother Alfie, who everyone called Spud because of the shape of his head, and last but not least, Dad's dog Ringo, who had mange and smelt of cheese, so someone should definitely pray for him. She'd added them all to the list, but now there were all these hungry children, too. She'd be there all night. That's when the angel turned up and said in a gentle, lullaby voice: 'Go to sleep, Byrdie Willis.'

She hadn't asked him to come. She hadn't had a clue how you got an angel's attention. She hadn't even seen him because, for one, her bedroom was dark except for the ladybird night light plug in the corner, and for two, he was invisible. There had been no glow of angel wings like in the school nativity the year before.

She'd known he hadn't wanted everyone to hear because he called her by her name and not her real name either, not 'Elizabeth', like the teachers at school, or 'our Beth' like her grandad, but 'Byrdie', her nickname. The one her friends used. She also knew it because Ringo didn't bark, and no one came in to check what was up. Mum would have heard the voice. Dad said she had ears like a bat.

It was because of this she realised he was an angel, and she shouldn't tell anyone about him because angels were bound to be fussy about things like that. If she went around telling everyone, there could be consequences. Mum talked a lot about consequences.

'If you don't do as I say right now, my girl, there will be consequences.'

So, she kept quiet about him, and although she kept expecting him, it was weeks before she thought of him again, then months, then years, until eventually, she almost forgot about him altogether.

Chapter One

2024

BETH STOPPED in the middle of the road, unable to place one foot in front of the other. Unable to go forward or back or sideways, umbrella half up, crying in the street like a fool, wishing the angel who spoke to her as a child would order her to walk to the pavement on the other side, the way she was meant to, the way she would have done had she not received the heart-squeezing news rooting her to the spot.

She had no idea why she remembered the angel now, but thought, if he spoke, she'd instantly recognise him, even above the din of the car horns and the man in a Mini Cooper shouting for her to; 'Get off the bloody zebra, you moron.'

Maybe the angel didn't know she'd grown up and had a daughter of her own now and that she wasn't Byrdie Willis anymore; she was Beth Matthews. Perhaps he needed to update his database.

She read the text again.

Elizabeth, this is your Auntie Freda. I'm texting to let you know your father is dead.

She wasn't sure how she made it home, but only there did she fully succumb to the weight of the wrecking-ball Freda had wielded with such precision.

What kind of person texts you with something like that?

She knew exactly what kind: her dad's sister, who had moved in the month after Mum left and had lived with Dad ever since in the family home in Cornwall. A stick-thin, nettle-tongued woman devoted to the Jehovah's Witnesses and *Countdown*, who had pinched her when she was little if she rustled her packet of crisps during the final conundrum.

'Angels don't need telescopes. You'd do well to remember that, my girl. They see everything no matter how hard you try to hide it. They will sniff you out. Your name won't be amongst the faithful, mark my words. Then how will you feel, eh?' *Pinch.* 'Eh?'

She had comforted herself back then with the knowledge her angel would never sniff anyone, and even if he did, she was pretty sure she smelt mostly of caramel wafers and not even an angel could take offence to that.

She rang Freda, who told her in a matter-of-fact way that the funeral would be delayed because the coroner would need to file a report as the death had been sudden.

'Waste of time. I could have told them exactly what was wrong with him if they'd bothered to ask me.'

'What *was* wrong with him?' Beth said, unaware her dad had been ill.

'Worry… that's what. Worry about you.'

'Me?'

'Yes, you. You've always been a worry to him. He spent half his life fretting about you.'

'But…'

6

'It's always a drama with you. Getting pregnant by some fly-by-night, then meeting someone else and running off to get married in Thailand. Then two months ago, dropping the bombshell you were getting divorced, and at your age too.'

She wanted to say she was only forty-six, hardly ancient, and that the divorce had not been her idea but didn't have the time or inclination to defend herself against the ridiculous wild child allegations. She'd hardly been a raving libertine. She hadn't got pregnant with her daughter Grace until she was over thirty, with a job and a flat of her own. She hadn't asked for a penny from her dad then or for her wedding five years later. In fact, she hadn't asked for handouts of any kind since she left home. She appreciated her marriage hadn't lasted, but the split with Liam was amicable, and they shared custody of Grace, who was a well-rounded thirteen-year-old.

'Oh, I know why he indulged you,' continued Freda, the bit well and truly between her teeth. 'It was because he felt guilty about that mother of yours. Well, the apple doesn't fall far from the tree I say, and just so we're clear, I'll be gone when you get here. My bags are packed. You've got your own key.'

She was ill-equipped in the state she was in to deal with Freda's vitriol. What's more, she was having difficulty interpreting the sub-text.

'I'm sorry, Freda, but are you saying you're not happy staying at the house on your own?'

'I've no intention of being your tenant if that's what you're asking. If your father's seen fit to leave you the house without a thought for me, so be it, but I won't be hanging around. To add insult to injury, he's being cremated. Apparently, he'd arranged a funeral plan and a plaque in the chapel of rest. I'll leave the details on the sideboard. You know very well I don't hold with cremation, so I won't be attending. The funeral director is lined up to pick up the body once the coroner's finished with it.'

Mind-numbing confusion fogged Beth's thought processes as she steadied herself against the kitchen units.

'When?' she managed to mumble.

'When what?' Freda said impatiently.

'When did Dad die?'

'Wednesday morning around ten o'clock. He had a heart attack at work. He died in the ambulance.'

'That was two days ago. Why didn't you call me before?'

'Well, pardon me for sorting things out before I bothered you.'

'Bothered me?'

Beth was angry now, tension ringing in her ears as she tried to hold herself together. 'I had a right to know,' she said choking back her tears, hurt and disbelief vying for space.

'What could you have done all those miles away? Better you didn't know until everything was sorted. I've left you a note. Everything you need to know is right there.'

The realisation she had gone about her business, done the shopping, had a Zoom meeting with her boss, oblivious to her dad's death, hit her. Fury bubbling like lava, she ended the call before she completely lost it and said something she might regret.

Chapter Two

Two months later

BETH'S FINGERS trembled as she levered the latch to the garden gate and made her way up the path. At this point, Dad would usually be standing on the threshold waiting with open arms, having heard her car pull up. The realisation she would never again feel his familiar embrace as he whispered, 'Welcome home, love,' caught in her throat as her nostrils stung with tears she thought she'd exhausted over the last few weeks.

It was her first time in the house since Dad's death. She and Grace had stayed at her Auntie Jean's the night of the funeral and headed back to London early the next morning. Setting her case down on the doorstep, she fumbled through her handbag for her key, hoping none of the neighbours spotted her and felt compelled to pass on their condolences. She'd managed to get through the funeral by the skin of her teeth. She'd strapped on her game face and, with Grace by her side, had just about coped with the sad little ceremony.

Had she been on her own, she thought she'd scream if one more person uttered, 'Sorry for your loss'.

A pile of post slid across the floor as she eased open the front door. She stooped to gather the charity envelopes and flyers for stairlifts. The rippling light from the stained-glass window at the foot of the stairs cast a kaleidoscope of memories with it. Thoughts of returning from holidays with Dad and Freda to find the house wrapped in musty silence and how they'd jumpstart it back to life with the arrival of the suitcases and the buzz of voices. Today was different. There was no one there but her. No Dad to rush upstairs bursting for the loo. No Freda filling the kettle for the longed-for cup of tea. She placed the post on the windowsill and closed the door.

Propping her case against the wall, she walked through to the kitchen. It too seemed sucked of life. All the surfaces had been cleared. The clock above the fridge echoed a melancholy tick above a picture hook where a donkey sanctuary calendar had hung every year for as long as she could remember. Freda's love of order and neatness had always been punctuated with an equal devotion for the cute. Kittens and puppies were cooed over with a sentimental fondness she had never thought deserved by Beth or other children, for that matter. Her dad had fought for the only photograph of her to remain on the wall despite Freda's protestations that it was dated and faded and should be replaced with something else, presumably with four paws and a wet nose.

Beth wondered why her most vivid memories of this house featured Freda rather than her mother before concluding it was hardly surprising. She had been so young when Mum left, and Freda had begun exorcising her sister-in-law from the house the minute she moved in. She had painted over the hand-sponged terracotta walls with puritanical fervour. Mum's patchwork throws and candles, referred to as 'dust gatherers' and 'fire hazards', had disappeared too. Her mum's clothes had soon followed. Tie-dyed skirts and halter-neck tops; even her favourite jeans had been bagged up and sent to the charity shop.

Freda had also endeavoured to eradicate Beth's memories as efficiently. If she ever asked when Mummy was coming home, she was bundled off with a flea in her ear. There were times when she heard Freda whispering with one of her JW friends about 'the floozy' who Beth gathered via tortuous means of deduction was her mum, but the conversation always came to an abrupt halt with a roll of the eyes and a knowing nod in her direction when Beth entered the room. It didn't help that no one at school mentioned her mum; not the teachers or the other children, when she went to their houses for parties. In fact, looking back, the only person who regularly talked about her was her Auntie Jean, Mum's sister. Whenever she was around at her house, Jean would try and get her on her own and ask questions about the night Mum left, but even that stopped once she realised she had nothing to add to the story she had told a hundred times before, first to her dad and afterwards to the police.

Mum had taken her to school and picked her up as usual. They'd had tea together, and she read her a story before she'd gone to sleep. She'd even told them she wandered downstairs to get a glass of water and about the TV being on. She never mentioned the angel, thinking she would be called a liar or, worse still, laughed at, but the rest she told as best she could remember for a six-year-old. With the passage of time, the memories became more and more jumbled, like bingo balls tumbling in an ever-spinning cage.

She'd thought Mum and Dad were upstairs together but the policewoman at the station who asked her the questions had said Dad had been at work all night. When he'd come home in the early hours of the morning after his shift, he'd found the sitting room lights on, her in bed fast asleep, and Mum gone.

'Gone?' Beth had asked. 'Gone where and when will she be back?'

The policewoman had looked at her blankly, rustled her papers, then with solemn eyes had admitted, 'We don't know, my love.'

No one had been able to answer the questions since.

Beth had barely spent a night in this house since she had left for university. The word 'home' had not conjured up feelings of anticipation and nostalgia for her the way it had for her fellow students. Freda was the hostess from hell, and her mother's loss clung to her dad like a cobweb.

Before Mum upped and left, he had been the life and soul of every party, and back then, being so young, Beth hadn't been able to fathom what had changed. Later, she realised Mum had been the catalyst for all the fun in their household. She'd hide cheek-reddening notes in Dad's lunchbox and play Wham! on high volume as she danced around the kitchen in her underwear, waiting for the tumble dryer to finish its cycle. She could diffuse an argument with a kiss, and when Beth had a grump on, she would tickle her until she giggled herself out of it. At weekends, she'd filled the house with friends and kids, and when they went on holidays, she invited complete strangers to look her up if they were ever in Cornwall. She was one of those people who made friendship look easy. Now, as Beth lay in her childhood bedroom staring at the ceiling, she wondered whether her mum was out there somewhere still kicking up her heels or whether she was dead, like Dad, and she was officially an orphan.

For years, she'd wanted to believe Mum was keeping tabs on her from afar, but for all she knew, she could have died years ago. She wondered if she should have announced her dad's death in a national newspaper so her mum might see it and turn up like in some cheesy soap, but what then? A teary reunion where all was forgiven; fuck that. She'd need answers, and they'd better be good.

Chapter Three

SHE WOKE to the sound of rain, the sort that was downright tropical, lashing in with the Atlantic wind, shredding café awnings and forcing dripping holidaymakers to mope around the shops in their slippery sliders, wishing they'd booked that flight to Alicante.

She needed to get some groceries in and could do with the fresh air, having suffocated in the car for hours the day before on the drive down to Flushing. She supposed she could pop to the corner shop for the basics, but she'd still have to go to the supermarket later for the rest and risk running into someone she knew when she wasn't in the mood for platitudes. Anyway, in this weather, she'd be drenched before she reached the garden gate, and the flat-packed boxes that she'd brought from the boot the evening before were beckoning. She'd make a start and hope the clouds cleared later.

She'd need the kitchen equipment for the duration of her stay, so it was probably best to begin with the bedrooms.

Freda's, then Dad's. Her own could wait. What she didn't dump from there, she'd take with her.

It was clear the minute she entered Freda's room that her aunt had stripped it to the point of Spartan starkness, so much so that she wondered whether she ought to find a duvet to drape over the bed in case would-be purchasers misconstrued and assumed someone had died in that room.

The first agent she'd called to book a valuation had asked her, without qualm, if her dad had died in the house, adding that some buyers found it off-putting. She had felt like saying, 'not as off-putting as an insensitive bastard talking about a man's death as if it were an interior design disaster'. She had put down the phone and called an agent more interested in commission percentages and sale boards than ghosts. It was laughable, really, given that if ever a house stood as proof you didn't need to die in a place to leave your spectre, this was it.

Convinced Freda had done her job for her, she headed across the landing, hesitating outside the door of her dad's room. Knowing he was gone didn't make her feel less of an intruder. She'd frequented this room often before Mum left but rarely after. It wasn't exactly off limits, not officially at least, but she had always known it was his space, the place where he retreated to grieve. It had been hard growing up knowing your father's heart was broken, and no matter what you did, it was not within your power to mend it. She turned the doorknob.

It was the one room Freda hadn't dared touch and it remained as she remembered it. Pale green ceiling and William Morris willow pattern wallpaper. She recalled the day Mum and Dad put it up. Mum measuring and cutting the sheets from the roll, Dad pasting and hanging, trying to seamlessly match the repeat in the pattern. How Dad had hung one gooey length upside down and had to strip it off again and chased Mum around the room with the paste-loaded brush when she teased him. Mum had bounced on the dust-sheeted bed and squealed when Dad grabbed her and kissed her on the neck.

Sniffing back a snotty tear, she peeled a black bag from the roll and headed for the wardrobe. Mum's side was empty. Dad's side held a couple of suits, covered in plastic from the dry cleaners since their last outing, probably another funeral. Freda had taken his best suit to the under-takers. It seemed strange to dress up to be cremated, but Freda had obviously thought it mattered. She'd mentioned it in her note, along with the fact she'd ironed him a shirt. She was pretty sure her dad would have thought his overalls were more appropriate.

Hanging at the far end was the pale-tan sheepskin coat she remembered snuggling into when she was little. Trousers pressed, jumpers stacked, except for his old jeans and the checked Timberland shirt he wore all the time. On the top shelf, shirts still in their wrappers; birthday and Christmas presents gratefully accepted but never worn. Why would he wear them? Who would he wear them for?

Beth tried not to look as she bagged them.

She did the same with the contents of the drawers until they were all empty, finishing with the mottle-mirrored dressing table. Freda's note had said she'd changed the bedding in case she wanted to sleep in the double bed rather than in her own single room. Beth couldn't imagine why. Perhaps as some sort of masochistic penance for what Freda perceived as her years of filial neglect. Or maybe her aunt thought that now she was single again, she'd be jumping into bed with the first man she came across and would need the space for all that sexual depravity. Who knew what went on in that buttoned-up brain of Freda's? Beth decided to leave it as it was.

She lifted the duvet cover to look underneath the bed to check for stray shoes or slippers. The space was clear of footwear, but she could see something lurking at the back, wedged behind the legs of the headboard. She straightened up and tried to slide the bed out, but it was too heavy to move on her own. She stood on the bed to get a better look. It could be a laptop case. She certainly didn't want to leave that for the house clearers to find.

She headed downstairs to search for something to hook it out with, but there was nothing long enough, so she decided to try the garage. Dad's tools were in there, waiting for Uncle Ron to collect them on Sunday. Lifting the garage key from its hook, she headed outside.

Dad was an engineer and meticulous with his tools. They hung on hooks around the walls or attached to the workbench at the rear of the garage, waiting for somebody competent enough to use them. Ron had already taken Dad's car back to the dealership where he'd bought it only six months before.

She scanned the gardening tools stacked in one corner, zooming in on a long-handled hoe, which looked ideal.

'What are you planning to do with that, my 'andsome?'

The voice made her jump. She turned. It was Ron. Looking beyond him, she could see his pick-up and trailer parked on the opposite side of the road.

'Because if you're worrying about the state of the back garden, I've already said to leave it to me. I'll make sure the lawn's mowed and the borders are tidy until the place is sold. I'll give the patio a power wash too. I noticed the slabs looked a bit grubby the other day.'

Ron's face was uncharacteristically stern. She could tell

he was concerned and would have no argument. He wouldn't get one from her. She had more than enough to do without worrying about the garden.

'Thanks. You and Jean have been brilliant with everything. I'm not sure I would have coped without you two. I'd like to do something to thank you both. A meal out maybe before I go back?'

Ron's face relaxed. 'Get on with you... we wouldn't dream of it,' he said, giving her one of his big bear hugs. The man was the gentlest of giants, tall and powerful though in his late sixties now. Dad always said none of the men down the dockyard could outwork him.

'Then at least let me get you a cup of tea.'

'Now you're talking.'

Beth led the way back into the house and put the kettle on.

'I thought you were coming around tomorrow?' she said.

'Your Auntie Jean's gone to a craft fair at the Falmouth Pavilions with her next door,' he answered, pausing to slip off his work boots before following her. 'There's nothing much in the way of sport on the telly except horse racing, and you know I'm not much for that, so I thought I might as well make a start today. I brought the trailer. I thought I'd take the power tools and the ladders and whatnot and leave the gardening stuff here for the time being.'

'Sounds like a plan,' she said, handing him his tea.

There was an uncomfortable pause. Given the circumstances, she guessed her naturally ebullient uncle probably didn't know how to pitch the conversation. He had been Dad's best friend since infant school. Jean had said he'd taken the loss hard, dealing with it the only way he knew how: by immersing himself in the practicalities. Beth decided to put him out of his misery.

'I'd better let you get on,' she said. 'Take the tea with you if you like.'

He drained his mug and handed it back to her. 'No need; this gob of mine is pure asbestos. What did you want that hoe for, out of interest?' he quizzed.

'Oh, nothing important. I needed a tool with a long handle to reach something stuck behind the headboard in Dad's room.'

'Do you need a hand to move the bed?'

'No, really, it's nothing. I'll do it later. I've got plenty of other things to do.'

She didn't know why she so readily turned down the offer of help. All she knew was she didn't want anyone there when she fished out the laptop.

She busied herself, taping up the boxes and loading them into the back of her car until Ron put his head around the door to shout his goodbyes. Only then did she head back to the garage to retrieve the hoe.

Upstairs, she balanced on the bed and slid it down behind the headboard using it to shove the case sideways until the handle was visible, and she could reach around the side and pull the thing out. It wasn't a laptop case. She knew exactly what it was, and for a second, she forgot to breathe as a gauzy memory filtered through.

When Mum left, their rainbow world had quickly turned monochrome, and on the darkest days, she walked on pins, worrying if she said the wrong thing, she'd send her dad spiralling into an abyss of despair. Little by little, she learnt it was best not to mention Mum, and although she continued to see her in her dreams and feel her presence like an amputee feels a lost leg, by the time she hit senior school, she kept her under lock and key; until one day, she'd slipped up and let her out.

She was sixteen, and Dad and her were in McDonald's when she'd absentmindedly blurted out, through a mouth full of fries, 'I wonder if Mum still loves cheeseburgers?' She had no idea then or now why she'd said it. She'd immediately buttoned her lip and wriggled deeper into the plastic-covered seat, hoping her dad hadn't heard.

'What did you just say?'

'Nothing,' she mumbled, eyes fixed on the mayonnaise.

'Look at me, Byrdie.'

She looked up at her dad, his face blanched under the lurid glare of the strip lights and knew he had heard her. Neither finished their burgers, and they left in silence, grief searching for a voice in the Ford Sierra all the way home. When they'd got there, he'd left her in the kitchen and gone upstairs, returning ten minutes later carrying a black briefcase. It was not the sort of thing her dad ever carried. He went to work with a toolbox and backpack.

'I'm giving you this now because you're old enough to understand what's in it and because you need to know I did all I could. I hoped this day would never come,' he said, swallowing hard. 'I hoped she'd come back, but I don't think we can wait any longer. It's not fair on either of us. So here,' he said, handing her the case. 'Take all the time you need. Auntie Freda's at the Kingdom Hall all afternoon. We both know she'd have forty fits if she knew about this, so let's keep it between ourselves.'

She'd looked at this man, spirit broken, face drawn and began to cry, her voice breaking as she screamed, 'I don't want to know, I don't want to know,' and threw the case on the floor.

It was the first and only time she'd seen it until today.

She wondered now if not talking about Mum for all those years had been easier than facing the fact her mother hadn't cared enough about them to stay. When Dad handed her the case, he'd said she was old enough to understand, implying it would reveal the truth, unpalatable as it may be. Would she ever be old enough to cope with that? Once these shadows were brought back to life, she'd be stuck with them.

She noticed the lock and, for a minute, felt a wave of relief that it couldn't be opened without the combination. But who was she kidding? Never opening the case was not an option. She lifted her phone and Googled *how to get into an old briefcase without the combination.* After fifteen mind-numbing minutes of watching and re-watching a guy called Ryan explain how all one thousand variations of combinations for a three-barrel lock could be tested in five minutes, she headed back to the garage, hoping Ron had left the chainsaw. She came back with a screwdriver and a hammer, and after a good deal of manoeuvring and a shedload of cursing, they did the trick.

Chapter Four

BETH WASN'T sure whether her heart was pounding because of the effort of unlocking the case or the dread coursing through her body like rocket fuel. She tried to get a grip of herself. After all, the case might contain nothing but old photographs or perhaps love letters between her parents tied with a red ribbon, testimony to her dad's love for her mum and, ergo, proof he naturally did everything in his power to find her.

'Just do it,' she told herself as she flipped open the lid and viewed the contents. As soon as she saw the 1984 calendar, its page folded to show its entries, she knew this wasn't going to be easy. She lifted the calendar from its resting place, noticing as she did, certain dates were ringed in red. Beth flipped back through the previous months to reveal more of the same. Unlike the other ringed dates, where words like 'dentist' or 'parent's evening' had been scrawled, there was nothing written against any of these regular red-ringed entries. Her parents had obviously needed to make a note of them, but at the same time, they knew already what they signified. She wondered for a second if it showed the dates her dad worked nights, but when there was no entry for the night of her mum's disappearance, she dismissed the theory. She knew he had been at the docks working because the police had said so all those years ago. So, if not her dad, maybe her mum? It would make sense; the dates she was working and could not pick her up from school. Mum worked at a hotel where the shifts varied with the seasons. She didn't work every day like Dad. She flipped the page forward to November, knowing if she was right, there would be no entries there. As she'd thought, there were no red rings in the month after Mum disappeared.

Placing the calendar on the bed, she lifted out the next item: a small red leather photo album she had a vague recollection of seeing before. She flicked through the cello-phane-covered pages. Holiday snaps of Mum and Dad, somewhere hot, their faces burnished with the glow of too much sun. Another of Mum with Auntie Jean, outside a club called Tall Trees, dressed to the nines, holding fishbowl glasses of florescent-coloured cocktails.

Beth settled down on the bed, wallowing in the cosy nostalgia, comforted by the snaps of her childhood taken when they were still a family. The final photo was of her sixth birthday party. Mum was standing behind her with Auntie Jean and Uncle Ron. Her cousins and school friends were laughing and clapping as she clutched the Care Bear she'd got from Mum and Dad and blew out the candles on her birthday cake. Dad wasn't in the photo, so she guessed he'd been the one behind the camera. Beth slammed the book shut, suddenly overwhelmed with the sadness of it.

She knew there were other photos, dozens of them arranged carefully in other albums. Her parents' wedding day. Others of her as a baby, Mum cradling her, Dad sitting on the arm of the chair, sporting a mullet and a Freddie Mercury moustache. They had the harried look of all new parents, frazzled but happy, but this was the last one Mum appeared in and the fact it ended so abruptly with this particular photo caught her off guard.

Heart aching, she decided to pack the album with all the others so it wouldn't go astray. She made a mental note to sit down with Grace and go through them. Albums were a novelty these days, real photos having been replaced by thousands of cloud-stored snaps no one seemed to look at after a few weeks of taking them. As she set the album aside, a folded slip of paper floated from its pages to the floor. Mum's smiling face stared up at her, but this was no family snap. It was a flyer. Above Mum's head was the word 'MISSING' and beneath, a phone number to call if the viewer had any information that might help the police find Suzanne Willis. It looked like something you might see in a Clint Eastwood western, minus the offer of a reward and the words 'DEAD or ALIVE'.

Beth bent to lift the flyer from the floor. The room swam. She gulped in air, hoping to quell the queasiness. She wasn't sure why the flyer had such an effect. It revealed nothing new. Her mum was missing, had been missing for years, but until this point, she had always thought of her as missing from their lives: hers and her dad's. This was different. The yellowing flyer she'd clutched in her sweaty hand made it official. Her mum was missing from the face of the earth, not just their little corner of Cornwall. This must be what her dad had wanted to show her all those years ago. He had wanted her to know that not only him but everyone, including the authorities, had been looking for her mum and still, despite all that, she couldn't be found.

She was glad she hadn't opened the case when she was

sixteen. It was hard enough to deal with now she was an adult and could rationalise what it meant – either her mum didn't want to be found, or she was dead. There was a growing realisation she may not be strong enough to revisit her loss without Dad to share the burden. She supposed she could pretend she'd never seen it. Nothing had changed after all, but was that fair? She had a daughter of her own. Perhaps she deserved to know her grandmother's story.

She put the flyer to one side and ventured into the case again, this time lifting a stack of newspaper cuttings, which she freed from their rusty bulldog clip and fanned out on the bed. The first was from a local paper, an interview with a neighbour. *The last person to see the young mother*, it said, *other than Beth, her six-year-old daughter who she'd put to bed that night*. How, in the neighbours' words, they were *a sweet young family*.

The next, from another regional paper, detailed her mother's last movements and how everyone agreed Suzanne Willis would never have left her daughter alone. She read the clippings one by one. *Oh yes. they were very happily married*, confirmed friends and family members, which ones, the article didn't say. When she'd read each one at least twice, she clipped the cuttings back together and lifted the next stack of paper, expecting it to be much the same. But, unlike the first, it did not feature faded photographs and reminiscences about her mother. It featured articles about the serial rapist Neville Savage. She'd heard of Savage, of course. The man had terrorised the southwest during the mid-eighties before extending his repertoire to murder and getting caught. He'd been the subject of any number of true crime podcasts and documentaries over the years, many of which speculated about possible undiscovered victims.

For a while, whenever a particularly brutal rape was

committed, his name had reappeared in the newspapers and on social media as clickbait for such atrocities. Beth paced the room, circling the cuttings littering the duvet cover like a soldier about to enter a minefield, before sitting herself back down on the bed, her hands shaking. Her instinct was to throw everything back into the briefcase and slam the lid shut, but one more document was lying in wait at the bottom of the case, and her methodical actuary's brain could not let it rest.

The thick, photocopied document was stapled together like a book and headed, 'The Green Shore Hotel'. Each page contained the handwritten addresses and signatures of hotel guests for the three months before her mum disappeared. Highlighted on three separate occasions was a name: 'N. Savage'. Beth's skin prickled as fear traced the back of her neck.

There was only one conclusion to draw from all this. Dad had believed there was a connection between her mother's disappearance and Savage. The question was why, and what was she supposed to do with that god-awful piece of information?

Chapter Five

BETH HAD an appointment with her dad's solicitor, Eden Gray, that morning to discuss the administration of his estate. After a weekend of fretful nights, she needed advice. She particularly wanted to discuss the possibility of splitting the proceeds from the sale of the house with Freda. She'd discussed her plan briefly with Jean the day before when she and Ron came around to finish clearing the garage. Jean had said she'd be mad to do it, her argument being that Freda had lived rent-free for years, and it had been her choice to stay on so long.

Beth saw things differently. No matter her motives, her dad would never have been able to cope on his own had Freda not moved in. Working nights would have been a nonstarter without an adult in the house to look after her and take her to school the next morning. Freda might not have shown her love; she didn't have a maternal bone in her body, but she had done the basics well. She'd always had clean clothes and hot meals. Freda had attended sports days and school fetes when her dad was working, and she'd tried to give her a moral compass of sorts, albeit one with a bigoted perspective. It stood to reason her aunt must have made sacrifices. Dropping everything to come and take care of them couldn't have been easy. In Beth's book, she deserved at least enough to see her through her old age. House prices in Cornwall were through the roof and a half-share of the house would give her plenty of money to buy a little flat with a bit to spare.

Beth had begun to work out the figures weeks ago but was worried there could be a problem if her mum miraculously turned up one day. As far as she was aware, her name was still on the deeds, so surely, she'd have a claim against the house. While she'd gladly give up any claim she had to have her mum back, she could hardly risk Freda having to do the same. It would be cruel to give with one hand only for it to be taken away with the other. She only wished she'd had this discussion with her dad when he was alive. Now that he was gone, it was all the more confusing. She hoped Eden Gray might be able to cast some light on the legalities of such an arrangement.

She wasn't sure whether she'd mentioned the Savage thing to Eden. After all, it wasn't strictly part of the estate administration, yet she couldn't help but think that her dad must have kept the case for a reason. He would have known that one way or another, it would fall into her hands. Then again, maybe had he not died suddenly, he would have thought better of it and dumped the bloody thing in the sea.

Why he'd pursued this for all these years, followed every snippet of information released about Savage from the moment he was arrested, was a quandary. There was nothing in any of the newspaper clippings linking the man to her mum's disappearance. Then again, her dad was not the sort to be led on some fool's errand, and the fact the name 'N. Savage' appeared in the hotel register was bound to set alarm bells ringing. Perhaps the contents of the case were only part of the picture. Maybe Dad had a hidden stash of Venn diagrams listing the names of Savage's victims and her mother's friends and acquaintances. Maybe there was an overlap that would give Beth the key to the mystery.

If such a document existed, she had no idea where it would be. She'd finished boxing up all the books, records and personal possessions she was aware of. Freda might have thrown others away, of course. She wouldn't put it past her to think she was doing her a favour, but in the absence of her owning up to a clear out, Beth was at a loss.

If she took the case to her meeting, she could at least tell the solicitor what she'd found. She felt she needed some official reassurance. It would be a relief to unburden herself. Eden Gray was the professional, after all. She might as well earn her fee.

Chapter Six

EDEN LEANED against the doorway of the beach house, watching the morning sun dot the sea with silver. She'd been out on her board at the crack of dawn and, despite having showered, still had the taste of salt water on her lips as she sipped her coffee. She wished she could have stayed out longer. The offshore wind had made for a clean swell, but she had to get to work, and the clock was ticking.

September had been a miserable month up until now, and weeks of squally rain and blustery onshore gales had made this summer one of the worst on record. The local news was full of depressing predictions about restaurants closing, and the tourist board was up in arms about greedy second homeowners letting out their properties on Airbnb destroying the hotel business.

As Eden scanned the deserted beach, none of that really mattered to her. Despite its precarious economy, extortionate house prices and the lack of well-paid employment opportunities, Cornwall was home. Every local she knew would rather be penniless here than rich anywhere else.

'So… have you had your saline fix?'

She felt his strong, tanned arms wrap around her waist, pulling her into him so that the back of her bare legs touched his.

'I could have done with another half an hour.'

'Busy day?'

'The usual,' she said. 'How about you? What time are you due back in chambers?'

'I've got some reading to do for a conference tomorrow, but I'm not in court again until Wednesday. I thought perhaps we could have a late breakfast at the Watering Hole or an early lunch if you'd prefer, and I'd fly back this afternoon.'

Tristan had taken a shine to the beach bar and restaurant hunkered in the sand dunes around the corner from Eden's place. It was a legend among the surfing community, and Eden secretly hoped he didn't blab to his city friends about it. An influx of the Soho House brigade would be the kiss of death to a gem like that.

'No can do. I've got appointments all day.'

'Anything juicy?' he said, spinning her around to face him.

'Nothing you'd be interested in. A custody mediation and an estate administration.'

'You're right there. Death and taxes and divorcee doldrums,' he grimaced. 'At least let me cook your breakfast,' he said, kissing her on the shoulder.

Even at this time of the morning, with his pillow-creased face and his hair sticking out at all angles, he was gorgeous. Not that looks were everything, but they had certainly oiled the wheels of this romance, not least because they helped her set aside her ingrained prejudice against men like Tristan Villiers.

He was the product of the establishment. Now she thought about it, even his name reeked of privilege, albeit with a dash of Celtic heroism. Father was a high court judge, Mother a retired QC. Top public school, then Oxford, before being shoehorned into his mother's London chambers. Nepotism or destiny, you could take your pick. Either way, he was not her usual type, and if she was honest, she was probably not his either, with her red-brick university degree and her arty left-wing parents who would have preferred her to become an anarchist rather than a successful lawyer.

They had met when, on recommendation from a colleague, she had instructed him on an assault case. A young fisherman accused of attacking his skipper with a metal chain. He had been the man for the job and the case had been dismissed when he was able to prove the false allegation came on the back of the boy's threat to report his boss for numerous breaches of health and safety regulations. He'd been thorough, confident and clever. Everything about him was polished. He was a class act.

Well-groomed and as smooth as silk, they had spent weeks working on the case via Zoom. Weeks of strictly business conversations that had turned flirtatious culminated in him arranging to travel to Cornwall to meet the client and discuss the case with her in person.

On the night before the trial, he had offered to take her to dinner to run through the brief one more time. They never made the restaurant. They worked long into the evening; heads bent over the papers strategizing. His breath on her cheek, the smell of his expensive aftershave in her nostrils as his fingertips grazed hers. She was no fool. She knew his strategy largely centred upon bedding her, but it had been exhilarating and dangerous. They had ended up having sex on the carpet and not just any old sex; fiery, sweaty, shout-it-from-the-rooftops sex.

It had been three years since her divorce, three years of near celibacy, and when the release came, it was explosive. Despite a well of shame that swept over her for a second as they'd dressed, she'd known they would do it again and why not? They were both single, and neither could deny the sexual chemistry. Furthermore, the man beneath the cocksure exterior was surprisingly gentle and giving, and the way they locked together body and mind was refreshingly easy.

Eden had not told anyone about the relationship, although she was pretty sure her assistant Molly had noticed she was spending way more time than usual on her mobile. She wanted to keep things low-key for the moment. She wasn't sure what this was or where it was going. They'd spent a couple of weekends together, one at his flat in London and one here in Cornwall, but other than that, their schedules had meant this had been a long-distance romance, and she wasn't sure it was sustainable. He would never leave the city, and she would never leave Cornwall. But for the moment, it was enough.

'I'll need my jumper back,' he smiled, tugging at the neckline of the baggy blue cashmere sweater Eden had pulled over her naked body after she'd showered.

'Well, I'd better take it off then,' Eden said provocatively, leading him back to the bedroom.

Chapter Seven

EDEN LEFT Tristan in the shower and headed into work, The Killers pumping through the car speakers as she tapped along. She felt an unexpected surge of happiness. True, it was Monday morning, and let's face it, nobody liked Mondays, but hers had started well. Surf, sex and scrambled eggs, could a girl ask for more? Even the drive was better now that Cornwall Highways had finally finished the work on the new dual carriageway. For months, her usual route into Truro had been closed, forcing her to loop several miles out of her way, adding time to the journey and often making her late. She was running a couple of claims for businesses affected by the diversions to the A30. To say it was slow going was an underestimation. As per usual, the council had not covered themselves in glory.

There was a faint smell of paint as she entered her office. A few successful cases had meant she'd been able to afford to have the place decorated throughout. She'd splashed out on new seating and new curtains in the reception. The painters had finished over a fortnight ago, but on warm days, you could still catch a whiff of turps.

Her first appointment was sitting in reception. Eden glanced up at the clock behind her secretary's desk. Beth Matthews was early. The woman had an old-style black briefcase on her lap, the kind that blew up in spy films or in which elderly people stored their papers. She guessed as the appointment was about Brian Willis's estate, it was the latter.

There was a cup of coffee going cold on the table beside the woman, who looked as if her mind was elsewhere. Her expression was one Eden had seen many times. A grief-induced fugue state where memory and regret supplanted the everyday.

Agnes hadn't looked up from her screen yet to acknowledge her arrival. It wasn't a good sign, and Eden began to wrack her brain for some minor misdemeanour she may have committed to justify her secretary's cold shoulder. She could think of nothing.

'Morning,' she said, deciding to force the issue. No one, including her temperamental secretary, was going to piss on her chips today.

To her relief, Agnes looked up with a broad smile. 'Good morning to you, Miss Gray,' she gushed.

Eden knew the 'Miss Gray' was for the client's benefit. It had taken over a year for Agnes to come to terms with calling her boss by her Christian name, but they'd got there in the end. Nevertheless, in the presence of clients, she adhered to her strict sense of propriety. Eden still hadn't cracked her secretary's mood swings or the under-the-breath tutting when things didn't go her way, but she'd learnt to live with the woman's foibles in return for efficiency. This morning's uncharacteristic enthusiasm for her boss was unnerving. It could be a trap. And was she imagining it, or was Agnes wearing lipstick? She never wore lipstick or any makeup, for that matter. And had she changed her hair? The cut was softer and the colour lighter, giving her a more youthful appearance.

Agnes was in her mid-fifties and had never shown the least bit of interest in fashion. Sensible was how Eden would describe her dress code although in the context of all those fifty-something women who passed through Eden's office: well-groomed, fighting fit and confident creatures, coming out of divorces with big bank balances and the promise of a new life ahead of them, Agnes seemed from a different era. She had spent much of her adult life looking after her ailing elderly mother. Her world had been small and lavender-scented, but for the first time, perhaps there was a hint of eau de cologne on the horizon. As she came out from behind her desk holding the Willis file, wearing a teal-coloured trouser suit, cinched in at the waist with a wide tan belt, Eden was certain of it. She made a mental note to ask Molly what was going on. Agnes had taken a shine to Molly the minute she joined the practice as a trainee, and if there was something afoot, her assistant would know about it.

Eden took the file without comment and turned to the client. 'Beth?' she said, holding out her hand. 'Eden Gray. Would you like to follow me?' Eden led the client through the newly panelled corridor to her office.

'I'm sorry, I should have asked if you wanted to bring your coffee through with you,' she said, gesturing to the seat opposite.

'No, I'm fine, thanks.'

Beth Willis was attractive with a tumble of chestnut hair

and green eyes, which would have been her best feature had they not been hollowed by what Eden suspected to be a lack of sleep and grief. Her ankle-grazing floral dress, teamed with trainers, made the black briefcase she was holding seem even more incongruous.

'I was sorry to hear about your dad. He was a lovely man.'

'Thank you, it's very good of you to say so.'

Eden noticed the woman didn't have an accent, which tied in with the information she had been given by Brian Willis when he made his will. He'd said his daughter had done well for herself and that she worked as an actuary in a large insurance firm in London, where she'd lived since she was eighteen. He told Eden she had a daughter of her own who was bright as a button, looking to follow in her mum's footsteps and head off to university in a few years' time. Eden thought she looked young to have a child that age and, for a moment, was reminded of her own biological clock ticking away.

It always felt strange meeting someone whose history you knew second-hand. You had to be aware the information could be inaccurate or tainted by prejudice, depending on the person telling their story. This was especially the case when drafting someone's will. Eden had lost count of how many times capricious testators had relayed their reasons for disinheriting this or that one, sometimes for the pettiest of misdemeanours. They may not have visited that month, or their latest Christmas present had not lived up to expectations. Other times, they had married the wrong person or pursued a disapproved lifestyle. On those occasions, there would be an unhealthy element of vendetta in the mix. A final show of power to regain control.

Other times, their reluctant reasoning was desperately sad. Their child was an addict or on the streets, or worse still, had disappeared from their lives completely. In short, they had broken their hearts.

Brian Willis had harboured none of these feelings about his daughter. He loved the bones of her, and his comments about her had been full of generosity and pride.

'You've probably already got a copy of your dad's will,' said Eden.

'I do,' Beth confirmed. 'I know I'll need a grant of probate to sell the house and get hold of Dad's National Savings bonds. I've already closed his bank account and notified his pension providers about his death.'

As one would expect, Beth Mathews was financially astute. Some relatives turned up frenzy-eyed, carrying bin bags full of ancient tax returns and bank statements. Clueless and desperate, they were glad to dump the whole lot on Eden's desk for her to sort. Beth was not one of those. Which begged the question, why did she look so anxious?

'I'd like you to apply for probate as soon as possible and to deal with the sale of Dad's house once I find a buyer. I'm in the process of clearing it to put it on the market.'

'You're very organised,' Eden said, thinking this was going to be a quick meeting.

Beth paused as if she was contemplating how to begin the next sentence. 'There are a couple of things upon which I need your advice.'

'Ask away,' said Eden, wondering if this was where the briefcase came in.

'Under the terms of Dad's will, I'm the sole beneficiary, but I want to know if I can share the proceeds of sale from the house with my Aunt Freda?'

Eden had a vague recollection that Brian Willis had mentioned his sister Freda lived with him. She had asked him if she was dependent upon him, and he'd said not.

'She looked after me and Dad after my mum left. She stayed on up until Dad's death, and I don't think it's fair she should have to pick up her life again without any financial assistance.'

How refreshing, thought Eden, *someone wanting to give something up*. She dealt with any number of bickering, money-grabbing relatives willing to fight each other over any worthless bit of tat, let alone a share of a house.

'It's perfectly possible,' said Eden. 'We can vary the terms of a will within two years of death if the existing beneficiaries agree. As you're the only beneficiary, it's completely down to you.'

'We'll do that then.'

'Are you sure you don't want to think it over? As I said, you've got two years. Things are still raw for you. I'm sure your father would have provided for his sister if he thought it was appropriate. He seemed a fair man.'

'I won't change my mind. I'd be grateful if you could draft up the variation as soon as we've got the probate. I'd prefer it if you let Freda know my plans. She's been a bit off with me since Dad died, and she might just cut off her nose to spite her face. Tell her it's for tax reasons if she starts banging on about not wanting my charity.'

'Of course, if you give me her address, I'll let her know.'

Beth slipped a piece of paper across the table.

'Is that all?'

'Not quite.'

Eden noticed Beth tighten her grip on the case.

'Is there something in the case concerning your father's estate I need to see?'

'Yes... I mean no, not about his estate... well, not directly.'

Eden could tell the woman was struggling to decide whether to show her the contents of the case.

'It's about my mum. I said earlier that Freda looked after Dad and I after Mum left. Well, that's not strictly the full picture. Mum disappeared when I was six years old. No one has seen or heard of her since. I'm not sure whether she is alive or not, and if she is, whether that prevents me from passing half the proceeds of sale to Freda. Mum and Dad owned the house jointly. I think Mum's name is still on the deeds.'

'I'm sorry, I assumed your dad told you,' Eden said.

'Told me what?'

Eden took a deep breath. What she had to say may not be easy to hear.

'Your dad had your mother declared deceased two years ago, around the same time as he made his will.'

'What do you mean, he had her declared deceased?'

'When a person has been missing for more than seven years, it's possible to make an application to the court for a declaration that they are presumed dead. The order has the same effect as a death certificate. The house passed on your mum's death to your dad as the sole surviving owner.'

Beth's face took on a grey pallor. 'I'm sorry,' she said, rising abruptly from her seat, I think I'm going to be sick.'

Eden, fearing she might faint and hit her head, rushed to help her out of the room towards reception, where Agnes, spotting them, came to their assistance.

'Now dear, take deep breaths,' Eden heard her say as she ushered Beth to the loo.

Eden went back to her room, assuming they'd have to rearrange the meeting for another day. She was about to pick up the case to deliver it back to Beth when Agnes came in.

'She's okay. She said to give her a minute.'

'Is she sure?'

'She's adamant.'

Just as Agnes had promised, Beth walked through the door five minutes later, looking washed out and embarrassed.

'I'm sorry. It was a shock, that's all… about Mum. I would have expected Dad to talk to me first about something like that.'

'We can reschedule if you like,' Eden offered, feeling uncomfortable. 'I appreciate this is terribly upsetting for you.'

'No, really, I'm fine. I'd like to go on. Your secretary kindly made me a cup of tea with two sugars, although I told her it wasn't necessary.'

'No point arguing with Agnes,' said Eden, smiling.

Eden could see Beth was making a mammoth effort to compose herself.

'I can drop you a letter with all the details about probate and the deed of variation. I've got all I need to begin the process,' Eden said, hoping Beth would take her up on the offer.

'There's something else,' Beth said, reaching down to retrieve the case from the floor where it had toppled when she'd had her turn. Placing it on the desk in front of her, she clicked it open and, in doing so, obscured Eden's view of the contents.

Eden knew clearing out a dead person's house could be a risky business, especially when the deceased died suddenly before they had time to sanitise their history. Skeletons really did lurk in cupboards and sideboards, not to mention chintz-covered ottomans and black briefcases. Gambling debts, a penchant for cross-dressing, kiddie porn on the computer, Eden had seen it all over the years and from the most unexpected sources. One case came to mind of a grieving wife who had discovered her husband of thirty years had a second family. A realisation made all the worse by the fact his second wife and three kids lived only twenty miles down the road. It had been the sheer audacity of the man that had almost broken the widow.

Eden watched Beth lift three plastic A4 wallets from the case before settling it back down on the floor.

'I thought it would be helpful if these were in date order,' she said, pushing them across the desk towards Eden.

The plastic wallets had handwritten stickers on the covers, the first dated 1984 to 1988, the second 1988 to 2024. Each seemed to be full of newspaper cuttings.

Eden was struggling to understand what she was looking at.

'Open them,' said Beth anxiously.

Eden unzipped the first, pulling free the contents. She could immediately see from the headlines they were related to Suzanne Willis's disappearance.

Brian Willis had gone into some detail when he'd asked her to obtain the declaration on his behalf, so the clippings were no surprise. He'd told her there had been an extensive search for his wife. Once the police had satisfied themselves, there was nothing to explain her leaving. No work difficulties, no mental health or emotional problems and no financial worries. Suzanne had no enemies. On the contrary, according to him, she had been universally liked, and the marriage had been a happy one. Eden knew from bitter experience that no one knew everything about their nearest and dearest. She'd learnt that lesson the hard way from her own marriage. No matter how transparent a person's character, everyone had secrets. Nevertheless, in this instance, it was not surprising Suzanne Willis's disappearance had been regarded as suspicious. It was an unusual case, but there was nothing to say she hadn't just up and left.

These days, the police could have traced her movements on CCTV or tracked her mobile phone, but back in the early eighties, these things didn't exist. People were not in constant communication with each other. Hardly anyone had a credit card. Today, it was nigh-on impossible to go off-grid, but back then, if a person was determined to disappear, with careful advance planning, it was possible. That said, the alternative had to be fully explored, and the clippings confirmed the police, in this instance, had done their job and had continued to actively investigate for a full two years after Suzanne disappeared.

Eden met Beth's eye. 'Your dad told me about your mum. I knew the police had treated her as a missing person and had made extensive enquiries.'

'You knew more than me then up until a few days ago,' Beth said, sounding understandably aggrieved.

'Try not to think badly of him. He needed to tell me because of the application. It formed part of the evidence of likelihood of death.' She knew she was making excuses for the man and that if she were in Beth's shoes, she'd feel let down too.

Beth looked away. 'I'm sorry, I didn't mean to sound churlish. I get Dad might have thought he was protecting me. We never talked about Mum's disappearance. It was too painful. He knew I hoped she'd come back, and when he tried to show me the contents of this case when I was a teenager, I didn't want to know. I suppose he didn't want to upset me again, but I think… no, I know, he left this lot for me to find after he'd gone.'

'To what end?' asked Eden.

'Well, as far as the file you're holding, I think to confirm what you said, that everyone did what they could to find Mum but as for the other stuff, I have no idea.'

Eden had supposed the other folders contained much the same as the first. She lifted the second file and slid out more clippings. She could see immediately that these were different. These were about Neville Savage.

'The ones in the last envelope are all about Savage too. They go right up to Dad's death. He collected anything he could find about the man.'

'And these were found in the case together with the articles about your mum?'

'Yes, so were these,' Beth said, handing Eden the 1984 calendar and the copy guestbook entry.

Eden took them, unsure what they signified. 'You think your father thought Savage had something to do with your mum's disappearance?'

'I don't know what to think. To be honest, my head has been spinning since I found all this. I brought them with me today in the hope you might be able to cast some light on what it means. I thought Dad might have said something to you about it?'

'No, nothing,' said Eden. 'We only discussed your mum's disappearance in the context of the declaration. He never mentioned anything about Savage to me.'

'Then did he leave anything for me? An envelope to be opened on his death or something similar?'

Eden could hear the desperation in the woman's voice. 'I'm afraid not. I hold the will and the deeds of the house, that's all.'

Beth looked deflated. 'Well, thanks anyway. I'm not sure what to do now. It's stupid, I know. To be truthful, I'd like to throw the whole lot on the bonfire and forget I ever saw it, but I can't help feeling Dad wanted me to do something with it, otherwise he would have got rid of the case long ago. I can't sleep thinking about that bloody monster and what he might have done to my mum.'

Beth began to cry, and Eden joined her on the other side of the desk to comfort her.

'I don't know what he expected me to do with this shit,' Beth sobbed.

'Look,' said Eden, sympathy welling, 'why don't you leave the case with me? Out of sight, out of mind. I know that sounds trite, but it might just hold true.'

'What are you going to do with it?'

Eden didn't have a clue, but she needed to offer something to this poor woman.

'I'll read everything, although I'm not sure I'll glean any more than you have. I make no promises, but a fresh pair of eyes might help. All this is overwhelming for you. I suggest you go home and try to put it out of your mind. If I find anything, I'll let you know. At least then, you can take comfort in the fact you've done all you can, and we can ditch the case together. In the meantime, it might be a good idea to ask those who might remember about your mum's movements in the weeks prior to her disappearance. Try to find out about her routine and if she deviated from it at all. Does that sound okay to you?'

Eden handed Beth a tissue and she dried her eyes. She showed her to the door, promising to call her in the next day or two.

As soon as she'd seen her out, a feeling of regret swept over her. Why on earth had she volunteered to share this woman's burden when she hadn't a clue how to discharge it? Her day had started so well.

'Funny how grief affects some people,' said Agnes, handing Eden a Blewett's Bakery bag as she passed through reception.

Something was going on with her secretary; that much was certain.

Chapter Eight

EDEN SETTLED back at her desk with a coffee and a jam doughnut. She had a couple of hours before she needed to leave for her mediation and decided to use the time to read through the cuttings about Savage. She had given them only the most cursory of reviews whilst Beth was with her and needed to scrutinise them more carefully before deciding what to do with them.

The early cuttings were contemporaneous with the crimes. They referred to the Bristol Beast, the identity of the attacker being unknown. The name had been coined at the very beginning of his spree in 1985 when he'd raped two women in one night in the city but seemed less and less relevant as he spread his net wider and the victim count rose. She imagined the gift the man's real name must have been to all those newsroom editors after his arrest in 1988.

The articles featured balaclava-clad identikit pictures drawn by police artists from the scant information provided by the survivors. Eden read how, as well as the mask, he wore black sportswear and gloves and, before the rape, callously added to the trauma of his victims by forcing them to sheath his erect penis with a condom, ensuring that at a time when DNA was barely talked about no evidence was left to test for blood type.

To be doubly sure, once he'd finished his assault, he frogmarched each victim to the bathroom and watched them shower or take a bath before he left. He brought the soap with him, Palmolive, as it happens, and a nail brush.

The later clippings, post-arrest, went into much greater detail. Centre-page features on his reign of terror and his life story; the identikit picture drawn from a description given by the neighbour of his second to last victim, who had seen a man loitering with no apparent reason in their cul-de-sac a couple of days before the rape. There was a remarkable likeness to his police mugshot. The short dark hair and designer stubble. The intelligent, wide-spaced eyes. Only the affable smile was missing. He was neither ugly nor handsome. Rather, he was run of the mill, a fact that seemed to make it all the more shocking.

His modus operandi had been to attack women in their own homes in the early hours of the morning. The victims were young mothers, often single or, if not, with husbands who regularly worked away. He'd break in by dislodging a window or forcing a lock, carefully choosing worse-for-wear properties without burglar alarms, security lights or double glazing. Once inside, he threatened the safety of his victims' children if they didn't comply.

His targets stretched along the M5, and this had led the police to believe the perpetrator worked as a lorry driver or commercial traveller. They'd been right. Savage had turned out to be a toy salesman, peddling his wares to the many small family-run emporiums existing back then before Toys R Us and Amazon.

He was in his early thirties and lived in a semi-detached in Taunton with his wife and two kids. When they waved him off on Monday mornings with a boot full of Transformers, they had no idea that he too, had an alter ego, one that raped and brutalised the women he targeted and followed from the toy shops he sold to.

He was personable and unassuming and, in the words of one of his regular retail customers, 'had a wonderful way with the mums and kiddies.' A talent he used to his advantage. His tactic was to engage a child and its mother with a free sample. In the time spent showing them how a toy worked, he'd dissect information and store it like a lab technician. He'd say how the box was damaged and they could keep the toy if he could take their name, address and phone number to contact them for feedback to relay back to the manufacturer. Excited kids and grateful mums let down their guard. He terrorised the southwest for three years before getting caught after choosing the wrong woman on the wrong night.

On the night of his capture, he had entered the home of a mother with a nine-year-old son who had been over the moon with the electronic Battleships game Savage had gifted him. He had read the rules on the back of the box while his mother, expertly prompted by Savage, divulged that 'No, her husband wouldn't get to play with his son that evening, as he worked nights every third week in the month. Savage had staked her out to check her story. What he hadn't reckoned on was the woman's twenty-year-old brother asking to bunk up on his sister's sofa. Woken in the early hours and believing they were being burgled, the young man waited until Savage climbed through the window and then met him with a heavy thwack to the back of the head with his nephew's cricket bat. When the police arrived, they were in no doubt the man being loaded into the ambulance with a cracked scull was the Bristol Beast.

In the boot of his car, along with the Cabbage Patch Kids, were cable ties, two bars of Palmolive soap and a box of condoms. In the glove compartment was a Polaroid camera and photographs of the victim and her son. When they'd searched his house, they'd found similar photographs of each of his victims hidden in the bottom of a large box of Lego, but it was what they found in the padlocked freezer in the garage that caused the greatest consternation. There, beneath the oven chips and the boxes of bargain burgers, was the body of a woman later identified as Melanie Rowse, a young mother with postpartum depression whose clothes had been found on the banks of the Tamar two miles from her home near Saltash two years before. Despite the body not being found, because of Melanie's history, suicide had been the conclusion. No one ever explored the possibility she had been taken and killed. The murder of the twenty-three-year-old mother raised other questions about women in the southwest who were missing; women thought to have walked out on their families.

Savage denied any involvement or knowledge of these women, adamant this was a planned rape which, just like his final attempt, had gone wrong. Rowse had been compliant at first, but when her baby began to cry, she had lashed out at him and ran to comfort the child. Savage had reached to grab her by the hair, missed, and she'd tripped on the landing, hitting her head on the newel post. In a state of panic, the baby screaming so loudly he could hardly think, his story was he'd bundled her into his car, aiming to dump her near Derriford hospital when he got out of Cornwall, but she'd died on the way. Unfortunately for Savage, his meticulous packaging skills and his freezer had done him no favours, and the pathologist's report concluded Melanie's head injury was not the cause of death. Her windpipe had been crushed.

Three days into the trial, Savage changed his plea to save his wife and girls from further distress. Devon and Cornwall Police had hit the jackpot, but his conviction had not quelled speculation about the possibility of other murder victims. It had clearly not put an end to any suspicions Beth's father had that Savage might have been involved in his wife's disappearance.

Eden paused, readdressing the evidence, realising it stood to reason that if Brian Willis was right, the chances were they would not be investigating Suzanne's disappearance but rather her murder. His rape victims, or at least all those the police knew about, survived. Had there been a trial, they would have given similar fact evidence. Only Melanie Rowse was regarded as a missing person like Suzanne Willis until, that is, she was found in Savage's freezer.

The final batch of cuttings focussed on articles about other possible victims yet undiscovered, along with reports on Savage's progress through the prison system. There was a piece about his wife's petition for divorce on the understated grounds of unreasonable behaviour. Eden studied the picture of Lindsay Savage leaving court with a blanket over her head.

There was an article written by one of Savage's sisters on what it was like to be branded the sibling of a monster and a self-serving interview with a newly released con who, when doing time with Savage, had beaten the rapist's face to a pulp resulting in an extended sentence for him and a spell in the prison infirmary for Savage.

Eden recalled there had been a piece in one of the

Sunday supplements several years ago about Savage's move from HMP Wakefield to a category B pseudo-psychiatric establishment referred to as a 'democratic therapeutic community'. There had been a hue and cry from his victims, outraged he was to get therapy, whereas most of them had not received any help with the insurmountable task of rebuilding their broken lives. The daughter of Melanie Rowse, the one whose cries had proved an unwanted distraction to her mother's murderer, had been one of the most vocal, saying it was an insult to the memory of her mother. In response, the criminal psychologists argued there had been little opportunity to analyse Savage at Wakefield, where he had spent a good deal of his time under threat from his fellow prisoners and confined to his cell. Now, with a zero-tolerance policy on violence in play, Savage would partake in group therapy with other inmates convicted of sex crimes, many of them lifers, and thus give valuable insights into the minds of men like him.

More had been written about HMP Fenton than any other prison in Europe. There was even a Channel 4 documentary about the place.

Piling the documents back into the case, Eden contemplated what to do. She doubted the police would be interested. They had enough on their plate as it was. Only last night the regional news had reported their resources were stretched because of the recent violent protests around the country. If they had drawn a blank all those years ago when the evidence and memories were fresh, what hope did Beth have of finding out what happened to her mother now, and how on earth could she help?

Then suddenly, as if Agnes's sugar-drenched doughnut had given her brain cells a boost, she thought of a solution. Picking up her mobile, she made the call.

Chapter Nine

BETH LEFT Eden's office a good deal lighter in body and spirit for having ditched her dad's briefcase but no wiser as to why he had left it for her to find.

Eden said she would look at the contents and, in the meantime, suggested she talk to anyone who might have information about her mum's movements in the weeks before her disappearance. That was easier said than done. She was pretty sure all those friends, neighbours and work-mates who were interviewed at the time had long since moved on, and her own knowledge was confined to what a six-year-old might be privy to – basically nothing.

She knew her mum went to work and picked her up from school. She was kind and fun and smelled of flowers, but that was about it. The only person she could think of who could give her a comprehensive and hopefully unedited version was her Auntie Jean. She was Mum's sister, after all. Beth found it hard to recall any social event when Jean wasn't around. Her and Mum shared the same interests and the same friends and were close even for sisters. She had no memories of Mum and Jean ever having words. She decided to call her. She looked at her watch; it was coming up for twelve. She wouldn't tell her about the briefcase or its contents, not until there was something to tell. It would only upset her.

Walking back to her car, she realised just how much Truro had changed. She remembered coming into the city in her early teens on the train with her mates to mooch around the shops and stake out the local boys. Boscawen Street was now car-free, and she imagined the wide cobbled road was teeming with tourists at the height of the holiday season, but today, on a Monday in late September, the place was dead, and she wondered if the pedestrianisation had knocked the stuffing out of it. There seemed to be a lot of charity shops and boarded-up buildings, although she noticed the Starbucks on the corner was busy. Then again, weren't they always?

Most of the little independent boutiques she remembered were gone, as was Roberts, the big family-run department store that had once dominated the city centre and sold everything from luggage to lacy underwear. They had all been replaced with the same old high street varieties you find everywhere.

She had no idea where the friends she had back then were now or what they were doing with their lives. It was natural, she supposed, given the limited career opportunities, that kids like her who left for university often never came back. Those who stayed to raise their own families grew distant and preoccupied. She knew, in her case, losing touch was partly down to not having a mum around who badgered her to visit. If she'd been there, she was sure Mum would have coerced her to keep in touch with her old friends. As it was, walking through this once familiar street, she didn't recognise a soul and felt suddenly lonely.

She retrieved her mobile from her jacket pocket and called Jean.

'Jean… is it alright if I come around for a chat? I've been to see Dad's solicitor this morning and could do with a friendly face to talk to. I'm in Truro, but I'm leaving right now.'

'Of course, my lover. Come when you like.'

———

BETH WAS HIT by the aroma of freshly baked pasties as Jean opened the door, apron on, teatowel in her hand.

'They smell good,' said Beth.

'Just out the oven. Ron's working around the corner at number eleven. He's laying a slab for their new greenhouse. I walked his pasty down to him just after you called so he won't disturb us.'

They went through to the kitchen, where two golden pasties sat on the table.

'I'll never eat all that. I'm not used to anything much at lunchtime,' she said, wondering what Jean would think of the healthy choice salads she bought from the Tesco Express on the way to work each day.

'Go on with you; it'll do you good, and what you don't eat, you can take home with you. I bet you've been living on ready meals since you arrived.'

'Cup a Soup mostly.'

'I thought as much. I told Ron we should have invited you for Sunday lunch yesterday.'

'I've not been that hungry, to be honest.'

Jean joined her at the table and began cutting into a

flaky crust, sending a delicious peppery waft of steam across the table.

'Do you want ketchup or brown sauce? I forget to ask. I don't have anything with mine. Damn sacrilege if you ask me, smothering a perfectly good pasty with ketchup, but both my kids and the grandchildren do it.'

'No, it's perfect as it is, thanks,' said Beth.

'So, how did you get on at the solicitors?'

'Fine, we discussed leaving a share of the house to Freda, and she said it was no problem.'

'Well, you know my feelings on that, but you must do what you think is right.'

Beth took a sip of water. 'She told me Dad had Mum declared dead around the time he made his will. Did you know about that?'

Jean's eyes fixed on her plate, her knife and fork paused.

'I did,' she said.

'Why didn't he tell me he was going to do it?'

Jean put down her cutlery and looked up at Beth, her expression serious.

'I told him it was best not to. I thought it wouldn't do any good raking up the past, but I knew as soon as your dad died, you'd have to be told. To be honest, I'm glad the solicitor did the job for me. It's been worrying me for weeks how I was going to broach the subject.'

'I must admit it came as a shock. I never thought Dad would accept she was dead.'

'I don't think he ever did. He was tidying things up for you, that's all.'

'What about you? Have you accepted it?'

Jean's face crumpled, her eyes glassy. 'Not really, to be honest. She was my baby sister. I still think she's going to walk through the door like the bloody whirlwind she always was. I still talk to her sometimes, in my head, when something good happens... you know, like when Ruby got pregnant. I thought *I'm going to be a grandmother. I've got to ring Suzy and tell her the news.* She was the first person I thought of. How ridiculous is that?'

'It's not ridiculous at all,' said Beth, reaching across to touch Jean's arm.

'You're lucky to have such fond memories of her. I have very few, and as I get older, they seem to become less and less clear,' said Beth. 'Sometimes I'm not sure they are my memories at all, or whether I've seen it in a photograph or heard you talking about something, and I'm projecting your recollections.'

It was Jean's job to comfort her now. She reached across and folded Beth's hands in hers.

'Your memories are as real as that pasty you're eating. Your mum was the best. She was a kind and wonderful mum... and the best sister anyone could wish for,' she said, her voice hoarse with emotion.

'Can you tell me something about her?'

Jean looked puzzled. 'What sort of thing?'

'You know, things about her other than mum things... about her job, her friends, what she liked to do when she wasn't being a wife and mother. What were her passions?'

Jean frowned. 'I hope you're not thinking of trying to find your mum because despite what I just said, I think your dad was right to put an end to all the questions by declaring her dead, and I'd hate for you to drive yourself mad the way he did for a while.'

'No, it's nothing like that,' Beth lied. 'I just feel I need to flesh her out in my mind. That if I knew a bit more about her as a woman, it might trigger some new memories.'

Jean got up and put the kettle on. 'Well, you already

know she worked at the Green Shore Hotel down the road. She went there straight from school. Started as a chamber-maid and worked her way up to deputy manager. She was always ambitious. I'm sure she would have become the manager of that place within a couple of years. She was smart. Had we had money, she would have gone to university like you. As it was, it wasn't an option for us, but whatever Suzy did, she made a success of it.'

'And Dad?'

'She met your dad when she was eighteen. He'd always lived in Flushing, whereas we were Falmouth girls, but he used to cross on the ferry every day to work at the dockyard. Ron worked on the docks too back then and had grown up with your dad. He introduced them one night when the three of us were out together clubbing.'

'Tall Trees?'

'How do you know about Tall Trees?' Jean laughed.

'I saw a photo of you and Mum outside it.'

'God, we loved Tall Trees. Your mum and I used to catch the train to Truro and then the bus to Newquay. She loved to party. That was before she met your dad. She was a hell of a dancer, I can tell you. It was all disco and soul then,' she smiled wistfully, clearly reconnecting with the crushes of her youth before shaking them free. 'She could have had her pick of the lads, but she chose your dad, and she chose right. It started with her waving to him from the hotel window as he crossed on the ferry and grew from there. They got married, and she had you. I'd already married Ron by then, who I'd known since I was fifteen. Everything was perfect.' She wiped away a tear. 'Have you finished, love?' she said, looking down at Beth's half-eaten pasty.

Beth nodded. 'Can I ask you something about Freda?'

Jean grimaced. 'If you must.'

'I remember hearing her refer to mum as "the floozy".'

Jean slammed the plates she was carrying down on the draining board. 'That bloody woman. I could knock her sanctimonious block off. She always was a vindictive bitch. She hated the fact your dad married someone outside her precious church.'

'But why would Dad marry a Jehovah's Witness?'

'Because he was raised as one. He left when he met your mum. Up until then, he'd never celebrated Christmas or had a birthday. He went to the Kingdom Hall twice on Sundays. Your mum told me when he was a kid, his mother carted him around door to door delivering *The Watchtower*. He'd been teased relentlessly at school, you can imagine.'

'I never knew. I always assumed Freda had joined later in life.'

'No... she thought your mum corrupted your dad. When your mum disappeared, she saw it as a chance to bring him and you back into the fold. Well, over my dead body. I fought her tooth and nail on that one, and so did your dad. In the end, he banned her from taking you to anything to do with the JWs. He said if she did, she'd be out on her ear.'

'So that was the reason for calling Mum a floozy?'

'That and the fact she'd probably got it into her head your mum had run off with another man.'

'Why did she think that?'

'No reason other than Suzy was so attractive and popular, and working at the hotel, she had plenty of chances to meet men. Back then, the place was full of commercial travellers during the week. Away from home and at a loose end. With the docks and port being so busy, they supplied all sorts. There were ships coming in all the time from all around the world.'

'Do you think Mum would ever have been tempted?'

'Never. She loved your dad. I'm not saying all her work-mates were as sensible. Your mum told me stories about some of the single girls working there that would make your hair curl. How they'd go for drinks with the salesmen, then go back to their room, but not Suzy.'

Beth decided to end it there. She'd taken up a good deal of Jean's time, and she really didn't want to raise her aunt's suspicion.

'Thanks for talking to me about her,' she said. 'It really helps.'

'You're welcome,' smiled Jean. 'I've wrapped your pasty in foil. Just pop it in the oven to warm it up this evening. Mind you do now, I'll be checking.'

Beth was about to reverse out of the drive when her phone rang. It was Eden.

'Hi Beth, is it a convenient time to talk?'

'Yes, fine,' said Beth, raising her hand to Jean, who was standing in her doorway, waving her off.

'I've been looking through the clippings you left with me, and to be honest, I'm not sure I can be of any help. I can obtain your mum's file from the police under the Freedom of Information Act, and that will reveal whether they explored the possibility that Savage might have been involved with her disappearance, but in the absence of new evidence, I can't see them re-opening the case.'

'I understand,' said Beth, finding it impossible to hide the disappointment in her voice. 'Thanks anyway.'

Beth sensed a moment of hesitation at the other end of the phone. 'Is there something else?' she asked.

'Well… there is another option. It's just a thought, and please feel free to dismiss it if it's of no interest to you.'

'Go on.'

'I have a couple of friends, a retired detective inspector and an ex-lawyer. They've recently set up in business as private investigators. They have experience in criminal investigations, and I wouldn't suggest this if I didn't trust them to do a thorough job. I haven't checked with them yet. I wanted to get your thoughts first, but I think they would be willing to help you explore this further if you're interested. I can arrange a meeting, and they can go through the procedure and the costs…'

Beth didn't need to hear more. 'Yes.'

'Yes, what?'

'Yes, arrange the meeting.'

Chapter Ten

ROSS HAD SPOTTED the office in Lemon Street in the 'To Let' pages of the *West Briton*. He'd decided to ring the agent and mooch around on his own before telling Claire about it. He appreciated they were partners now, but she was still finding her feet. Life had brought changes for her over the last couple of years, not least a spell behind bars for a fraud that had also seen her struck off the solicitors' roll. He was relieved she'd finally realised he had chosen her as a partner because she would bring her years of legal expertise to the team and help with the business side of things rather than out of pity. His wife Karenza was willing to do her bit, but she had the family pub to run in St. Ives, and that, by anyone's reckoning, was a full-time job. In any event, this was his baby, his chance to prove he had done the right thing when he'd resigned from the force.

He trusted his record as an investigator. He, like Claire, had served his time. In his case, as a detective in the Devon and Cornwall Police, albeit less conventionally than his superiors would have liked. Claire was a perfect foil for what many regarded as his seat-of-the-pants style. She was methodical, with an eye for detail, and people unburdened to her in a way they wouldn't necessarily confide in an ex-policeman. She had warmth, a way of putting people at ease and letting them know she was on their side.

Back in the day, this had come across as doggedness bordering on obsession with her job, but lately, her resolve had evaporated along with her self-esteem. Life had dealt her more than her fair share of blows. A failed marriage. A diagnosis of terminal cancer and her beloved mother's decline into dementia had pushed her over the edge. She'd forged an elderly client's will so that the woman's only relative and longtime carer, abused for years, was not left homeless. She had acted out of pity without any thought for herself, and there had been extenuating circumstances, not least of which was the fact she had been told by her deranged oncologist she was dying.

Those she had represented over the years had stood by her, and that counted for something. They'd read her story in the tabloids and, despite the headlines, defended her on their social media platforms. Ross knew what she'd done was wrong and misguided, but there were worse people out there, and he hadn't found it hard to forgive her. Whether she could so easily forgive herself remained to be seen.

He had picked her up from prison on the day of her release and driven her back to Cornwall. He'd been shaken by her appearance. He had always thought Claire beautiful. She had been his first proper girlfriend. He was happily married now to Karenza, and no one, not even Claire McBride, could induce him to fuck up his marriage for a second time, but there was a picture of his first love lodged firmly in his heart. Sea-damp curls and eyes the colour of a summer sky. He had never truly shaken off the image, nor did he want to. It was a thing of wonder to be cherished like a pearl in an oyster shell.

Prison may have temporarily dulled Claire's shine, but he knew he could help her get it back. He had intended to ask her about joining him in his new venture on the journey home, but he'd bitten his tongue, sensing it would only add to her anxiety and might lead to her rejecting the idea out of hand. Karenza had counselled him before he'd left home not to push Claire, and for once, he'd taken her advice and waited a full month before broaching the subject. She'd said she'd think about it and had done so for a further nail-biting month before saying yes.

During the hiatus, he'd managed to attract a stream of enquiries via a website put together by a friend of his daughter Livvy, and now he had five ongoing files. Nothing earth-shattering, but a start. He had worried he'd be inundated with requests from spurned wives and jealous husbands, but with no-fault divorce and the wealth of information on the internet on phone tracking and catfishing, your average PI was redundant in that field. He wasn't sorry. He imagined that kind of work to be as dull as dishwater, not to mention depressing.

His cases had turned out to be less tawdry and predictable. For a start, he would never have guessed that they would involve issues that, in his book, should be police matters. Indeed, two of the cases had been reported to the police, but no further action had been taken.

Ross guessed this was down to lack of funding or personnel or both.

The first of these concerned a local restaurant owner who was convinced the tumble in his profits was due to his bookkeeper cooking the books. Ross, having investigated it, thought he had good cause to be suspicious given the place was always heaving, but despite an independent audit, he could find no direct evidence and was frankly stumped.

The second concerned an elderly couple terrorised by their neighbour. The man was a viperous bully, and Ross was pretty sure if he dug deep enough, he'd find the couple weren't his only victims.

The client who gave him the most grief, however, was a middle-aged woman convinced her thirty-year-old son had been the subject of gang recruitment and was involved in a county lines operation. Ross had tried to explain this was unlikely given the man's age and had suggested his change in behaviour, the staying out overnight and complete reworking of his wardrobe might be down to a love interest rather than him being recruited by the local hood, but she'd have none of it and rang daily for updates. All in all, Claire would have plenty to occupy her when she joined him.

Standing with Karenza in the middle of the space that would become the waiting room, he could tell by the look on her face she wasn't impressed.

'Did you check the broadband speed with the agent? I'm assuming it's fibre?'

'I assumed that as it looked newly decorated and the previous tenants operated a business from here, it would be.'

'Mmm.'

Her frown and the downturn of her mouth, along with the note she made in the pad she carried, told him he had made his first cock-up.

'The carpets are new,' he said optimistically, hoping to distract her.

Karenza glanced down and gave a little kick to the navy cord with the toe of her boot. 'Pity they didn't think to keep the dust sheets down until they'd finished painting the ceiling.'

Ross spotted the minuscule splatter of white paint by her left foot.

'I suppose we can cover it with a mat,' she sighed, scribbling.

Ross felt sweat bead on the back of his neck.

'What time did Claire say she'd be here?' said Karenza, finally closing her notepad and looking up.

'Eleven-thirty.'

'You get the vacuum cleaner out of the back of the car and give the place a once over before she arrives. I'll pop around the corner to get some teabags and a pint of milk.'

Ross looked at her blankly.

'Please tell me you've bought a kettle.'

Karenza swiped her handbag from the floor and then, throwing the car keys and a look that could curdle cream in his direction, headed for the door.

'Thanks, love,' he called feebly after her.

Once he was sure she was gone, he took the stairs two at a time up to the first-floor office he'd share with Claire. Their desks were already in place. Hers in the bay window facing inwards, his on the back wall facing hers. They could bounce ideas off each other. Be a real team. An image of Mulder and Scully came to mind.

To the rear of the building was a smaller room where they could interview clients. He thought it was right to call them clients rather than customers. He was used to inter- viewing suspects or witnesses, both of which he'd been trained to test and scrutinise. Things would be different now that he was no longer part of that merry band of brothers and sisters known colloquially by any number of colourful epithets, the old bill, the filth, or his personal favourite, the dibble. The people he interviewed in this office would need to be treated differently. He'd have to assume they were telling the truth, and if that was not novelty enough, they'd also be paying for his time. Politeness and professionalism would be the order of the day, and he could do that, but first, he needed to vacuum; otherwise, it would be blood, not paint, on the carpet when Karenza got back.

Chapter Eleven

CLAIRE SAT opposite Karenza at a corner table in Mannings restaurant. She'd come prepared to begin work that morning, armed with her laptop, but had been whisked away by Karenza the minute she'd finished the tour of the new office, leaving Ross looking like the only puppy left in the pound.

'So, what's the plan then?' said Karenza.

'Plan?'

'Well, you've seen the office, and despite my initial misgivings, I think Ross has done a pretty good job, although please don't tell him I said that.'

'He has,' smiled Claire.

'Claire, I apologise in advance for asking you this, but if I don't do this now, it'll only niggle, and I don't want it to.'

Claire wondered what on earth was coming next.

'I know that you and Ross had a fling years ago, long before he ever looked at me. I need to know all that's in the past, that there is no chance of anything being rekindled because of this new partnership.'

Claire's cheeks glowed with embarrassment as Karenza continued.

'Look at you, you're gorgeous. Most women wouldn't let you within a mile of their husbands. Ross and I have had our ups and downs. We've been married and divorced, and to some, we must seem a bit of a car crash, but now we've decided to give it another go, I can't risk putting my kids through more upset and frankly, my heart won't stand being broken again.'

'You have nothing to worry about, I swear. Ross and I were teenagers when we were together. We are different people now. What you two have is the real deal, hard-fought, not romantic kids' stuff. You have nothing to fear from me.'

'Good, then we'll say nothing more about it,' sighed Karenza, clearing her throat of emotion. 'So, now the past is put to bed. What about the rest of your life?'

'I've not really thought about it.'

Claire had found reconnecting difficult since her release. Ross and her best friend Sarah had visited her regularly in prison, and it made it easier to pick up where they'd left off, but with many other friends and acquaintances, the reunion had been clunky, to say the least.

She couldn't blame them. She could hardly expect congratulations. If she could have claimed a miscarriage of justice, maybe things would be different. But she'd pleaded guilty to forging a client's will, and if her ex-husband Daniel had not refused to press charges, they could have added criminal damage to the list for torching his car. The best she could offer her critics was she'd served her time. Everyone knew she'd not benefitted herself, and she had not been responsible for the old lady's death. She was no Shipman, but there was no such thing as a victimless crime. As the will was rendered invalid, the client had died intestate and the church she had chosen to benefit missed out, even if her long-suffering and wholly deserving niece scooped the pot. Add to that the sensational publicity that had plastered the front pages for months about Dr Issy Moran, the serial killer who had murdered the old lady and who had tried to add Claire to her list of unworthy patients primed for execution; you hardly had a recipe for small talk.

There were those who balanced precariously on the back of the elephant in the room, frightened they might tumble and land on their backsides with a slip of the tongue. Others, like poachers on the prowl for ivory, set traps. 'Claire, how lovely to see you. My, you're looking so thin. I can't imagine what it must have been like. Of course, we read about it in the papers... shocking, truly shocking and poor you, prison... I mean, you hear so much about it, don't you, the drugs and the violence?'

Just ask me, she'd think, as they poked and prodded her with their spears. *Just ask me what you want to know, and I'll tell you. The food was crap, and I look like shit because of it. No, I didn't console myself with drugs or take the opportunity to have a lesbian affair because, frankly, I was too busy being terrified, and yes, I do realise I've ruined my entire fucking life.*

She was jolted from her reverie by Karenza.

'I've spoken to Sarah and Eden, and we want to throw you a welcome home party.'

Sarah was her best friend in the world. As for Karenza and Eden, she'd known them for years. Ross was, of course, the glue that bound them. The wife, the surfing buddy, and the... what exactly was she to him? The old flame? The new business partner? Either description was factually correct, but only one had a future. As she had just confirmed, whatever there had been between them in the past had to be confined to the mists of time if their new venture was to work, and she wanted, needed it to work. As for Eden and Karenza, the pair were chalk and cheese. Eden was a fellow lawyer. She had a reputation for clear-headed reason in the face of whatever catastrophe came her way. She was a formidable advocate with a soft spot for the underdog. Claire was certainly that: a convicted felon and struck-off solicitor. She was walking testimony to how far a person could plummet before hitting rock bottom.

'I'm not sure that's such a good idea,' she said.

'Rubbish. This way, you get it over and done with in one fell swoop. Just friends, past and present and a few old colleagues. Eden will help on that score, and it can double up as a celebration party for the new business as well.'

'I don't think I have enough friends left to warrant a party,' said Claire.

'Well, they were all over it when they thought you'd drowned, and Sarah held that memorial service. Are you seriously saying they'd admit to being up for celebrating your death but not the fact you're alive? Because if you are, they're not worth worrying about. Move on with the people who care about you. The rest can go to hell.' Karenza slammed the table with this last comment.

Claire wished she had some of Karenza's spirit. The memorial service was yet another cause of embarrassment as far as she was concerned. When her clothes were found on Penmorvah beach, it was assumed she'd committed suicide. The assumption had not been far off the mark. It had been her intention to drown herself. She had not wanted to die in a hospice. She had wanted a blaze of glory, and she'd got it, just not in the way she'd imagined. She had planned every last detail, stealing Daniel's car and setting fire to it on the clifftop so it burned like a beacon for all to see, but what she hadn't planned for was her rescue and imprisonment by Issy Moran.

'You can't hide yourself away,' continued Karenza, popping an olive into her mouth. 'This is Cornwall. I've seen at least five people I know pass by the window in the twenty minutes we've been sitting here. What are you going to do? Spend the rest of your life ducking into shop doorways to avoid them?'

'I suppose not,' replied Claire, thinking that was probably a fair estimation of what she envisaged.

'I thought Saturday would be good,' said Karenza. 'The season's over, so only my regulars' noses will be put out of joint if I close the pub for the night. I can make it up to them the next evening. A free pint and a portion of chips should do it.'

'Isn't it a bit short notice?'

'Not at all. This way, you won't have time to back out. I'll put out a WhatsApp, and I'll tell you what, I'll get Piran's band to play a session.'

'Oh, no need for that,' said Claire, feeling panicky and that it might be getting out of hand.

'Hey, if we're having a party, we're having a party. Leave it to me. All you've got to do is turn up. Now, where's our order? I'm starving.'

Chapter Twelve

CLAIRE ARRIVED home shell-shocked and exhausted. She'd decided to go along with Karenza's party plans rather than argue the toss in the restaurant, but she still had misgivings. She accepted that perhaps her friend was right, and she should stop worrying about what others thought and concentrate on her own needs, but did her needs really extend to a pub bash with a band? She wasn't convinced.

She'd be eternally grateful to Ross for giving her this opportunity. It had forced her to start thinking about her future. She'd come to realise over the last few months that if left to her own devices, she was at risk of becoming a recluse.

During her incarceration, she had longed for freedom. She had dreamt of long walks along the clifftops of her beloved Cornwall, of feeling the warm sand between her toes and the sea air in her lungs, but during the first couple of months home, she'd barely been outside the door.

She had spent the summer in her garden, having convinced herself that the plants had run amok during her absence and desperately needed her undivided attention now she was back. She began early when the grass was wet with dew, finding comfort in the warm earth and the drone of honeybees. Lopping and pruning beneath the shifting shadows of the day, she'd work until sundown with only the birds and the occasional squirrel for company. The weather was no obstacle. When fine, she'd fill wheelbarrow after wheelbarrow with brambles and weeds, which she set light to in the evening, sitting by the bonfire until the embers died. On stormy days, she'd slip on her wellies and tackle the slick greenery to the steady drip of the rain rolling off the leaves of the Rhododendrons. She had found solace in the garden; it wrapped around her like a thick green blanket.

She had gone along like that for months, turning down invitations and shutting out the world. When Ross offered her the job, her initial instinct was to say no. It had been Sarah who had shaken her out of her malaise and had talked her around. She'd turned up unannounced one Sunday afternoon and, unable to get a response at the front door, had guessed where Claire was and come around the side of the house to the back garden.

'I might have guessed you'd be here,' she said. 'Now listen, it's a gorgeous day and Ben's working, so me and the girls are off to Perranporth, and we all decided you're coming too.'

'I hadn't planned to go out. I've set aside today for staking the tomatoes in the greenhouse.'

Sarah's face darkened. 'Enough,' she said, frowning. 'The bloody garden can wait. You need to get out of here. You're in danger of disappearing in the undergrowth.'

'I think you're being unfair. I'm just getting things straight,' Claire said defensively.

'Are you sure that's what you're doing because from where I'm standing, it looks like you're hiding? You might not be sitting in the house with the curtains pulled and the phone disconnected, but this is just as bad. You're burying yourself in this jungle. Look at you; you're covered in mud, and when did you last wash your hair? There is literally nothing more to do here. It looks like something you'd see at Chelsea. It's an excuse, Claire, an excuse and some sort of penance.'

'You've got no right to talk to me like that,' Claire shouted, genuinely shocked at her friend's brazen honesty.

'I've every right. You're like a sister to me, and I won't let you bury yourself in the dirt. This ends here. Now put that bloody trowel down before I throw it over the fence and you with it.'

She had gone to the beach that day with Sarah and her girls and had, for the first time since her release, swam and felt free. On the way home, she confided in Sarah about Ross's offer of partnership. Sarah had told her that, in no uncertain terms, she would be mad to turn it down. She'd called him the next morning to accept the job, but until today, when she'd taken the tour of the office and sat at her new desk, none of it had seemed real.

Claire poured herself a glass of Rioja and looked down at the file Ross had given her to read. Her first assignment. Michael and Irene Henshaw, an elderly couple being terrorised by one Kelvin Harvey. She took the file and the wine out to the patio. The garden was bathed in the lazy glow of the late afternoon sun. Soon, the trees would start wearing their autumn coats. There was something reassuringly familiar about the scene. Sitting with a glass of wine, a client file open on the table. She could almost close her eyes and imagine the last few years of her life had not happened and that she was still a lawyer.

She had so much to be thankful for. Three years ago, she had thought she was dying of cancer. She had become obsessed with righting wrongs while she had the chance. Well, maybe she still had a chance to do that with Ross in this new venture. Perhaps, in some small way, she could still make a difference to people's lives. She took a sip of wine and breathed in the heady scent of the late summer garden, the jasmine and the last of the roses, blighted by black spot and battered by rain all summer. It was a relief to be free. It was good to be alive.

Her mobile rang. It was Ross.

'Hi, how was lunch?' he said.

'Delicious,' she replied, deciding not to mention her heart-to-heart with Karenza. She need not have bothered being coy. It was clear Ross had already caught up with his wife and had been made aware of their conversation and her none-too-enthusiastic reaction to the party.

'Look, I know Karenza can be a bit full-on, and to be honest, I'm embarrassed she felt it necessary to ask you about… you know.'

'What, whether I intend to seduce you?'

'Yeah, that… ridiculous, I know,' he coughed. 'But I think she's right about the party. It would be nice for you to catch up with old mates, not to mention good for business. Talking of which, I picked up a new case while you two ladies were lunching,' continued Ross, clearly wanting to swiftly move on.

'Really?'

'Yeah. Eden called. A client of hers has died, and the daughter wants to investigate her mother's disappearance now her dad's gone. He left a case full of papers. I'm not sure of the details other than... now get this, the woman thinks Neville Savage might be involved in some way or other.'

'Savage? You mean the Bristol Beast? But wasn't he convicted in the eighties?'

'Yeah, that's when the mum disappeared, 1984, when the daughter was a kid.'

'How on earth are we meant to investigate something that old?'

'Police records, witness testimony... same as we would with a new missing person case.'

'You're assuming the evidence still exists.'

'Well, Savage still exists for a start. The old bastard's at HMP Fenton with the rest of the nut jobs.'

'Are you suggesting we just... what, go along and ask him if he had something to do with this woman's disappearance?'

'Why not?'

'Because you're not police and I'm not a lawyer anymore. Even if we were to get clearance, which is unlikely, and Savage was to agree to the visitor's order, he's not likely to confess, is he?'

'True, but sometimes it's what people don't say that betrays them.'

Claire sighed. She could tell Ross was excited at the prospect of interrogating someone like Savage. It was within his comfort zone, but they had a duty to the client, not only to tell her the good news but also the bad. As a lawyer, she was used to managing clients' expectations. Ross was all about the chase. He left the outcome to the courts.

'All I'm saying is, let's take things easy and assess the evidence the woman has first. I assume Eden has spoken to the client about us?' said Claire.

'Yeah, she went back to her after speaking with me and checking out our costs. Beth Matthews, that's the client, is happy to pay our fees.'

'Okay, then let's meet with her and take it from there, but let's not give her false hope. We need to be cautious.'

'Oh ye of little faith,' chided Ross.

'What about our other cases? They're all in the early stages. Isn't there a danger we stretch ourselves too thinly?'

'They're small fry compared to this. Imagine if we were to discover a new victim of Neville Savage. It would be huge. Work would flood in. We can't miss an opportunity like this. We can handle the other cases between the two of us, no problem. Trust me, this is great for us.'

Claire wasn't so sure, and as she ended the call, a greasy unease churned her stomach. She knew there was no way she would be able to step back inside a prison gate, not even as a visitor. The very thought of it made her blood run cold. If Ross wanted to interview Savage, he'd be on his own.

Chapter Thirteen

ROSS WAS SLEEPLESS IN ST. Ives. He'd been tossing and turning all night thinking about Neville Savage. This level of disturbed rest had in the past been reserved for criminals he was trying to catch. He knew the phone wasn't going to ring the way it routinely had when he was in the force. He had lived for years in a high state of anxiety, the surge of cortisol pricking his skin. All that was meant to be a thing of the past. But he felt jumpy, nettled as if he were on the brink of something.

He shouldn't be. Savage was already behind bars. His was a well-thumbed horror story. They'd caught the bad man, but there was this niggling feeling that the bastard had got away with something and was right this minute lying in his cell, reliving crimes he'd never paid for.

The apprehension of Savage was the biggest feather in the Devon and Cornwall force's history. Ross remembered his dad talking about it back in the day. He'd been in the force when they made the arrest. He had never seen his father so pumped. Ross had had his moments, but nothing as big, no international headlines. To think he might get a bite at that cherry gave him chills.

Claire, as expected, was the voice of reason. She was right; he wasn't police anymore. His resources would be limited to the information in the public domain, although there was a possibility they might be able to tap into the National Archives or get the Courts and Tribunal Service records, but it would take months. The criminal justice system was in a shambolic state, and all government departments were notoriously slow post-COVID. Their best chance was to get to see Savage in the flesh. He wasn't sure just how they'd do that, and until he met the client, he couldn't be sure how far she was willing to go to get to the truth. Nevertheless, they had crossed the first hurdle. Beth Matthews wanted to meet with them. They'd arranged an appointment for Wednesday morning, and Ross couldn't wait.

Chapter Fourteen

TUESDAY MORNING, Claire headed out to interview the Henshaws. The couple lived in a semi-detached in a quiet cul-de-sac in the Highertown district of Truro. Built in the 1960s before land was at a premium, whilst the houses were modest, they had sizable gardens and plenty of room to park.

The Henshaws lived at number thirteen, their neighbour from hell next door. Claire noted that his property, unlike the clients', looked tired, with its dirty windows and neglected garden. The couple were clearly watching out for her. Michael Henshaw opened the door before she had time to ring the bell. He was a tall, distinguished-looking man with a shock of white hair. He wore tan cords and a matching cardigan with leather-covered buttons. His round wire-rimmed specs gave him the look of an ageing Atticus Finch, and Claire immediately warmed to him.

She introduced herself, and he invited her in.

'Irene is in the sitting room at the end of the hall,' he said, bending to grab the collar of the dachshund running circles around Claire's feet. 'Don't mind Byron. His bark is worse than his bite.'

Claire bent to greet the dog, who immediately ceased yapping and rolled onto his back, hoping for his belly to be tickled. She gladly obliged before following the dog and his master through to a small but comfortable sitting room overlooking the back garden.

Irene Henshaw sat in a high-backed electric recliner Claire recognised as the type she'd seen in the care home her mum moved to shortly before she died. She knew from the file that the Henshaws were in their late seventies. Irene looked frail but had one of those faces that would remain beautiful no matter her age. Byron had settled on his mistress's lap. Claire noticed, as she stroked the dog, the woman's fingers were knotted with arthritis and surmised that might be the reason for the chair.

'Can Mike get you a cup of something before we start?' she said.

'Not for me thanks, I'm fine.'

Michael Henshaw took up his position in the chair next to his wife. 'I must tell you from the outset this was my wife's idea. We're very private people, and the idea of strangers poking about our dirty linen doesn't come easy. Not to mention the cost of all this.'

'I've told him we haven't got a choice. Once upon a time, we could have dealt with this ourselves, but not now; we're too old. Mike has a heart condition, and as you can see, I have severe mobility problems. He might not be keen on the idea, but things can't carry on as they are.'

'It's not a matter of being keen or not. I'm not convinced it will change anything. No disrespect to you, Ms McBride, or your agency, but if the police can't sort this, I'm not sure what you can do.'

Claire had her doubts too. They were obviously sitting in what her mum would have called the best room. Though impeccably clean and tidy, she noticed the furniture was dated and the carpet was faded. These people were on a budget.

'Look, I promise you, if after this meeting I don't think we can help, I will let you know. I appreciate you haven't got money to burn... who has these days?'

The man's face relaxed a little.

Claire reached into her bag and pulled out her dictating machine to record the conversation. 'Do you mind if I use my machine?' she said, placing it on the coffee table in front of her. 'It saves me writing everything down.'

What she really meant was that it enabled her to watch as they spoke, checking for changes in expression or moments of hesitation, which might indicate they were hiding something or disagreed with the other's interpretation of events. Experience had taught her over the years that it was often the small details that proved to be key to unravelling the truth. Things forgotten or misunderstood.

'No, that's fine,' said Irene.

'Before I turn it on, I want you to know I've read the file and noticed that whilst it covers your neighbour's behaviour and the actions you've taken to put a stop to it, it doesn't mention how all this began.'

The couple looked at each other in a way that Claire found hard to read.

'Don't get me wrong,' she said, suddenly worried they might have thought she was blaming them in some way or another. Nothing could be further from the truth. 'I'm not suggesting for one moment there is any justification for Mr Harvey's behaviour. It may well be he's picked on you purely and simply because you are the closest in proximity or… please don't take offence at this… or because you're more vulnerable due to your age, but if there is any other reason you can think of you need to let me know.'

Whilst her husband's expression remained impassive, Irene's bottom lip began to tremble.

'We have to tell her, Mike. You heard what she said. She needs to know everything if she's going to get to the bottom of this.'

The woman reached for her husband's hand, but he pulled it away.

'I told you before, I will not involve her in this mess… not again.'

Claire wanted to ask who he meant but said nothing.

'But Mike, we had none of this before she arrived.'

Michael Henshaw rocketed from his chair. 'If that's the case, I want nothing to do with this. I've told you that girl has been through enough. None of this is her fault.'

He stormed out of the room, leaving Claire wondering whether she, too, should pick up and go. She looked to slip the recorder back into her bag.

'No,' said Irene.

Claire heard the front door slam. 'Should I go after him?' she said, realising it would be difficult for Irene to mobilise quickly.

'No, let him be. He'll be back. Now let's get on with this.'

Irene took a deep breath. 'This all started when Tegan moved in with us.'

'Tegan?' said Claire, trawling the notes in her memory for the name.

'Our granddaughter. She split up with her partner and had nowhere else to go. She's got a little boy, Noah, a dear little chap… five years old.'

'Her parents?'

'Her mother died when she was thirteen, breast cancer. My son remarried, and his new wife... well, I don't like to say it, but my son's a weak man. His new wife is not much older than Tegan and a right madam. She spends money like water, going away on this and that holiday... buying designer shoes and posting photos of them on Facebook. They've got two kids of their own, a boy and a girl. We get to see them once in a blue moon. There was no way that woman was going to let Tegan and Noah move in with them, so Tegan turned to us, and we were glad to have her. She was like a breath of fresh air, especially for me, stuck in the house most days. Tegan's a wonderful girl. She's hard-working and paid her way, and we've got plenty of room. It was all going well until he moved in next door.'

Claire switched on the recorder. 'You're talking about Kelvin Harvey?'

'Yes. His great-aunt left him the house. She moved into a care home years ago. The place has been rented out ever since, but there's never been any trouble from any of them. We heard she'd died and that her nephew had been left the property but thought nothing of it. In fact, we were glad, thinking it would be nice to have a permanent neighbour again.'

'Did the trouble start right away?'

'Not at all. When he first moved in, butter wouldn't melt. He came and introduced himself, apologised in advance for any inconvenience or disruption caused whilst he was doing up the place. We were delighted. The house had deteriorated since his aunt moved out. Tenants never look after property the way owners do. Everything was fine until he became interested in Tegan.'

'You mean romantically?' said Claire.

Irene nodded. 'It started innocently enough. He'd talk to her in passing, ask her how she was getting on. He came around one day with a football for Noah. He said he'd found it while clearing his back garden. It was all very neighbourly, but then he asked Tegan out on a date.'

'She said no?' pre-empted Claire.

'She told him she wasn't ready for dating and needed to concentrate on Noah.'

'And he reacted badly?'

'No, not then, that's why what came later was such a surprise. He said he fully understood and that he had come out of a bad relationship recently and knew these things took time. Then, within a couple of days, the flowers started to arrive. Tegan began to find flowers on the doorstep every morning. They were never there when Mike locked up at night. At weekends, there would be a gift on the boot of her car, a box of chocolates or a bottle of perfume. One time, there was a necklace. It was all a bit of a joke at first, and Mike and I thought Tegan was overreacting when she said he was stalking her. We thought he was a bit old-fashioned, that's all, acting more like someone back in the days when Mike and I were first courting. Now it's all texting, and if you believe the telly, inappropriate photos of body parts constitute showing an interest. Then he asked Tegan out again.'

'How long was this after the first time she'd turned him down?' asked Claire.

'Oh, only about a month, not time enough for anything to have changed as far as Tegan was concerned.'

'What did she say the second time?'

Up until this point, Irene had been stroking the dog, sitting contentedly on her lap, but now, she picked him up and placed him on the floor, her face pinched with worry.

'That was our fault. You see, Mike and I could see no real harm in him. He seemed like a nice lad. He's the right age and a good-looking boy... polite, with his own gardening business and the house, of course, and we felt sorry for Tegan staying in night after night with a young child. We persuaded her to go. We told her to just go for the meal to see how they got on. We told her it didn't have to be any more than that... a bit of company her own age, that's all.'

'She went on the date?'

'Yes, more's the pity. He took her to a fancy restaurant in town, and she told him again that she didn't want anything more than friendship.'

Claire knew the end of this story and it was no Mills and Boon.

'He screamed the place down, accusing her of leading him on... of spending his money. He called her a slut in front of everyone in the restaurant. She came home in floods of tears, and from then on, things went from bad to worse. He started bad-mouthing her to anyone who would listen. A couple of the neighbours told me what he was saying... terrible things. He said Noah was neglected and that Tegan's last boyfriend had left her when he found her in bed with someone else. Awful, wicked lies. In the end, Mike went round to have words with him. He thought the lad had taken the rejection badly and could be made to see sense. You see, Mike taught for years in an inner city comprehensive before we retired to Cornwall. He thought he knew how to deal with young men with issues like this.'

'What did Harvey say?'

'He denied it all. The flowers, the gifts. He even denied asking Tegan out. He said it was all in her imagination. Mike was taken aback by his reaction. He must have known we could check with the restaurant and that we knew our granddaughter well enough to know she wouldn't lie. We thought maybe he was embarrassed or shocked at being confronted and that he'd stop.'

'But he didn't?' said Claire.

'No, it got worse. He started following Tegan and telephoning her workplace, telling them she was a thief… that she'd stolen a piece of his aunt's jewellery from the house. It was all nonsense, of course. She'd given every one of those gifts back. Then, one day, she went to pick Noah up from school, and he was there. That was the last straw. She told us she was moving out. She put in for a transfer at work and found a new school for Noah. We couldn't blame her. She'd suffered four months of hell, but I can tell you it was a terrible blow for us. We'd got so used to them being around.'

Irene began to cry. Claire grabbed a tissue from her bag.

'The only consolation,' Irene continued, dabbing her eyes, 'was we thought that would be the end of it, but once she'd left, he turned his attention to us, saying we were the reason she'd gone, that Mike and I had split them up.'

Claire already knew about the loud music at all hours, the relentless banging on the pretext of work on the house that never materialised, and the rubbish dumped over the fence into the back garden. Dog shit through the letterbox. The usual vindictive intimidation from narcissistic losers like Kelvin Harvey Claire had seen often in her career as a lawyer from narcissistic losers like Kelvin Harvey.

'And the police?'

'We reported him, but they said they could do nothing unless we could prove it was him doing these things. So, we bought one of those cameras and had it connected to the back shed so it would catch him on film if he threw stuff over the hedge or came into the garden. Then he reported us.'

'What?' Claire said incredulously.

'He called the police and said we were interfering with his privacy. He insisted they come around here and look at the camera. He told them that it was trained on his property and that we were spying on him.'

'What was their response?'

'They told us to take it down, or else they'd be forced to take further action. So we did. What else could we do?'

Claire could not believe her ears.

'That's when Mike became really depressed about everything. We're thinking about putting the house on the market and moving back up country, closer to Tegan and Noah. She has no idea all this is still going on. That's why Mike is concerned about me telling you about her.'

'It's not right you should have to leave,' said Claire, infuriated by the unfairness of the couple's situation and the police apathy.

'We wouldn't want to. Moving to Cornwall when we retired was our dream come true. We've lived here for nigh-on fifteen years. It's our home, but what choice do we have? We're even scared to let the dog into the back garden in case he's put down broken glass or poison to harm him.'

Claire felt so sorry for this poor woman.

'I saw your advert, and I called and talked to Mr Trenear. When he told me he was an ex-detective inspector, I thought maybe, just maybe, he'd be able to sort this out. We're at the end of our tether. To be honest, you're our last hope.'

The dog ran from the room, yapping as the front door opened. A couple of minutes later, Mike Henshaw entered the room. He looked pale and contrite. He walked over to his wife.

'I'm so sorry, love. I shouldn't have stormed out like that.'

He turned to face Claire. 'And my apologies to you, Ms McBride. My behaviour was boorish and inexcusable.'

'Please, don't worry about it. You are both under a lot of stress.'

'I daresay Irene has told you the whole story. You know about Tegan?'

'Yes, but rest assured I have no intention of contacting her. The agency will be concentrating on Harvey and whether he has a history for this sort of thing.'

'Do you think you can help us?'

'All I can say is that we will try our level best to put a stop to this.'

Claire meant what she said. She knew that Ross would feel the same once she'd told him the whole story. 'I'll be in touch,' she said to Mike Henshaw as they parted on the doorstep. 'One more thing before I go. What's the name of Harvey's gardening business?'

'Harvey's Horticultural Services, it says HH Services on his van.'

Chapter Fifteen

BY THE TIME Claire arrived back at the office, she had a plan she was pretty sure Ross would go for if she sold it well.

She'd play him her interview with the Henshaws and appeal to his sense of justice. The way she saw it, the police weren't going to assist the couple unless they had proof that Harvey had committed a crime. Harvey had been astute enough to spot their rigging of a camera in their garden as an attempt to do just that and had stopped them in their tracks by calling the police himself.

That kind of savvy didn't miraculously come to you. Most normal people would have taken the cue to adjust their behaviour rather than turn the tables. His actions showed the kind of audacity that came from knowledge. The man was someone who enjoyed toying with people, whether those people were the authorities or a vulnerable elderly couple. He saw this as one big game. In Claire's experience, to be that good at gaming, you needed practice. She was sure Harvey had done this before, but that didn't mean he'd ever been caught for it. They could search his criminal records, but she wouldn't mind betting he had no previous.

She could, of course, advise the Henshaws to take the civil route, mount an action for nuisance, obtain an injunction and claim damages, but they would still need proof. The couple were adamant they did not want to involve their granddaughter, but without her evidence, Harvey's harassment would seem random and unbelievable. He would not come across as an unhinged thug. The couple themselves admitted they'd initially fallen for his charms. A judge might do the same and throw the case out. They were not flush, and a civil action would take money they could ill afford with no guarantee of success.

Claire assumed Harvey would be extra careful as far as they were concerned after the police involvement, but whether he had been so careful in the past or had other victims in his sights who he still felt weren't on to him yet would only be revealed with a bit of digging. Claire had thought of just the place to sink the shovel.

Harvey seemed to have a sound little enterprise going with his gardening business. Either he was a completely different animal as far as work was concerned, or there were other people out there he'd worked for who'd been on the receiving end of his abuse.

Ross listened intently to the interview.

'Little shit,' he said.

'Exactly my sentiments,' said Claire, silencing the recording.

'I'm disappointed the police didn't see through him,' said Ross. 'I can only assume they sent someone junior, but even so…'

'I think he's clever at covering his tracks and playing the innocent. You heard how he spread this information about their granddaughter among the Henshaws's neighbours. His tactic is clearly to throw mud before it's thrown at him in the hope that some of it sticks. The problem is if the police aren't interested, I'm not sure there's any other viable route. I don't think a civil action is going to get off the ground. If I did, I'd point them in Eden's direction.'

'So, what do you suggest?'

'I'm going to employ him as my gardener.'

Ross frowned. 'I'm not sure that's a good idea. What if he takes a shine to you the way he did to the grand-daughter?'

Claire laughed. 'I'm way too old for him,' she smiled.

Ross looked unsure. 'I don't quite get how this is going to work.'

'Well, put it this way, I'm a very particular gardener. I'm not going to employ anyone without getting references first, and I'm going to want to talk to his customers personally face-to-face and see his handiwork before I let him get his hands on my greenery.'

'Clever,' Ross said, impressed, 'but what if there's nothing untoward going on? What excuse are you going to give for not employing him?'

'Don't worry. I wouldn't employ him if he was the second Monty Don. The man's a creep. I'll say my old gardener changed his mind, and I felt duty-bound to have him back.'

Ross gave a sigh of relief; 'That's okay then. I wouldn't feel happy about him being around your place any longer than is necessary, given what we know he's capable of. I wouldn't think he'd be an easy person to sack.'

'No,' said Claire.

'You know I'd rather be the one putting out the feelers, don't you?' said Ross.

'Yes, but you're lacking something essential.'

'What's that?' said Ross, looking confused.

'A garden, you fool.'

'Oh, yes,' said Ross, relieved she wasn't thinking of anything else.

'Anyway, this is my first case, and I want to help the client. If there's a chance of that, I'm happy to use my herbaceous borders to do it.'

'Fine, but you need to keep me in the loop on everything. From the sound of it, this bloke is a nasty piece of work. You need to be careful.'

'I agree, and if it becomes clear that there is nothing beneath the surface early on, we stop digging. The clients are on a limited budget in any case, and we can't afford for one of our first cases to be a freebie.'

'You're right there, leastways not while Karenza's doing our accounts.'

'So, can I make the call?'

'Be my guest,' said Ross, holding up his hands in a gesture of surrender.

'I need to look up the number,' said Claire, tapping Harvey's company name into Google.

Ross sat back, pen poised, waiting for her to shout the number out so he could jot it down.

'Can't you find it?' he said when it wasn't forthcoming.

'It's not that,' she said, a frown creeping across her brow. 'Look at this.'

Claire tilted her computer screen so Ross could see Harvey's website.

'But I thought you said he was a gardener?' he commented, wondering why he was looking at photographs of gravestones.

'It says here that their speciality is the construction of pet memorials.'

'Pet cemeteries… creepy,' said Ross. 'What a weirdo.'

'There are dozens of them. Who would have thought there would be such a demand and some of these memorials are elaborate? They must cost a bomb.'

Ross crossed the room to take a better look. 'Is that one marble?'

'Carrara, apparently. Look at this one with the lifesize statue of a Beagle carved in green granite.'

'You know what, I wouldn't mind betting that most of these have been bought by elderly people with biggish gardens?' said Ross.

'Why… you think they love their pets more?'

'I'm not saying they love them more, but they're more likely not to replace them and to want to have something solid to remember them by. When I was a kid, we had a succession of pets: dogs, cats, guinea pigs… goldfish. When they got ill or old, they ended their days at the vets. We didn't have the room for home burials… apart from the goldfish, who returned to his maker via the U-bend. We certainly never had a memorial erected, but Mum's last dog sits in an urn on the mantlepiece. She never wanted another. She said it wasn't fair because she couldn't guarantee she'd outlive it, and somehow, that made the old Labrador special; that and the fact she'd kept her company after Dad died. I'm just saying it was a definite age thing with my mum.'

'You might be right. Are you saying that makes them vulnerable… that Harvey's targeting them? Taking advantage of them at a time of grief?'

'It's a possibility. He's the type who would.'

'It leaves me with a problem, doesn't it?'

'What's that?'

'I may have a garden, but I haven't got a dead pet.'

'You don't need one. All you need is an urn full of ashes.'

'I haven't got one of those either.'

'No, but I know a woman who has. Dial the number, but remember we're seeing Eden's client about Neville Savage tomorrow. We could be busy working on that, so best arrange the meeting for next week.'

Ten minutes later, Claire put down the phone, having arranged for Kelvin Harvey to come to her house the following Monday with the aim of providing a quote for a memorial grotto.

Chapter Sixteen

ROSS AND CLAIRE were on tenterhooks waiting for Beth Matthews to arrive on Wednesday afternoon. Knowing Eden thought there was something to all of this too, excited the pair. She had phoned earlier to confirm she'd attend with the client for her first meeting to introduce them and that she'd read through the documents Beth had left with her and, on the back of that, had requested Suzanne Willis's file under the provisions of the Freedom of Information Act.

Ross spent the morning trying to distract himself with the report to his restauranteur client. He was deeply disappointed to have drawn a blank so early on in his career as a private investigator, but there it was. He'd had to admit defeat plenty of times as a policeman. The statistics spoke for themselves. According to the most up-to-date figures, only ten per cent of crimes were solved in the UK. It was stark comfort. He hated the taste of failure.

The upside was, with Claire working on the Henshaw case, he'd be able to give Beth Matthews his full attention.

That was if there was anything to investigate. He hoped Eden's confidence stemmed from the fact she had established a link between Savage and Suzanne. It wasn't necessarily the case. It was unlikely she'd found anything earth-shattering without Suzanne's file or Savage's trial records. It would be a miracle if Beth's dad had been able to join the dots without all the information.

Savage wasn't a name on anyone's lips when Suzanne disappeared. It had taken another four years for the police to catch him. Until then, the task force was pursuing a rapist, not a murderer. They would never have looked for clues about his identity amongst their missing persons files.

By the time Eden and the client arrived, Ross was itching to get things started, and after the briefest of introductions, he marshalled them upstairs to the interview room, leaving Claire to follow once she'd locked the front door. Until they hired a receptionist, they had no choice but to operate on an appointment-only basis.

Eden took the lead. 'The good news is I've been told Suzanne's file is available. We can wait for a copy to be posted, which I don't recommend, or we can ask for it to be scanned to us. I could try and call in a couple of favours, but even then, it could take weeks. In the meantime, we'll have to make do with the contents of Beth's dad's briefcase. Are you happy for me to talk Ross and Claire through it, Beth?' Eden asked.

Beth nodded.

'It's clear from the documents that Brian Willis thought Savage had something to do with his wife's disappearance, and if we take the documents at face value, he may well have had good cause for suspicion. Setting aside the news-paper cuttings for the moment, there are these,' she said, placing the 1984 calendar and the photocopied guest list down on the desk.

Ross picked up the calendar. 'What are we looking at?'

Beth chipped in. 'I think the red circles record the days that Mum was working at the Green Shore Hotel. She didn't work full-time; her hours varied week by week depending on the season and how busy the hotel was. I remember she had to arrange for someone to pick me up from school when she couldn't be there. Dad would collect me sometimes on the weeks he was working nights or my Auntie Jean or Dad's sister Freda if Mum was desperate.'

'Makes sense,' said Claire, picking up the photocopied document from the table. 'And this?'

'A copy of the hotel's guest book for the three months leading up to Suzanne's disappearance,' said Eden.

Claire skimmed the pages of addresses and signatures, letting out a sharp cry of surprise when she came across Savage's highlighted name. 'Look at this,' she said, passing the paper to Ross.

'Bloody hell.... sorry, it's just I didn't expect that,' he said, looking at Beth.

'Don't worry. I felt the same way when I saw it the first time,' she said.

'Savage definitely stayed there then?' said Ross.

'Seems so, and more than once,' said Eden, pointing out the other two highlighted entries. 'And you can see from the overlap of the dates that Suzanne could well have run into Savage while he was staying there.'

'Do we know when your dad made the copy.' Claire asked Beth.

'Unfortunately not.'

'We have to assume after Savage was caught, don't we?' offered Eden. 'Otherwise, why would he have highlighted the man's name? Until Savage became notorious, his name would have had no particular relevance. He would have been just another regular guest.'

'That's true,' said Beth. 'I had a conversation with Mum's sister. She told me there were loads of commercial travellers staying at the hotel back then.'

'I wonder why he thought of checking after Savage was arrested?' said Claire.

'I suppose by then everyone knew that Savage operated in the southwest and what he did for a living,' said Eden.

'Not to mention that he wasn't only a rapist. He was also a killer,' said Ross.

'It makes you wonder if the police thought of the connection too?' said Claire.

'If Dad told them of his suspicions and was able to show them this, they must have looked at it surely?' said Beth.

Ross raised an eyebrow in Eden's direction. 'We won't know for sure until we have your mum's file,' he said.

'I wish we had some way of finding out if the hotel staff were questioned after Savage was arrested. Is there anybody who worked at the hotel at the same time as your mum?' asked Claire.

'I doubt it. It was so long ago. I dare say most of them have retired, and a lot of them would have been part-time workers. They'd all be on zero-hour contracts these days. There would have been a fair share of foreign students as well during the holiday season,' replied Beth.

'So, where do we go from here?' said Eden.

'We must be realistic. The fact Savage stayed at the hotel where Suzanne worked is evidence of nothing other than just that. We know he was a commercial traveller, and there are toy shops in the area he could have supplied. It doesn't mean he had anything to do with her going missing. It's not like we have a body,' said Ross.

Claire coughed, reminding him not to be quite as blunt as he might have been in a police incident room.

'There's another problem,' said Eden. 'Savage wasn't staying at the hotel the night of Suzanne's disappearance or the night before. For all we know, he was at home in Taunton with his wife and kids or somewhere else. He could have a rock-solid alibi.'

'We're not going to know for sure without his police file or from the court records, and getting copies of those could take a while through official channels,' said Claire.

'Unless we pull some strings,' said Ross.

Eden raised a disapproving eyebrow.

'I've been thinking. What if I was to write to Savage?' said Beth.

There was a pause from the room.

'I'm not sure that's such a good idea,' said Claire. 'The man's a clever manipulator. You only need to look at how long he was able to commit all those assaults without being caught to know that. He was able to fool his friends and workmates. Even his wife didn't have a clue. He's not only a ruthless, sadistic killer. He's also an accomplished liar. Without corroborative evidence either way, how will we ever know if he's telling us the truth?'

Claire knew what Ross was thinking. *We'd know if we found Suzanne's body.* She glared at him before he had the chance to open his mouth.

Eden nodded in agreement. 'I think you need to slow down, Beth. You've just lost your dad, and are you sure you want to know the truth? If Savage had anything to do with your mum's disappearance, the likelihood is she's dead. Are you going to be able to cope with that? Remember how upset you were when you found out your father applied for your mum to be pronounced dead by the court? This would be much worse, and there is bound to be media interest, and most of it would be centred on you,' warned Eden.

'I think I would be able to cope... I must be able to. I can't forget what I've seen. Before I opened that briefcase, I always thought Mum might be out there somewhere, but now the question will be there, lurking like an undiagnosed disease... the way it did with my dad. I need to know.'

'I'm with you on this,' said Ross, turning to Beth. 'I think you should write to Savage, but you need to be careful what you write. Men like him have massive egos. They love the limelight, and he might use the opportunity to position himself in the tabloids. If you're going to write to him, we need to sit down and do it together.'

Claire moved to interrupt him.

'You heard Beth, Claire,' countered Ross before she got a word in. 'She needs to know the truth, and who better to hear it from than the horse's mouth. Our role is to decipher his response. If he doesn't outright deny it, we stop the correspondence, and you and I will talk to him face-to-face. I'll know if the bastard's lying. I'm sure of it.'

Claire's face reddened. She wasn't going to admit in front of the client that she couldn't possibly do what Ross was volunteering them for.

'Let's cross that bridge when we come to it,' she said.

'I'm not sure I agree with what you're proposing,' said Eden. 'I think it's risky, but if this is what you want, Beth, I will do everything in my power to help you.'

Chapter Seventeen

ROSS AND KARENZA spent the whole of Saturday preparing for the party. There was a minor panic first thing. Karenza and Loveday Soloman, one of her closest friends, sat on the picnic tables outside the pub looking over a mist-shrouded St. Ives Bay, wondering what the hell they were going to do with all those people if it rained and they could not spill outside.

Karenza's father, Gill Martin, sauntered over and cast a fisherman's eye across the water.

'Don't fret, maid, that lot will disappear by midday,' he said sagely as if it were a foregone conclusion.

He had been right, of course, to everyone's relief.

Loveday was joined later by her wife, Josie, and the pair stayed to help prep the food. Karenza was adamant that they only serve finger food. The kitchen would stay well and truly closed that evening. She intended to have a good time.

At three o'clock, Piran and his band turned up in their van to set up their gear, and Piran's wife, Carly, set about decorating the place. Karenza was the first to admit she had no skills in that direction, but Carly, a talented artist, had more than enough for both. By the time she'd worked her creative magic, the beams were festooned with twinkling fairy lights and greenery and looked incredible.

Ross had been charged with ensuring they had enough chairs and tables outside and that they wouldn't run out of booze. He had no idea why Karenza was getting herself in such a spin. They ran a pub, for god's sake. They were used to the place thronging with demanding tourists for weeks on end. This was small beer in comparison.

'It's not the same,' Karenza pointed out when he questioned her. 'These people are our friends. It's years since we've thrown a proper party. They'll be expecting a good do, and I intend to deliver.'

Women, and Karenza in particular, continued to be a complete mystery to Ross. It had been her idea to throw the party for Claire, who hadn't even been keen. Why on earth was she putting herself through the wringer like this? As far as he was concerned, the best parties were impromptu affairs on the beach: a fire pit, a burger and a couple of beers, simple, but this had grown into a different animal altogether.

He realised he may not have helped matters by being a tad free and easy with the invites. But could he help it if he knew so many people? It stood to reason that word would get out in a town like St. Ives, and if someone stopped him in the street and said they'd heard Karenza and him were having a party at the pub on Saturday night, he could hardly not invite them.

Karenza had asked him as they lay in bed the night before how many he'd invited, and he'd had to admit he didn't have a clue.

'This is typical of you,' she said. 'Thank goodness Claire's given me a list.'

Well, bully for Claire, he thought.

By six-thirty that evening, they could do no more. The pub looked great, the food was prepared, there was plenty of booze, and their guests were arriving in half an hour. Gill and Carly were all set to help behind the bar and to cap it all, there was a wonderful sunset across the bay. As far as Ross was concerned all was right with the world. When Karenza came downstairs wearing a white dress, tanned and glowing from the shower, her dark hair falling around her shoulders, he could not imagine anything more perfect.

He pulled her to him, kissing her hard on the lips.

'Hey, watch the makeup,' she said.

'What makeup? You don't wear makeup?'

'You fool. It takes me hours to make it look that way.'

'I like the dress,' he said, running his hands down her hips. 'What material is that?'

'Broderie anglaise, for your information. But you and I both know the only thing on your mind at the moment is where the zip is.'

Ross grinned. She knew him too well.

'Nice to see you've made an effort,' she said, poking a finger at his faded Quiksilver T-shirt.

'I'm in charge of the BBQ; no point me dressing up.'

'Lucky I didn't marry you for your sartorial elegance.'

'No, you married me for my sexual magnetism and phenomenal good looks,' he grinned.

For once, Karenza didn't argue.

Ross had chalked *Private Party* on the menu board outside, so when they heard the door open, they knew it was likely to be one of their guests. It was Claire. Her friend, Sarah, and her husband Ben, were with her.

'Oh no, we're not the first, are we?' said Sarah. 'You can tell how eager we are to be invited to a party. That's what having kids does for you.'

'It's only right the party girl is here before her guests arrive,' said Karenza, smiling at Claire, who looked stunning in a pale green silk dress. A perfect fit for her slender frame.

Claire blushed.

Piran and Carly were the next to arrive, and after that, a steady stream trickled through the door. Familiar faces, all looking to party.

Eden and her new fella were among the last to arrive.

Ross knew nothing about him other than, by all accounts, he was a top defence barrister who batted out of London chambers. He had a look of money about him. For starters, he was dressed from top to toe in designer gear, not the obvious labels but the understated brands only the seriously minted could run to. He seemed pleasant enough, and Eden looked happier than he'd seen her in ages. He was no judge of what made for a good match, but it helped in their line of work if your partner understood how much it took out of you. His old boss had arrived on his own and was lurking on the periphery. If he got the chance, he intended to take Luke Parish to one side and ask him what the chances were of getting his hands on Neville Savage's police file. He was about to head across with a beer when he saw Luke cross the room to speak to Eden.

Ross decided to stay where he was and take notes. He wouldn't be able to hear what they were saying, but he could watch their body language. He had an inkling Luke would not be so laid back about Eden's choice of boyfriend.

Chapter Eighteen

'HAVE you seen your mum and dad lately?' asked Luke.

Tristan carried on heading for the bar.

'About three weeks ago. I've been busy,' replied Eden.

The corners of Luke's mouth turned down, forming an expression that looked very much like a grimace to Eden. 'With Tristan Villiers?'

'No, not particularly, just busy generally with work and stuff.'

Luke's eyes zoomed in on Tristan's back as if he were a suspect under surveillance.

'I see. It's just that I've heard two are an item. Maybe I heard wrong.'

'Depends on what you mean by an item?' said Eden defensively.

Luke snorted and took a large swig from his bottle of Peroni.

'Anyway, forget about what I've been doing. What were you saying about Mum and Dad?'

Eden was determined not to be drawn into a conversation with Luke about her love life. He'd obviously heard about her and Tristan. She wandered from whom? They'd tried to keep their relationship low-key, but it was nigh-on impossible in the small legal pond in which they swam. Since Luke had managed to arrange after-school activities for her niece Flora and cover for the holidays, she hadn't seen so much of him, although their paths continued to cross when he dropped Flora off with her parents. She was their only grandchild, and they, like her, were keen to see her whenever possible.

'Let's just say they're going through a bumpy patch.'

'In what sense?' said Eden, wondering if the small-holding was getting too much for them or if the income they earned through letting the caravans in the bottom field had been affected by the poor weather.

'In a matrimonial sense,' said Luke.

Eden looked up at him, eyes widening in disbelief. 'Marriage problems... Mum and Dad?'

'No one's immune, you know. Relationships are complicated things for most of us, although apparently, for some, it's plain sailing.' Once again, he cast his disparaging glare in Tristan's direction.

'How come you know all this, and why hasn't anyone told me about this *bumpy patch*?'

'Probably because you're too busy to listen,' he said pointedly.

'Who told you?'

'Your sister. Your mum called her a couple of days ago.'

'Mum told Thea?'

A wave of indignation swept through Eden at the thought her mother would confide in Thea rather than her. Thea was a walking disaster as far as relationships were concerned. Luke was one of many discarded partners.

114

When Eden had told Thea that her husband Andrew, was leaving her for another woman, her one piece of sisterly advice had been that she get herself tested for STDs.

'Thea told me because she knew I'd be dropping Flora over to your parents the next day, and she wanted to warn me that there might be a frosty atmosphere.'

'It's probably something of nothing. Mum and Dad argue all the time over politics and art and Mum's cooking skills or lack of them. It'll blow over in a few days,' Eden said dismissively, not wanting to show she'd been wounded.

'Possibly, but it must be quite bad for your dad to have moved out.'

'What... moved out... when?'

'Last Friday.'

Eden had the urge to swipe the smug look off Luke's face but wanted to know more. She was just about to quiz him further when Tristan looked over and beckoned her to join him at the bar.

'Your boyfriend's summoning you,' said Luke, tipping his bottle in Tristan's direction. 'Better not keep learned counsel waiting. I've heard he's a stickler for protocol.'

Eden could feel her hackles rising. *Boyfriend! What were they, fourteen?*

She was determined not to give Luke the impression she was at Tristan's beck and call. 'I'm sure he'll manage without me. He doesn't know many people here, but he can charm the birds out of the trees.'

'That'll be all that public school training and supper parties with Mummy and Daddy's posh friends,' said Luke sarcastically.

Eden could feel her cheeks reddening. He was totally out of order. Her private life was none of his business. Granted, they were close. In fact, for the last few years, since

Thea moved to Scotland and he'd been bringing up Flora on his own, they'd drifted into a pattern of pseudo-domesticity, but that didn't give him the right to think he could say what he liked to her with impurity.

She decided to cut her losses before they had a full-blown row. She scanned the room for someone less judgmental and spotted Ross standing on his own by the band, an expression of pride blazing across his face as he tapped his foot to his son's rendition of 'Smells Like Teen Spirit'. Piran had obviously been told to pick a set that would go down well with the forty-something audience. They'd already covered a couple of Oasis numbers and given a pretty good rendition of Pulp's 'Common People' that had everyone dancing.

Eden wound her way through the crowd, stopping to clink bottles with her mates as she headed towards the proud, middle-aged groupie.

'Hey, buddy. How's it hanging?' said Ross.

Eden and he habitually engaged in surfing lingo when they were off duty. They did it firstly in tribute to their common love of the waves and secondly, because it annoyed the hell out of people not in the know, especially legal types who became bemused and panicky when they strayed from the accepted norms of conversation. They could keep it up for hours when maximum aggravation was required. It was, in effect, a kind of code between two mavericks with an anarchic streak.

'Looking Rad, Miss Gray,' said Ross, planting a kiss on Eden's cheek. 'I only usually see you in your work gear or in a rubber one-piece.'

'Hey, don't say that too loudly. People might get the wrong idea,' she smiled.

'My ex-gaffer looks none too happy. You two looked as

if you were about to wrestle each other to the ground just now.'

'I don't know who's put a weed up his ass, but he's being really snarky about Tristan.'

'The dude's jealous.'

'Jealous of what?'

'You and him, of course,' replied Ross, nodding in the barrister's direction.

'That's ridiculous.'

'Maybe DCI Parish has his own idea about who you should be dating?'

'I don't know why he thinks I need his permission for anything. Having once been my sister's partner and being my niece's dad doesn't make him my keeper. There's never been anything between us that should give him that idea.'

Ross had insinuated a romantic connection between her and Luke once before. She had never taken it seriously, but the way Luke was behaving was certainly odd.

'I'm just saying,' said Ross, holding up his hands.

Eden looked over her shoulder and saw Luke had moved outside and was now standing against the railings, looking moodily out over the harbour.

'He looks lovesick to me,' said Ross. 'I'm telling you straight, I'm not going in after him if he decides to jump in.'

'Oh, shut up,' Eden laughed. 'Change of subject.'

'Okay,' said Ross. 'How do you fancy coming with me and a couple of the guys to the Cribbar tomorrow? I can pick you up if you like?'

The Cribbar was the reef off Towan Head. It was known for huge waves at certain times of the year when the wind and the swell were just right.

'The Fistral boys have been watching the sets for the last couple of days, and they reckon it could be big.'

Eden looked across at Tristan. 'I'm not sure. I've got company for the weekend.'

'Bring him with you, let him see you in the wet and wild,' Ross grinned, displaying a perfect set of white teeth.

'Okay,' said Eden, unable to resist the prospect of a big swell, 'but we'll make our own way.'

'Awesome,' said Ross, fist-bumping his friend.

'Now I'd better go out there and comfort your cast off,' he said,

He watched Eden, tall and elegant as any runway model, sashay across the room to join Tristan at the bar. They certainly made a handsome couple. Then, grabbing a couple of bottles, he headed out to where Luke stood hunched over the harbour railings.

'Enjoying yourself?' He resisted the urge to call him 'Sir'.

Luke turned to face him. 'Yes, thanks, great party… great crowd.'

Ross, having watched his altercation with Eden, was sceptical, and when Luke rejected the beer he offered, saying he was driving, he knew he'd be a hard sell.

'How's life outside the force treating you?' asked Luke.

'Good, I've got a few cases on the go, and now Claire's joined me, I'm hoping we can take on more work. As a matter of fact, I wouldn't mind having a word about one of them sometime.'

'No time like the present,' said Luke.

'It's a cold case. We've been asked by a client to investigate the disappearance of their mother back in 1984.'

'I hate to break it to you, but the trail might just have gone cold by now.'

'Oh, very funny,' said Ross. 'It was high profile in Cornwall at the time, and there's something unusual. The woman thinks Neville Savage might have been involved.'

Luke looked more interested in the introduction of the man's name. 'Savage was a rapist, wasn't he?'

'Primarily, but he went down for murder.'

Luke's thick, dark eyebrows knitted into a frown. 'Now you mention it... wasn't a girl found in his freezer?'

'Yeah, and there's been speculation since, and the mum's disappearance was around the same time.'

'One swallow doesn't make a summer,' said Luke.

Ross, who had just taken a sip of beer, almost spat it out. 'Listen to you, Captain Sensible, but I'll definitely use that one in the future, and I'm happy to give you credit for it if anyone asks.'

Luke gave a broad grin. It was the first Ross had seen him give all evening. The DCI had a great smile. Karenza always commented that it was his best feature and it was a shame he didn't use it more often.

'The client's dad recently died, leaving her a briefcase full of cuttings about Savage. That's why she thinks there's a link.'

'Tenuous at best,' said Luke.

'I know, but I've got a feeling about this one.'

Luke lifted his eyes to the heavens. 'Please, God, save us from Ross Trenear's gut,' he shouted.

Ross glanced over his shoulder to see if anyone had heard and could tell by the giggles coming from a group of girls sitting on the pub wall that they had.

'I know from bitter experience what one of your feelings can get you,' said Luke.

'A conviction?' said Ross, pleased with his comeback.

'Sacked more like.'

'I wasn't sacked. I resigned.'

Luke smiled. 'If you say so.'

'So, what are the chances of getting my hands on Savage's file?'

'Zero.'

Ross took a step back and scrutinised his old governor's face. 'You're serious, aren't you?'

'What did you expect that I'd walk into records and lift a whole shelf full of files just because you had a feeling?'

'No, but I thought you might be able to give me the heads up on the highlights.'

'Mate, you're not a policeman anymore, and that comes with advantages and disadvantages. Not having routine access to police records is one of the latter. The former is you don't need to answer to me anymore because if you did, I wouldn't be sanctioning wasting public money on this. As you are your own boss now, with a client stupid enough to pay you, it's none of my concern, and I'd like to keep it that way.'

Ross's heart sank. 'Is this because of Eden?'

Luke's smile slid from his face. 'Why the hell would this be because of Eden?'

Ross thought better of alleging Luke's bad temper was down to the green-eyed monster.

'She's the one who recommended us to the client,' he parried, thinking on his feet.

'I know nothing about that, and like I said, it's not my business.'

Luke glanced at his watch. 'Look, it's getting late. I've hired a babysitter for Flora. Like I said, great party mate and I wish you and Claire all the best.'

Ross could have kicked himself. He'd known Luke was pissed about Villiers, and he'd still gone ahead and asked for a favour. If only he'd bided his time, the answer might have been different. He'd been an idiot. 'Fuck,' he muttered under his breath.

Karenza came to the door of the pub and shouted across to him. 'What are you doing out here? Come in and have a dance with us.'

The music was pumping, and he could see Claire and Sarah dancing like a couple of carefree teenagers. Claire was clearly enjoying herself, and he was relieved the party had done the trick. Placing his beer on the bar, he grabbed Karenza's hand and dragged her onto the dance floor.

Chapter Nineteen

THE PARTY eventually broke up around one in the morning. Eden did the rounds, saying her goodbyes. She thanked Karenza for a great evening and shouted over her shoulder to Ross as she left.

'See you tomorrow, mate.'

'Looking forward to it,' he shouted back.

She and Tristan began the steep walk from the quay up to the island car park. The narrow streets were deserted apart from the party stragglers dispersing. Tristan was silent, and Eden noticed he was swaying slightly, so she linked her arm through his to steady him.

She hadn't kept an eye on what he was drinking. She'd been on Gordon's Zero all evening. Getting a taxi home from St. Ives was nigh-on impossible out of season, and she'd decided from the outset she was going to drive. So had Sarah's husband, Ben, by the look of it. He was ahead of them, trying to marshal Claire and Sarah, into the back seat as they passed.

'Great night,' Eden shouted across to him.

Claire paused by the car door. 'Thanks for coming,' she yelled before crossing the tarmac to give Eden a hug.

'What the hell are you carrying?' Eden said, looking at the ornamental urn tucked under Claire's left arm.

'It's Honey the Labrador,' she said. 'Ross handed her to me as I was leaving... don't ask. It's a long story.'

'I won't,' said Eden, pleased to see her friend back on form. Claire had looked nervous early in the evening, clinging to the walls, unwilling to mingle. Then the music began, and Sarah had dragged her onto the dance floor.

'Are you coming or what?' Ben shouted across. 'I'm having trouble keeping this one in the car. She wants to go skinny dipping,' he said, grappling with a giggly Sarah.

'Come on, the beach is just down there,' Sarah yelled, pointing in the general direction of the sea. 'We always go skinny dipping after a night out,' she said.

'Yeah, when we were eighteen,' Claire shouted back, smiling at her tipsy friend. 'Better go and help,' she said, kissing Eden on the cheek before turning to Tristan. 'Nice to meet you,' she said, turning and running back to join Ben and Sarah.

Tristan swayed. 'I can't bear to see women drunk.'

Eden glared at him, flabbergasted by the comment. 'And what about men?'

'THAT'S DIFFERENT.'

'Really?' Eden said, looking straight at him as he dumped himself into her passenger seat.

He shrugged. 'It's unseemly. That's all I'm saying.'

'And that's all you're saying, is it? Well, I think that's more than enough, saying there's one rule for you lot and another for us.'

'No need to get tetchy,' he said, leaning forward and turning on the music.

Eden reached across and turned it off.

He stared at her bleary-eyed for a second, then put his head back on the headrest and closed his eyes.

Eden wasn't about to have a full-blown row. He'd obviously had too much to drink. She was happy to drive in silence and let him sleep it off. She'd save her challenge until tomorrow morning.

She put the car in gear and reversed out of her space, beeping the horn one last time as she passed Ben, who was putting the funeral urn in the boot. She wound her way through the impossibly narrow streets, climbing past the Tate Gallery and out of town. Rounding the corner, she glanced to her right across the inky water off Porthmeor, the surfers' beach of choice. Ross was right. The wind was getting up, the breakers frothy, like white lace against black velvet in the twinkling lights of the town.

'What was that you said about tomorrow?' mumbled Tristan, making Eden jump. She thought he was asleep.

Eden cleared her throat. 'I said we'd meet Ross in Newquay. They're expecting a big swell, and I thought we could go take a look.'

Tristan peeled open his eyes and sat upright. 'Why the fuck did you volunteer us for that?'

Eden was taken aback by his tone. 'I thought it would be nice to get out and about. You haven't exactly seen much of the county up until now.'

'I've seen as much as I want to, and even if I wanted to explore, what makes you think I'd want to do it with your surfing buddies?'

Eden was trying hard to concentrate on the road.

'Didn't you think to ask whether I'd want to spend my

day off with a load of ageing beach bums?' Tristan sneered, his plummy accent becoming more pronounced with every sentence.

Eden could feel her hands beginning to sweat as she gripped the steering wheel tightly.

'Who is this Ross bloke to you anyway?'

She felt her face flush with annoyance. 'He's a good friend,' she said resenting the fact he was questioning her, but at the same time not knowing quite what to do. She did not want this to escalate.

'Well, I guessed that much,' he said, swallowing the words in a hiccup. 'You were talking to him for half the evening. The other half, you were talking to that moody bugger in the cheap jacket who spent the night giving me evils.'

Eden was furious, but she did not want to stop the car in the middle of nowhere. There were no other cars on the quiet country road. She could, pull over and tell him to get out, but what if he wouldn't? Or, worse still, what if he did and wandered off somewhere? That could be dangerous. She had no wish to abandon him to the elements, not in the condition he was in. Anything could happen.

'It was fucking rude, that's what it was, leaving me to make small talk with a bunch of yokels I didn't know. You bloody ignored me all evening.'

Eden could hold her tongue no longer. 'I did not ignore you all evening. Ross was our host, after all. It was common courtesy to talk to him, and Luke needed to talk to me about my parents. You could have come across and joined in. You've got a lot in common. They both work in the justice system. Luke's a DCI, and Ross is a retired detective inspector with his own PI business.

'Oh, real intellectuals then,' Tristan sneered sarcastically. The charming debonair barrister he had been at the beginning of the evening had morphed into a boorish, spoilt child.

'You don't need to come tomorrow if you think it's beneath you,' Eden barked. 'I'm sure my beach bum friends won't miss you. Neither will I, for that matter.'

She expected him to answer back, but as she looked across at him, she saw he was fast asleep and snoring. When she got home, she didn't wake him. She locked him in the car. He wasn't coming anywhere near her, that was for sure. She couldn't trust herself not to push him over the cliff edge.

Chapter Twenty

EDEN WOKE at 5am on Sunday in a panic, fearing Tristan might wake and, in a fury, break her car window, setting off the alarm or worse still, call the police on his mobile. She could lie and say she'd mistakenly locked him in, but it would be embarrassing. She could imagine the hours of entertainment it would give them down at the station. The titters and the quips about her doing anything to keep a man.

Shouldering on her coat, she grabbed her car keys and headed downstairs.

She needn't have worried. Tristan was fast asleep where she'd left him. She pressed the release button on her key fob, hoping he wouldn't wake. He didn't. Back inside, she packed his bag and placed it by the door.

She decided not to go back to bed. Pulling on her jeans and a jumper, she grabbed a blanket and curled up on the sofa. If there was going to be an altercation when Tristan woke, she wouldn't be having it in her pyjamas.

She hoped, having slept off the alcohol, he would have

calmed down. She, on the other hand, had become anxious once she'd gone to bed. Sleep had proved evasive as she lay stewing in her anger, imagining all the things she'd say to him the next day. It was a shame he'd turned out to be such a dickhead. They'd hit it off, and the sex was great, but none of it was worth tying herself to a misogynistic narcissist who seemed to think he was a cut above her friends, and her, for that matter. Luke's words rang in her ears.

'I hear he's a stickler for protocol.' Talking of self-righteous pricks, there was another.

Tristan had said she'd been rude for leaving him on his own for most of the night. Had she been? She wondered how she would have felt if the boot was on the other foot. If he'd taken her to one of his snooty London parties full of old school chums talking about jolly japes in the dorm and skiing holidays in Courchevel. What if he'd left her at the bar to make small talk with the varsity girls? She had to admit she would have been furious, too.

She lit the wood burner and brewed a pot of coffee, pouring one for herself and, with a pang of contrition, one for him. She had to knock twice on the window before he stirred. He stared bleary-eyed at her through condensation-misted glass. His face crumpled and confused; he reminded her of the family dog Castro when he'd forgotten where he'd buried his bone.

He slowly opened the door.

'I brought you a coffee,' Eden said, handing him the steaming mug.

'What time is it?' he asked groggily. 'Have I been here all night?'

'It's nearly seven, and yes, you have. You fell asleep on the drive back.'

He shivered. She didn't blame him. There was a thick sea mist, and the air had a definite autumnal chill.

'Can you hold it for me?' he said, handing her back the mug. 'My back is killing me. You might need a hoist to get me out of this thing,' he grimaced, holding onto the car door for leverage. 'Why didn't you wake me when we got back?'

She wanted to say *because you were a drunken asshole and I had no intention of letting you into my home, let alone my bed.* 'You looked so peaceful,' she lied.

'I don't remember the drive home.'

'That's probably a good thing. I'd prefer to forget it myself.'

Tristan crawled out of the passenger seat and straightened up slowly. He was obviously in pain, and Eden winced in sympathy when he gave out a little squeal as he pitched his foot and his back spasmed.

'Don't worry. I'll be fine once I get going,' he said, hobbling like Quasimodo up the pathway to the beach house, Eden following with the coffee.

He paused as he entered the open door. 'What's my bag doing here?' he said.

'I packed it for you. Come inside and warm up while I call you a taxi.'

'Am I missing something here?' he said, turning to face her. 'I thought we had today together. I've bought a return ticket for tomorrow morning.'

Eden closed the door and steered him towards the sofa as if he were one of her elderly clients.

'Take a seat,' she said. She handed him his coffee before walking to the kitchen to fetch a glass of water and some paracetamol.

'Thanks,' he mumbled, still shivering as he popped the tablets in his mouth.

'You really don't remember anything, do you?' she said, passing him the blanket to put around his shoulders.

'I remember leaving the party and your friend, the pretty one in the green dress, coming over and giving you a hug. Did I imagine it, or was she carrying a funeral urn... anyway I don't remember anything much after that.'

'Well, let me fill you in. I remember every obnoxious word you uttered.'

'Oh god. What did I say?' he said, his previously ashen face flushing crimson.

'Where do I start? Shall we begin with the bit where you accused me of talking to too many men or the bit where you made it perfectly clear that you thought my friends were morons?'

Tristan's eyes were downcast as he chewed his bottom lip.

At least he has the good grace to look shamefaced, thought Eden.

'I'd had too much to drink,' he stuttered.

'You think?' said Eden, sarcastically.

'I know it's no excuse, but I get nervous in situations I'm not used to. I'm not as confident as you might think. I find meeting new people stressful, and when I stress out, I drink too much. Sometimes it helps me relax, but other times... well, you've obviously experienced firsthand what happens other times.'

'You're right, it's no excuse.'

'Have I completely fucked this whole thing up?' he said, desperation flashing in his eyes.

'Pretty much,' said Eden.

'I don't remember what I said, but whatever it was, I'm so sorry. You must think I'm a complete waste of space.' He was on his feet now. He seemed to have forgotten his pain as he moved towards her.

'Tristan, I know you were drunk, but in my experience, that's often when people let their guard down and say what they really feel. You see my friends as a bunch of country bumpkins. And if that's the case, you're not the man for me. I will not apologise for the way I live or the people I choose to live it with. I wouldn't swap my life for anything, particularly not a sterile, soulless existence in the city. I don't give a crap about an apartment near Chancery Lane or securing a booking at a Michelin-star restaurant. We're from different worlds, and I like mine better than I like yours.'

'Have you quite finished?' he said sternly.

'Yes, I think I have,' she said, releasing a sigh.

An hour later, Eden found herself alone, a stony-faced Tristan having departed in a taxi. She opened the door. The mist had cleared. She filled her lungs with the crisp ocean air and felt relieved and a little bit excited. The surf looked clean, and she had a date in Newquay with a bunch of ageing beach bums.

Chapter Twenty-One

ALL THINGS CONSIDERED, Claire felt remarkably fresh on Sunday morning, which is more than could probably be said for Sarah, who she imagined would be nursing a humdinger of a hangover.

She felt oddly exhilarated. Despite her misgivings, she'd had a great time at the party. She had been amazed at how many of her old friends and colleagues had turned up, and not one of them had mentioned prison, even in passing. She felt as if she had finally moved on and could face the world without the need to constantly look and feel repentant.

She was starving and decided to pop into Truro and treat herself to a full English, complete with a slice of hog's pudding in true Cornish tradition. She wolfed it back, enjoying every morsel, but once she'd finished her second cup of tea, she felt at a loose end and wondered what on earth she was going to do with herself for the rest of the day. Until recently, she had been content to skulk around the house, but now, she could not think of a single thing that needed her attention, inside or out.

Her preparations for Kelvin Harvey's visit the following day were complete. The final touch had been the urn full of ashes handed to her by Ross the night before. She assumed his mum had given permission for her beloved Honey to act as bait but couldn't guarantee it. Ross was just as likely to have sneaked the urn out, hoping his mum wouldn't notice. It had worked for him when he stole her Crème de Menth when they were fifteen. Why not now?

She'd received a catalogue from Harvey with illustrations of his previous memorials. They were much the same as on his website, ranging from the tastefully understated to the downright gaudy. She decided she probably ought to air on the side of flamboyance if she was to convince him she needed to inspect his handiwork before she committed. The fact he'd not been able to fit her in sooner led her to believe the man had a full diary. She hoped he wouldn't have time to accompany her when she visited his past customers, figuring they'd never give up his secrets if he was breathing down their necks.

She looked at her phone. No messages. It was only eleven-thirty. She wouldn't need to eat again until supper time so there was no point traipsing around the supermarket for something to tickle her tastebuds. What did single people do on Sunday afternoons?

She'd overheard Eden and Ross talking about surfing in Newquay. In a region where they gave out the surf conditions at the end of the weather forecast, it was difficult not to have dabbled in the sport, but she had long ago decided she preferred to swim without the paraphernalia of a wet suit and a board.

She found herself wondering what Beth Matthews was up to. She knew she had relatives in Cornwall but nevertheless, it must be hard to be seconded down here without her daughter and her friends. She remembered clearing her mother's bungalow when she went into the care home. It had been exhausting and emotional. Add to that the trauma of finding her father's papers and the thought of corresponding with a serial rapist... well, this was no holiday for Beth, that was for sure. Claire wondered if it would be an imposition to call her. She hesitated, then punched in her number.

'Hello?'

'Hi, it's Claire. From the detective agency?' she added when the pause on the other end stretched a little too long.

'Claire... yes, of course, I'm sorry, I didn't expect to hear from you on a Sunday.'

This was a mistake, thought Claire.

'I'm sorry I didn't mean to impose.'

'You're not. I'm glad for an excuse to down tools. Did you need to ask me something?'

'Nothing specific. I was just wondering if you have made a start on that letter to Neville Savage or whether you might like some help?'

Further hesitation, then, 'Really? You'd give up your Sunday to help me do that?'

Claire felt guilty. She was giving up nothing.

'To be honest, I'm at a bit of a loose end,' she admitted. 'Please say if you've made plans. The letter can wait.'

'No, no... I'd be glad of the help. I haven't a clue what to say. Eden said you used to be a solicitor. You're bound to be better with words than me. I'm a numbers person. Give me a probability to work out and I'm in my element, but words, they're an anathema to me. I've bought a writing pad, but that's as far as I've got.'

'That's great,' said Claire. 'I'll come to you.'

'You have the address?'

'Yes,' Claire said, picking up her bag and making her way to the till to pay. 'When would you like me to come?'

'Now is as good a time as any.'

'Now's fine with me,' said Claire.

'I thought it would look better if it was handwritten.'

'I agree.'

'Perfect, I'll get the Basildon Bond out.'

———

IT HAD BEEN years since Claire had visited the waterside village of Flushing. She'd forgotten how picturesque it was. Not in the quaint fisherman's cottage way associated with the county. The place had more than a touch of grandeur about it and was a magnet to the sailing fraternity. Parking was a nightmare, and anticipating the tiny car park on the quay would be full, she decided to park on the outskirts and walk the rest of the way.

Most of the houses on the main street were three-storey villas built in the Queen Anne style. They would have once been owned by wealthy sea captains who preferred the genteel living a dockside house in Falmouth couldn't offer. That is when they weren't sailing off to the far-flung colonies of the British Empire. These days, the colonies came to them. The place was awash with foreign tourists.

Claire noticed that none of the massive houses had garages, and she imagined tempers were fraught when the locals got home from work to find the space outside their house occupied by a Volvo with a Frankfurt numberplate. Passing the pub, Claire remembered drinking there with her mates during regatta week when the bar was heaving with fit-looking gig rowers. The place looked as if it had undergone a revamp and a change of name. She made a mental note to have a look at the menu on the walk back to the car. She found Beth's house easily enough and was reassured by the broad smile on her client's face when she answered the door.

'It's great you can spare the time to help me with this,' Beth said, leading her through to the kitchen. 'It's been playing on my mind since our meeting. I know Ross offered to ring next week to go through it but to be honest, the thought of another night lying awake trying to come up with the right pitch fills me with horror. It's the stuff of nightmares when you stop to think about it, and the more I turn it over in my head, the more awful it seems. After all, I'm writing to the man who might have killed my mum.'

Before Claire had met a real-life serial killer in the form of Issy Moran, the doctor who had tried her level best to add her to a list of victims, she too would have feared any contact with a killer of any type. Women who corresponded with men like Savage had a screw loose as far as she was concerned. Trying to fathom how you gained the upper hand and maintained your sanity when engaging with such creatures was a challenge. Killers like Savage and Moran were cannibals with endless appetites for misery. How Beth phrased this letter was crucial, not only because they wanted to get information from the man but also because they didn't want her to unwittingly reveal anything about her personal life for him to feed on. You did not give these people a pathway to your soul.

While Beth made the coffee, Claire stared out of the window at the long, thin garden sloping upwards from the house in a series of narrow terraces laid with gravel and planted with hardy sea-side varieties she couldn't grow in her own garden. She particularly liked the Victorian blue glass buoys strung together with rope dotted about the place, although the water feature on the patio made from two granite troughs reminded her of her meeting with Kelvin Harvey tomorrow, and she turned away.

After coffee, they made a start. Beth's pen hovered above the paper, her eyes glued to Claire as she waited for her to begin dictating.

'Let's take a breath,' said Claire, feeling under pressure. 'We need to establish what we want to achieve first.'

'I hate to say it because of what it will mean,' said Beth, 'but a confession, I suppose?'

'I agree, but if we press too hard, there's a chance Savage won't reply or will forward the letter to his solicitor for a formal response. If they close ranks, the whole thing will be a complete waste of time.'

'So, what do you suggest?'

'I think we need to apply a light touch and appeal to his better nature, not that I think he has one. Remember what Ross said, men like Savage are narcissists. They need to believe they hold all the power. We need him to think you are at your wit's end, and he's in the driving seat.'

'Which he is,' said Beth.

'At the same time, we have to impress upon him that you're not seeking retribution.'

'I stress I'm looking for closure?' said Beth.

'Exactly, and I think it might be a good move to drop your dad into the conversation. Savage is a father, after all. He had two young daughters when he committed his crimes.'

'Hardly father of the year,' quipped Beth.

'Not in our eyes, but I dare say he doesn't see things the way we do. I wouldn't mind betting he saw himself as a family man. Men like Savage compartmentalise. They have to, otherwise they betray themselves to their nearest and dearest. I bet he would have been horrified if his wife had been assaulted the way he assaulted those women. I wouldn't even be surprised if he didn't go home at night and talk to her about the atrocities being committed by the Bristol Beast. I've read Peter Sutliffe warned his wife against taking unnecessary risks with the Ripper around. Why should Savage be any different? It's all part of the mind games they play.'

'So… appeal to his paternal side.'

'It's a good start, but remember, don't reveal too much about yourself. I'm not even certain you should give your mum's name at this stage. Treat this letter as a fishing exercise. All we're doing is baiting the hook. If Savage bites, we can reassess how we reel him in.'

'I'm so glad you're helping me. If it had been left to me, I would have told him everything: about Mum, her disappearance, the briefcase… everything.'

Claire liked Beth. She was reasonable and willing to take advice despite the emotionally charged quagmire in which she was sinking. Not all clients were so willing to bow to experience.'

'What about Ross? Won't he want to see the letter?' asked Beth.

'He'll be fine if I've helped draft it. I'd like to get it posted as soon as possible, and I'm not in the office tomorrow. He's busy on another case, too. He's going around to break the news to a local restaurant owner that he's drawn a blank trying to find out why he's losing money hand over fist when the place is always busy.'

'Surely that's more up my street than his… hasn't the man got an accountant?'

'I think he has, and Ross has had another accountant look at it, but neither could work it out.'

'In that business, it's usually one of two things: some-one's nicking money from the till, which is difficult when everyone pays by card, and the tills are automatic, or the chef is over-ordering.'

'Over-ordering?'

'It's a common scam. Chefs these days are demigods. They dictate their terms because good ones are in demand, especially somewhere like Cornwall. Look at them the wrong way and they'll walk, more than likely joining a competitor the same day. No restaurant owner is going to risk challenging his chef for paying too much for his ingre-dients or delving into his supply chain. If they are chal-lenged, they're likely to deny it, putting it down to spoilage or a lack of portion control when, in fact, they're selling half of the goods on.'

'You ought to become a detective. You're good at this.'

'I already am in a way,' said Beth, smiling. 'It's my job to analyse risk and effect. Figures have their own undeniable logic. When they don't add up, it's usually down to human intervention of one kind or another. Sometimes innocent, sometimes not. Get Ross to tell the owner to keep an eye on his chef.'

'I will,' said Claire, grinning. 'Right, let's get this letter written.'

An hour and a half and several cups of coffee later, they had constructed a letter they believed would do the job.

Dear Mr Savage,

Writing this letter is not easy, and if someone had told me a year ago that I would be asking you for help, I would have told them they were mad, but here I am doing just that.

142

Up until a few weeks ago, I knew little about you. But having read a lot lately, I feel I know you a little better. I know, for instance, that you are a father and that for the last few years, you have been undergoing therapy to help you come to terms with your past. My own past has taken on a new shape since my father died. Dad raised me alone. He had little choice in that because in 1984 when I was six years old, my mother disappeared from our home in Cornwall. Whilst I was sorting through my father's belongings, it became very clear to me that he thought you might have had something to do with my mum's disappearance all those years ago. I have no idea whether you did or not. I only know my dad spent his life trying to protect me from his suspicions. But I know I will never be able to truly lay him or my mother to rest until I know the truth.

I'm appealing to you as a father and a man with a past you may wish you could change. It is not my wish to punish you further. I know you will spend the rest of your life in prison, no matter what.

All I am asking for is closure. Perhaps the truth will free you too.

Please write care of my solicitor Eden Gray (address included). She is dealing with my father's estate and suggested I write to you.

Yours sincerely
Beth Matthews

Chapter Twenty-Two

EDEN SPENT the rest of Sunday morning in Newquay watching others surf. She resisted going in herself. Usually, surfing was a release. It was liberating, letting intellect give way to sensation. When others asked what it felt like to ride a wave, she could never adequately describe it. The nearest she came to it was telling them it was like riding a unicycle on a rollercoaster. Most found that a terrifying prospect. Those who didn't were good candidates to give it a go. She never found surfing terrifying, other than when the waves were titanic and unpredictable like they had been off the Cribbar. To surf waves like that, you not only required nerves of steel and exceptional technique, but you also needed concentration, which was sadly lacking in her today. For her to surf in her frame of mind would be reckless. She could break bones or worse. So, she watched while Ross and the others battled with the surge and churn of water, pitting their wits and their bodies against Mother Nature in her most unforgiving guise.

She had received five texts and two voicemails from

Tristan at the beach, all of which she deleted. His bruised ego was the least of her worries. Luke's revelation the night before about her parents had been playing on her mind, and instead of heading home for a well-earned warm in front of the log burner, she headed for her parents' chilly smallholding.

She was temporarily thrown when she saw Luke's car parked outside. If she'd thought this through, she would have realised he might be there. He often took Flora to see her grandparents on a Sunday when he wasn't on duty, and since he'd made DCI, he had more free weekends. She couldn't criticise him for doing the right thing as far as his daughter was concerned. Her parents doted on Flora, as did she. Any embarrassment she felt about the night before, whilst not extinguished, was dampened by the thought of seeing her niece. She was greeted by Castro. She watched him haul himself from his blanket and walk on arthritic legs towards her, tail wagging.

'Hello, boy,' she said, giving him a scratch that made his back leg jumpstart an invisible motorbike. 'Who's a lovely boy then… yes you are… yes who are.'

Luke walked into the kitchen carrying two empty mugs. She guessed he'd come from the sitting room where she supposed Flora and her mum were.

'I didn't expect to see you here,' he said.

'Last time I looked, my parents lived here, although apparently, it's now a broken home.'

'Don't shoot the messenger,' he said, putting down the mugs.

'Is Mum next door with Flora?' she asked, avoiding further reference to the previous evening. It might lead to a question about Tristan.

'They're finishing off a game of Hangman. It helps Flora with her spelling.'

'Nice,' said Eden. 'Haven't they thought of something a little less politically incorrect, like I Spy or Scrabble?

'If you can't be politically incorrect at eight, there's not much hope for the rest of us,' Luke grimaced.

'True,' Eden said.

'I'll go and chivvy them along. I imagine you want to talk to your mum in private?'

'I do, but don't rush them. I'd like to cadge five minutes with Flora. I miss her now she has her after-school clubs, and you've got the holidays covered.'

'She's doing well and loves all the activities, but I know she'd prefer to spend time with you. You're the closest thing she has to a mother figure. We both know we can't count Thea. I have my limitations. I never know how to dress Barbie so she doesn't look like a sex worker. You could pick her up from school one Friday if you like for a sleepover. Although I don't want to step on anyone's designer brogues.'

There it was. She knew he'd get a dig in about Tristan sooner or later.

'If you're asking whether I have plans next weekend, the answer is no. Tristan and I have parted ways.'

'Really?' he said, a look of genuine surprise and not a little pleasure sweeping across his face.

She didn't respond. Instead, she left him standing in the kitchen with Castro and walked through to the sitting room where Flora and her mother were cuddling up on the sofa.

'Good timing,' said Eden's mother. 'We've finished, haven't we, darling? Flora is very good at finding the words. The villain was strung up in no time, wasn't he?' she said, giving Flora an affectionate squeeze.

'Alright, Pierrepoint,' said Eden. 'I thought you were against capital punishment.'

'Who is Pierre Point?' asked Flora.

'No one you need worry about,' grinned Eden, flopping down beside Flora and giving her a hug. 'Hello, monkey. Your dad said you can stay with me at the beach house next Friday if you want. Do you fancy a movie night?'

'Can we have popcorn?'

'Of course, and you get to choose the film.'

'Easy, *The Greatest Showman*,' Flora yelled.

At least she's moved on from Annie, Eden thought. She wondered where Flora's love of musicals came from. It certainly wasn't her mother. Thea hated anything theatrical unless she was playing the leading role.

'It's a date,' she said.

'Come on, Flora, time to go,' said Luke from the doorway.

'What… not staying for lunch?' Eden said tongue-in-cheek.

Luke's Adam's apple bobbed with the thought of her mother's culinary catastrophes past and present.

'No… no, you're alright. Five minutes to get your things together, Flora,' he said before turning to Eden and grimacing. 'Can I have a quick word?'

'Sure,' said Eden, assuming Luke wanted to talk about her parents.

'Ross collared me at the party about a case his agency is working on. The disappearance of a woman called Suzanne Willis?'

Eden had no idea Ross had spoken to him about Suzanne. Given the mood Luke was in last night, she assumed he'd given him short shrift.

'I suppose he told you Neville Savage might be involved?'

'He told me your client's late father thought he could be, which is something quite different. He wanted Savage's case files.'

'And presumably a truck to carry them in?' said Eden, imagining the files would fill an incident room.

'Exactly,' said Luke, pleased Eden instinctively knew how impossible the request was. 'I think I was a bit harsh on reflection. I gave him a dressing down about him not being in the force anymore and it being a waste of time and money.'

'I can see it would be like searching for a needle in a haystack,' said Eden.

'Acres of haystacks, crossing several counties,' said Luke.

'All those police forces, with a vested interest,' said Eden.

'I wanted you to know I wasn't being obstructive. I can't help… not on such flimsy evidence, but I can give you this.'

He lifted a thin lever arch file from the kitchen worktop.

'This is Suzanne Willis's file. I saw you put in a request. I thought I'd speed things up for you and appease Ross in the bargain.'

Eden took the file. Luke must have made the effort to collect it that morning.

'Thanks,' she said, genuinely grateful. 'I'm not sure how much help it'll be.'

'I have to admit I thumbed through it when I picked it up. The initial investigation hit dead end after dead end. Then again, it was 1984. I'm surprised they dedicated as much time as they did. I think that must have been down to the persistence of her husband and the local press.'

'Does Savage come up anywhere?'

With that, Flora ran into the kitchen, Castro, ever game, at her heel.

'Bits are interesting. I'll leave it to you to make of it what you will. All I ask is you promise you'll keep me in the loop. Devon and Cornwall collared Savage. I'm loathed to let one of the other forces in the mix get first dibs on any new intelligence.'

'Don't worry. I promise you'll be the first to know if this comes to anything.'

'Right then, Flora, in the car,' said Luke, pausing at the kitchen door to say to Eden, 'Don't be hard on your mum. She's feeling fragile.'

That's nothing to how she'll be feeling when I've finished with her, Eden thought. Certain that if anyone was at fault here, it would be her scatty, evangelically liberal mother. She would have read an article on the servitude of marriage or decided that after over forty years together, her and her dad's chakras weren't aligned.

'Bye, Grandma,' Flora shouted. 'Give my love to Grandad when he gets home.'

Eden was grateful to Flora for the unsolicited cue, and as soon as Luke and her niece had gone, she joined her mother in the sitting room and waded in.

'What on earth is going on with you and Dad? Luke told me he's moved out?'

'That's right.'

'Why on earth has he done that?'

Her mother gave a long, dramatic sigh. 'Your father is having an affair, darling. He's gone and shacked up… that's the phrase, isn't it?… with a younger woman.'

'You've got to be joking… you must have got it wrong. You're in your seventies, for god's sake. You've been married for over forty years.'

'Time counts for nothing, apparently. Not once the testosterone starts pumping.'

'Where did he meet this… this younger woman?'

'She's one of his pottery students.'

The idea of her father seducing some long-legged ingénue was incomprehensible to Eden.

'One of the girls from college?'

'No, of course not. Your father isn't a pervert. With someone from his evening class, one of his tertiary students. She's in her fifties.'

'Are you sure about this, Mum? You haven't put two and two together and made five?'

'I might be old, darling, but I'm not stupid. A wife can sense these things. I've seen that film.'

'What film?'

'That one with Demi thingy and Patrick Soiree.' Her mother's pronunciation of Swayze left Eden struggling to keep a straight face.

'I know the sort of thing that can happen when a man and a woman get together over a potter's wheel. Clay is a very sensual material.'

Eden couldn't help herself; she laughed out loud this time.

'I don't know what you find so funny; this is partly your fault.'

'My fault?' said Eden, stifling a guffaw.

'Well, from what I understand, you're the one who introduced them by getting that woman to sign up for his class.'

'Me?'

'Yes, you.'

'Hang on a minute, who exactly are we talking about here?'

'Agnes, that woman from your office. He's moved in with Agnes. There, you're not laughing now, are you?'

———

EDEN ARRIVED home in the dark in more ways than one. Her mother must have got her wires crossed. The idea of her father shacking up with Agnes was inconceivable. Then again, Agnes had upped her game recently with a new look, and she'd been uncharacteristically pleasant of late, which, given her performance since Eden took over the business, was suspicious for a start.

Could it be that she felt she had to mollify her because she was her father's daughter in a way she had never felt pressured to do when she was merely her boss?

What was her father thinking? There was no denying her mother had her faults. She'd be the first to admit she could be infuriating, but talk about out of the frying pan and into the fire. Agnes made her mum look like Mother Teresa. At least her mother was optimistic and charitable, whereas Agnes was prickly and loved to find fault. She appreciated it was not entirely her secretary's fault. From what she could gather, she'd been raised by an emotional vampire, a pathological pessimist who sucked the joy out of every pleasure. Maybe Agnes had decided to throw caution to the wind and make up for lost time?

By the time she got to the beach house, Eden was fuming. Her father had put her in an impossible situation. She was pretty sure having an affair with your boss's father was not a sackable offence, and raising the subject had its risks. She could hardly warn Agnes off. Her secretary might argue she had no alternative but to walk, and she could find herself at the end of a constructive dismissal claim. She decided to call her dad and talk some sense into him instead.

After three attempts going straight to answerphone, she left a voicemail for him to call back.

Retrieving one of the expensive bottles of red Tristan had brought with him for the weekend; she poured herself a large glass which she knocked back in one, partly because life was crap and partly because she knew it would annoy her ex no end if he could see her. Refilling her glass, she grabbed the Willis file and headed for the sofa, deciding work was a better option than trying to second-guess the motivations of the men in her life. Opening her laptop, she noticed she had an email from Claire, attaching a copy of the letter Beth intended to send to Savage. This thing was travelling at a pace. She'd better get on board, or she might be left behind.

She laid the contents of the file out on the table. It was subdivided into various witness statements, all handwritten by what looked like the same hand. It was not uncommon back then for the interviewing officer to make a contemporaneous note and then get a witness to sign. She had to keep reminding herself that 1984 was the year the Police and Criminal Evidence Act, more commonly referred to by the acronym PACE, came into force. Before then, taping interviews would not have been routine. No doubt, Devon and Cornwall Constabulary, like the rest of the forces in England and Wales, would have been coming to grips with the new codes of practice. The changes that came on the back of high-profile miscarriages of justice like the Birmingham Six and the Guildford Four and media exposés of widespread corruption in the Met changed policing forever. She remembered her criminal law lecturer at university getting very excited when telling them that prior to PACE, remaining silent could indicate guilt, admissions had not required corroborative evidence, and there had been no right to legal representation during interview. She imagined most police officers had to keep a copy handy for the first year or so and that a hard core clung to the good old days when they could act like they were in an episode of *The Sweeney* and get a pat on the back.

She tended to review every file from a defence lawyer's perspective, but that was hardly useful in this case, where there were no suspects other than the one who always came to mind when a woman went missing. Her husband. He, according to the file, had a cast iron alibi for the night of Suzanne's disappearance. She could see what Luke had meant when he said the police had met dead end after dead end.

Statements from neighbours and friends supported the impression she'd gathered from the newspaper cuttings kept by Willis. Nothing new to report here.

The most interesting thing about the investigation was Brian Willis's dogged persistence. He did not let the matter go. He had contacted the police almost daily for the first three months, then once a week and then, despite being told time and time again there were no new leads, once a month for two years. The poor man must have been in a desperate state.

There was no copy of the calendar or the guest list from the Green Shore on the file, which Eden found strange. Surely, as part of the investigation, the police would have wanted to know who Suzanne had been in contact with in the weeks before her disappearance, and that included the hotel guests. Of course, it could have been a matter of resources. A missing person case with no evidence of foul play had to fight for a place at the top of the list today when investigations benefitted from CCTV and computerised telephone, social security and banking records, all of which could reveal a person's location at the press of a button. Back then, the main weapon would have been door-to-door inquiries, costly and time-consuming. Dirty words to a superintendent with a budget to manage.

Her phone rang. She assumed it was her father ringing back, but it was Luke.

'Hi, how did you get on with your mum?' he asked.

'If I tell you something, do you promise not to laugh?' said Eden.

'What?'

'Promise,' Eden said.

'All right… ALRIGHT, I promise,' Luke said, already sounding too jovial for Eden's liking.

'I can't believe I'm saying this out loud,' said Eden, taking a deep breath. 'Dad is having an affair with Agnes.'

There was a burst of laughter at the other end of the phone.

'You promised,' reproached Eden.

'Yeah, but that was before I knew what you were going to say. I mean *Agnes*?' He began laughing again.

'It's not funny.'

'But it is, though. You've got to admit it… Agnes, are you sure?'

'According to Mum. He's moved out and she's convinced. I've tried calling him and he's not picking up.'

'Perhaps he's busy… getting jiggy.'

'Oh please,' said Eden 'I don't want to think about it.'

'Will you have to call her Mummy if they get married?' Luke snorted.

'That's it. I'm putting the phone down.'

'No, wait. I won't say anything else; I promise. Change of subject. Have you had a chance to read the file?'

'Just finished, for what it's worth. The investigation seems a bit half-hearted, to tell you the truth.'

'Yeah, that's what I thought. After I left you, I rang Jake Fairchild. I miss having him as custody sergeant. He's the font of all information on old cases. Since he's retired, I have to look things up. Anyway, I gave him a call, and he was happy to help. It seems half the force were away in Yorkshire or South Wales helping police the miners' strike in '84. Not that they were very effective, apparently. He said that a lot of the boys back then were ex-miners or the sons of them, and loyalties were split. The strikers called them daffodil soldiers because they wore yellow high-vis vests. First in the country, apparently.'

'It would explain why they didn't bother reviewing the guest list at the hotel where Suzanne worked. It would have been a mammoth task tracking down all those names from across the country. It's a shame, though. They might have cottoned on to Savage earlier if they had.'

'What guest list?'

Eden had assumed Ross had told him about the copy guest list.

'Brian Willis had a copy of the register among his personal files. Savage is on there. He stayed several times. Willis also had loads of newspaper cuttings about Savage after his arrest.'

'That's what Ross was referring to when he said your client's father thought Savage was involved.'

'Yes, I suppose he made the connection in '88 when Savage was caught. Anyone would.'

'But there's nothing on the file to indicate he shared his suspicions with the police.'

'I know, that's odd, don't you think? The obvious thing would have been to go to them armed with the copy guest list, assuming they'd interview Savage. They were the force in charge of the wider investigation. They would have jumped at the chance of yet another feather in their cap.'

'Why didn't he?' said Luke, the question hanging in the air.

'Unless he did and was ignored.'

'Again, why?'

'I don't know. All I know is that now Willis is dead, the only way to get to the truth is to hear it from the horse's mouth.'

'You mean Savage?'

'Ross plans to get Willis's daughter Beth to write Savage a heartfelt letter. If the response is favourable, Ross and Claire intend to interview him at Fenton.'

'No wonder the little sod was so excited last night. He would love to solve a murder the force missed.'

'You love him really,' said Eden. 'You wouldn't be so interested in watching what he's doing if you didn't.'

'I watch Ross the way I watch the monkeys at the zoo. I find them entertaining, but I know enough not to put my fingers in the cage.'

'So, do you still want to be kept in the loop?'

'Of course, the zoo's my favourite place, and who doesn't like the monkeys best?'

Chapter Twenty-Three

EDEN WAS NOT LOOKING FORWARD to facing Agnes that Monday morning. Whilst she was not convinced she was the scarlet woman in this melodrama, she was complicit in her silence. There had been plenty of opportunities for Agnes to take her to one side and say her father had moved in, but her secretary had said nothing. Could it be that she thought she already knew and had been waiting for her to raise the subject? It was a possibility. Either way, she would have to raise the issue with her today. Given her father had seemingly gone to ground, she would have to go around to Agnes's house and confront him. She could hardly do that without the woman's permission.

Her father had no business going rogue at his age. The implications were unthinkable, not only because his relationship with Agnes could topple the carefully constructed balance of her working relationship with the woman but also because, in his absence, she would be expected to carry the full weight of her mother's idiosyncratic ego. Thea may well have been the first to know about her parents' marital problems, but experience told Eden she'd be the last to volunteer to help.

Eden imagined her phone ringing every hour with requests from her mother for one thing or another as she staggered from crisis to crisis. She loved her, but god almighty, love had its limits. If this didn't get resolved soon, at best, it would play out like a P. G. Wodehouse farce and, at worst, like a Greek tragedy with a good deal of beating of breasts and gnashing of teeth. One way or another, she'd end up the villain. It was she who had commissioned the script to this drama by signing Agnes up for pottery lessons.

The morning was dismal, like her mood. She thought about Tristan and their pot-holed romance. She knew despite everything, she'd miss their weekends together and his daily calls. It would have been so much easier had their breakup happened in the summer. The clocks would go back soon, but it would do little to lift her spirits. There was no light to surf before or after her working day; its loss forcing her inside. This time of year, her evenings dragged.

Agnes was at her desk when she arrived, but there was no sign of Molly yet. Today, her secretary was wearing a green knitted dress with a colourful scarf jauntily tied at the neck. Eden glanced critically down at her own drab work-suit and thought she'd have to up her game if things carried on like this. She decided not to say anything about her father until she'd had the chance to raise the subject with Molly. Agnes was sure to have confided in her assistant, and Eden needed more information before she opened this can of worms.

When Molly arrived fifteen minutes later, she invited her into her office on the pretext of reviewing a file.

'What file do you want to look at?' said Molly chirpily as she entered Eden's room.

'Can you close the door? I need to talk about a private matter.'

Molly's brows furrowed into an uncharacteristic frown. 'You're not ill, are you?' she asked, her dark eyes bright with concern.

'No, nothing like that. It's about Agnes,' said Eden.

'Agnes?'

'Has she spoken to you about my dad?'

The girl's face flushed. 'You mean about him moving in with her?' she said.

'So, you do know,' said Eden, trying not to make it sound like an accusation.

'Yes,' said Molly sheepishly.

'Well then, perhaps you can tell me what's going on?'

'I know he's moved in and that Agnes is very worried about it.'

'Worried?' Eden said, raising her voice.

'Uncomfortable, I suppose that's a better word to describe how she feels.'

'Uncomfortable!'

Eden was annoyed that she seemed unable to string two words together, such was her irritation.

'Yes, with him being your father and you being her boss. She knows it's bound to upset someone.'

'She should have thought about that before she started the affair.'

'Affair?' said Molly, eyes widening. 'Gosh, no... you've got that wrong. Agnes and your dad aren't having an affair.'

'But... the fact he's moved in and the way she's changed her appearance and she's being so... well, unusually nice.'

'That's not because she's having an affair with your dad. Agnes *is* in a relationship, but it's with Hugh, the chap who lives next door. The one who bought the house from her friend Pinkie. He's the reason she's smartened herself up. She's being nice to you because she hopes you'll be able to help her get rid of your dad before he ruins everything.'

'How is he likely to ruin everything if he's not in a relationship with her?'

'Because he joins her and her gentleman friend for dinner every evening, and he's taken to playing chess with Hugh afterwards. This weekend, they're going fishing together, and they've started going to the pub on Friday evenings. Agnes feels she isn't getting a look in. To be honest, she's at her wits' end. No disrespect, but your father's hardly conventional, and he's driving her mad. She says he's untidy and she's sick to death of washing all his clay-covered overalls. He keeps telling her her meals are bland, and apparently, he objects to her not buying organic. He plays his music too loudly, he has holes in his socks and doesn't wear slippers. I could go on…'

'No, please don't,' said Eden, mortified that her father was being an almighty pain in the backside. 'Why did she let him move in in the first place?'

'Apparently, he told her he'd had a falling out with your mother and needed a place to stay for a couple of nights. She'd mentioned to him some time ago that she had a room to let to one of his college students, so she didn't have an excuse when he asked if he could stay.'

'Thanks for letting me know, Molly.'

'What are you going to do?'

'I'll have to go around there and talk to him.'

'It will be good to put Agnes's mind at rest. She's worried that if she turfs your dad out, he'll head next door, and she'll never get to spend time with Hugh on her own.'

'Don't worry. I'll sort it, I promise,' said Eden.

———

LATER THAT AFTERNOON, Eden took Agnes aside for a chat. The look of relief on her secretary's face told her everything Molly had said was spot on. She told her she'd leave early and catch her dad when he got home from college around four-thirty. That way, Agnes would not have to suffer the embarrassment of being there. Eden decided not to call her father first, in case he tried to avoid her. The look on his face when he answered the door suggested she'd made the right choice.

'Eden… I wasn't expecting to see you here.'

'Really… well, if you listened to your messages, you know I've been trying to get hold of you.'

'I've been rather busy.'

'So, I've heard. Are you going to invite me in?'

'Yes, of course,' her father said, holding open the door.

'Why are you here, Dad?'

'Your mother and I had a little disagreement, and we've decided to have some time out.'

'Time out for what?'

'Time to rethink our relationship.'

'Mum thinks you're having an affair with Agnes.'

Her father's face took on a blank expression. 'That's ridiculous.'

'What's she supposed to think when you've moved in with her?'

'Nothing… there's nothing to think. I'm renting a room from a friend, that's it.'

'A friend who thought you were only staying for a couple of days.'

'I am paying to stay here, you know.'

'That's hardly the point. You know that Agnes is conservative in her ways. She's bound to feel compromised having you as a lodger. I'm pretty sure that when she told you she had a room to rent for someone from the college, she didn't expect it to be you.'

Her father frowned.

'She never said. And I've become good friends with Hugh next door. He's surprisingly broad-minded for an ex-military man. We have some very enlightening conversations despite his questionable politics. He's not as opinionated as your mother.'

'That's another thing. Before you came along, Agnes and Hugh were getting together.'

'They're still getting together. He comes over for dinner regularly and to play chess with me.'

'By getting together, I mean romantically.'

'Oh…' he said. This was clearly a revelation to him.

'You are well and truly the third wheel, and neither one of them has the heart to tell you. Eden wasn't sure what Hugh's thoughts were on this, but she didn't want to give her father any wriggle room to manoeuvre himself under the poor man's roof the way Agnes feared. What's more, Mum is devastated. She misses you and Castro's pining.'

'Is he? Dear old Castro,' said her father, sniffing back a tear.

Eden rose from her seat. 'Time to go home, Dad. Whatever differences you and Mum have won't get sorted whilst you're here. Think of Flora. Think of Castro, and frankly, I can't be responsible for Mum. We'll kill each other.'

Her father walked towards her and gathered her into his arms.

'There… there. It's all right, I'll pack my bag. I wouldn't want to outstay my welcome, and truth be known, I miss my own cooking. Agnes is rather traditional when it comes to spice. I don't think the woman has the capacity to let rip.'

Eden knew Agnes would have a far better chance of spicing things up once her father moved out. As she bundled him and his possessions into the car, she felt a certain comfort in returning Castro's master to him and the realisation that whilst her own love life was dead in the water, for others, the promise of romance still held boundless possibilities. She had a feeling she'd made two old dogs very happy.

Chapter Twenty-Four

CLAIRE WATCHED Kelvin Harvey's van pull up as arranged on Tuesday morning. The vehicle was elaborately decorated. A leafy background with roses and daffodils sprouting from the wheel arches. She took a deep breath and headed for the door. The man walking up the garden path with a clipboard and an engaging smile was not the same creature the Henshaws talked about. Or rather, he was the man they described when they first met him before he turned into a manipulative stalker.

'Good morning, Mr Harvey,' said Claire. 'I spotted your van. Nice artwork.'

'Glad you like it,' he said, smile still intact, though Claire noticed it didn't quite extend to his eyes.

'After you,' he said, carefully wiping his feet on the mat before motioning her to lead the way. Well-practised tokens of respect, no doubt designed to win over his more manner-conscious elderly clients.

She wanted to start things in the sitting room where she

had placed the urn containing Honey's ashes on the mantlepiece.

'What a lovely room,' he said, scanning the artwork. 'Do you live here alone?'

'No, I live here with my aunt. She's at the daycare centre right now. Can I offer you coffee?'

'Not for me, thanks. I have a bottle of water in the van. I try to avoid stimulants.'

'Good for you,' Claire smiled, thinking, *no, you'd prefer to drive others to drink.*

She gestured to the sofa by the window, which faced the mantlepiece. She watched his eyes fix on the well-positioned urn, an expression bordering on funereal reverence sweeping across his face.

'I see you've spotted dear Honey,' she said, looking suitably moved. 'She's been there since she passed away last year, but we think it's time for a more suitable memorial for her. She wasn't a lap dog, you see. She was very much an outdoors girl. When we weren't out walking on the beach or in Idless Woods, she was out in the garden. We originally thought we might scatter her ashes around some of her favourite haunts, but we've got used to her being with us and don't think we could bear to let her go. It's a comfort having her around. That's what made us decide on a garden memorial. It seemed like fate when I saw your advert on your website.'

'It sounds like you had a wonderful friendship. I often think that the purest of all loves is that between man and his best friend,' he said sycophantically. 'Animals are so trusting. They give the kind of unconditional commitment you don't see among people these days.'

Claire almost laughed out loud. The man had a fawning, obsequious quality, unsettling in one so young. Whilst he looked like he'd walked straight off the set of a TV dating show, all bleached white teeth and shiny hair, there was something positively Dickensian about his mannerisms. She half expected that any moment he'd offer his *very 'umble opinion*.

'I've been looking through your brochure,' Claire said, resisting a shiver. 'I'm very impressed.'

'Thank you,' he said, preening.

'We've decided on something in marble, and I think it's important it's big enough to be able to take other pets in time should I choose to have them. My aunt is adamant that she wants no more, but I'm hoping to be able to talk her around. Right now, the loss is a little raw, but in due course, who knows.'

His face lit up with the mention of the words *marble* and *large*.

'My aunt and I would very much like to incorporate a portrait of Honey, just her head, but not a photograph, something more permanent like an etching. Less obvious, don't you think? Maybe in slate or bronze. Do you have someone who could do something like that?'

'Of course. I have any number of artisans I can call upon for special jobs, but these things do increase the cost, you understand?'

'Oh yes, but in this instance it's not so much about the cost, more the quality.'

Harvey shuffled in his seat.

Claire knew she was laying it on a bit thick, but she was enjoying controlling the little creep just like he'd enjoyed controlling the Henshaws. The difference was she was using the thrall of money rather than intimidation.

'Would you like to see the garden now?' she said. 'You probably need to measure up.'

'Of course,' he replied, rising from his seat, clipboard still gripped in his sweaty hands.

Claire led him through the kitchen and out through the patio doors into her pristine garden. His face dropped. She guessed he'd been hoping for the disarray of eccentricity.

'It's beautiful,' he said, his permanent smile stiffening a little.

'Yes, it is. It's such a shame our gardener has had to give up. I'm not sure what we'll do now. I do a bit myself, of course, when I can, but I'm not good with the heavy manual stuff.'

Nothing was further from the truth. Claire loved to get her hands dirty and was as good as anyone with a shovel and a pair of tree loppers. She knew in her heart she shouldn't be straying into helpless female mode. Ross had been worried Harvey would latch on to her the way he had to the Henshaw's granddaughter, but she was beginning to get into the role, and it was hard to pull back now she'd thrown herself into it, and what did it matter? It wasn't as if she was actually going to let him near her borders.

'You know I run a gardening business as well as the memorial side of things, don't you?'

'Really? That's very interesting,' she said, feigning ignorance.

'I'd love to get my hands on something like this,' he said, wandering along the pathway towards the greenhouse.

I bet you would, thought Claire.

'I have a horticultural degree, but usually, I'm stuck with mowing lawns and replanting pots as the seasons change. If I'm lucky, I get to prune a few roses. This… this,' he said, spinning around like a child in a playground, 'would look great on my website. I could see my socials going through the roof if I posted a video of this place.'

Claire imagined he had delusions of Gardeners' World-type weekly visits.

'Over there is where we'd like the memorial,' she said, bringing him back from la la land. 'It's a dark corner, I know, but the magnolia is beautiful in the spring, and I thought I could put a little bench under it so that my aunt and I could sit with Honey.'

'Yes,' he said, mind ticking as he whipped out his tape measure, 'and there's plenty of room for something quite spectacular,' he chortled. 'Maybe even a bed of violets around the bottom.'

Claire disliked violets and had none in her garden. They were melancholic, funeral little flowers that skulked in the darkest of corners. She understood why Harvey would choose them; they were like him. She preferred daffodils. Now there was a flower that celebrated life.

'Maybe a water feature, instead?'

'Yes, of course,' he replied, no doubt totting up the extra charges. 'Now, I just need to take a few measurements, if I may, and then I'll get some samples from the van so you can choose the marble.'

'Maybe we'll leave the samples for another day when my aunt is around. Honey was her dog, after all. Oh, and one other thing. It is our practice to always get references from tradesmen who work for us. I know it's rather old-fashioned, but my aunt insists. She always says that there is no better recommendation than a satisfied customer.'

Harvey's metal tape measure ricocheted back into its case.

'You don't mind, do you?' Claire asked, her face a picture of sincerity.

'No... no, of course not. I'll email you some details when I get back to the office.'

'And they won't mind me going over to their gardens to have a look at the monument in situ?'

He looked concerned at the prospect. 'I don't think there's any great need for that. I have photos.'

'Yes, but it's not the same as seeing something up close, is it, and this memorial is going to be a lot of money? I'm sure, given its size and our requirements, you can appreciate we need to be absolutely sure you are the right firm for the job.'

His expression darkened. 'Of course, I'm sure they won't mind. I'm assuming a couple of clients will do?'

'I was thinking more like three or four.'

'Three or four?' he said, his lip twisting with annoyance.

'Is that a problem?'

'No… it's fine,' he said sulkily.

'Good, then that's settled. I'll expect them later today.'

Claire was relieved. Everything had gone to plan.

———

FOUR NAMES CAME through by email as promised that evening. Claire had no doubt Harvey had cherry-picked the clients he'd given her to contact. She would lay money on it that they would respond with glowing references and an invite, but she had a plan of her own.

She saved the email and headed off to bed, giving a respectful pat to Honey's urn as she passed.

Chapter Twenty-Five

THE NEXT MORNING at around eleven o'clock, Claire took a chance and called Harvey's office.

'Arveys Orticultural Services,' announced the woman on the other end of the phone. The H drop was regrettable, given the name of the company, but it gave Claire hope that she might not be dealing with the sharpest tool in the shed.

'Good morning, I do hope you can help.'

Claire had rehearsed her fictitious aunt's cadence several times before calling, but when faced with the real deal, her voice seemed to have morphed into a mid-Atlantic accent somewhere between Downton Abbey dowager and Dolly Parton. She tried to pull it together.

'Mr Harvey met with my niece yesterday to measure for one of his lovely memorials and kindly emailed a list of his past customers so that we could contact them for references. I've been tasked with the job, but silly old fool that I am, I have managed to delete the email whilst trying to print it off. I know I should have waited for my niece to do it, but she's a busy girl, and I so wanted to speed things along. Would you be a dear and email the list through again?'

'I've not got access to Kelvin's emails, and he's out on a job most of the day.'

'Oh, that is a bother. It would be so nice to get things moving. You see, it's rather a big memorial we're thinking of, so the sooner we get the references, the sooner your boss will get his money. If only you could email me your customer list. We could get things moving.'

'Well, I suppose I could. He does like to get his deposits in promptly.'

'I cannot tell you how grateful I'd be, and Mr Harvey and my niece need never know. It'll be our little secret. What's your name, dear? I'd like to drop you off a box of chocolates for your trouble.'

'Darci, like the ballet dancer, only mine's got an *I* on the end of it, and *I* like soft centres,' the girl said.

'Thank you, Darci, you're a lifesaver.'

Claire immediately set to work ringing the numbers, beginning with the four Harvey had provided. As expected, they had nothing but praise for the man. According to them, he had been professional, considerate, on budget and excellent value for money. Five-star reviews all around. Claire didn't believe a word of it and was proved right when she began randomly phoning the numbers provided by Darci.

With these clients, it was a different story. Many were clearly upset to hear Harvey's name mentioned. They slammed down the phone or told her they didn't want to discuss the man with anyone. There was an element of fear in some of the voices that Claire found alarming, given most seemed to be of advanced years.

Much as she would have loved to press them in the hope

they might give up more information, she didn't have the heart to cause them additional distress. Furthermore, she didn't have time for persuasion. There was a chance Darci would spill the beans when Harvey got back to the office and Claire had no idea how he'd react.

After making half a dozen calls to people unwilling to engage, she finally struck gold.

Ralph Philpott told her, in no uncertain terms, that he thought Harvey was a conman and that he and his wife would be happy to elaborate if she would like to call on them. It was an offer Claire couldn't refuse.

The couple lived in Grampound, a picturesque village just outside Truro, and they were waiting for her when she arrived at their quaint thatched cottage opposite the village school. She was ushered into a low-beamed kitchen with a view across the village green. A fire was blazing.

'We've been waiting for someone to call about Kelvin Harvey for a long time,' said Ralph Philpott, nodding to his wife, Edna, to pour the tea.

Thinking they might think she was from trading standards or some consumer watchdog, Claire said, 'I'm sorry if I gave the wrong impression on the phone. I'm not on official business in that sense. I don't represent any government agency or anything like that. I'm a private investigator. My client has had dealings with Mr Harvey, and I'm trying to ascertain whether his bad behaviour is part of a pattern.'

'Don't worry, love, we've given up on that crowd and the police for that matter. No beggar wants to know these days. People like us are on our own.' Edna Philpott said. 'We thought when we saw you pull up, you were a bit young to be one of his victims. He likes the old crocks like us, who he thinks will be too scared to give him any grief.'

'My clients are elderly too,' Claire said. 'Their dealings

with him are on a slightly different footing, but I had an inkling he might have targeted people like them through his business.'

'You're right there. I'm pretty sure we're not the only ones. He as much told Ralph that when he went around to his office to complain. "You old timers never know when you're beaten," he had said.'

'Do you mind if I ask what your complaint was about?' said Claire.

Ralph Philpot took the lead. 'We wanted a memorial for our dog... something small and discreet, not showy but something to remember him by. Harvey measured up and gave a quote, which we agreed to. We liked him at first. He seemed genuine and wasn't shy of hard work. He told us he was a startup, and we were among his first customers. He said he hadn't been able to set up trade accounts yet, so he'd need money up front for materials. It seemed reasonable to us. We thought good on him for trying to make a go of it. We gave him the thousand pounds he asked for so he could order the stone.'

'Don't tell me, he took the money, and you didn't see hide nor hair of him again?'

'If only. Looking back, that would have been a good result.'

'So, what happened?' asked Claire, intrigued.

'He began removing vegetation in the corner where the memorial was to go, and we were pleased he was getting on with it while he was waiting for the stone to arrive. We had no complaints until the second day when he came in from the garden saying he had dug up something he believed was asbestos roofing from an old outbuilding. He said he'd fetched a sample and was taking it off to get it tested. He warned us that neither we nor anyone else should go near it.

He said he wouldn't be able to start work again until the tests were back and he was certain it was safe. About a week later, he told us the test was positive and that our garden was contaminated. He said it substantially devalued our property, and if the environmental agency got involved, they might insist we remove it at a cost of thousands and thousands of pounds. Well, you can imagine we were devastated, and when he offered to clear it at a cut price, we jumped at the offer.'

'How much?'

'Five thousand for cash. He said he had a team who would deal with it quickly, and no one would ever know.'

'You agreed?'

'We were too worried not to. This house is all we've got. When the time was right, our intention was to downsize and put the surplus in the bank to supplement our pensions and pay for our care. From what he said, we reckoned we'd have nothing spare. That's if we could sell the place at all.'

'So, did he come and take the asbestos away?'

'Yes, he came with a van and four men dressed up in hazmat suits and masks. They put the stuff in special sacks with a skull and crossbones on the side... you know, like you see on pesticides and such.'

Claire was pretty sure that if Harvey were licenced to remove contaminated waste, he'd be advertising it on his website.

'When did you become concerned things weren't as they seemed?'

'It was a little thing at first. Harvey told us he couldn't put the memorial where we wanted it and that he couldn't dig up anywhere else just in case he found more asbestos. He said that if the stuff remained intact underground, it had no danger, but if it was disturbed, it was deadly. We understood and said that was fine, and if he could just give us our money back for the stone, we'd call it quits. He said he couldn't do that because it was a non-refundable deposit. Well, we'd never agreed to that. You can imagine what with the five thousand, it had made a hefty dent in our savings.'

'Things got worse,' said Edna. 'It was my fault, really. I'd told my friend that we were having a memorial for our dog, and she asked how it was going. I confided in her. I said about the asbestos and what had happened, and she told her husband. He came round to see us and told us it was impossible for us to have asbestos because the gardens at the back of the cottages had been the same since the 1800s. He said the part of the garden in question had belonged to his granddad and his father before that. He said there had never been a building where Harvey had said because it was the exact position of an old oak tree lost in the 1987 storm. You know the one the weathermen missed? He took us out into the garden and dug. There were no buildings, no tiles, only old tree roots just like he said there would be.'

'Did you get your money back?' asked Claire.

'I confronted Harvey... said I knew it was a scam and that I'd report him. He said if I did, he'd tell the authorities I called him and asked him to remove asbestos illegally. I was so angry. I called his bluff and told him to do it. He got nasty then. He came round here and threatened us. He said we'd wake one night and find this place on fire, or if we didn't have asbestos now, he'd make damn sure we did have and dump some in the garden. He said if we wanted to sleep at night, we had better back off.'

'Peace of mind is worth more to us than the money,' said Edna.

'What if I were to find other elderly people like you who

he's conned? Would you be willing to take action against Harvey then?'

Ralph looked at Edna. 'I don't know. I suppose if there were more of us. There's strength in numbers, but surely Harvey's not stupid enough to be doing this regularly?'

'I'm sure he's not stupid at all,' said Claire. 'Ruthless, corrupt and morally redundant but not stupid. It's not right that this man has taken your savings and terrorised you. Are you happy if I come back to you if I find others?'

'Be careful, love. He's a nasty piece of work when you cross him. I'm not a cowardly man, but there's a vicious streak in him that scares the life out of me.'

'I'll be careful,' said Claire, her mind firmly fixed on calling all those customers who were reluctant to talk. When they answered, she'd have one word to say to them: asbestos.

Chapter Twenty-Six

THAT EVENING, Claire rang Ross and told him the news.

'I've called the other customers, the ones who blew me off earlier in the day. He did the same with all of them. He convinced them their land was contaminated, then fleeced them on the pretext of removing hazardous waste. In one case, he got inventive. He told the couple there was evidence of an uncapped mineshaft in their garden. He took ten grand off them to cap it.'

'No way,' said Ross.

'It goes to show you can fool a lot of the people a lot of the time, as long as those people are gullible and trusting.'

'Or you're brazen enough,' said Ross.

Ross knew from experience good thieves invariably had brass necks and that good liars always span an element of truth into their deceit. The county was riddled with uncharted mine shafts and sink holes, many of which were in people's back gardens. It was a miracle more didn't open up. It wouldn't be too hard to convince someone you discovered the makings of one and, knowing the impact it would have, talk them into a miracle cure.

'So, what now?' he asked.

'I've convinced the victims to club together and report the matter to the police. I'm also going to put them in touch with Eden so she can mount a civil suit for misrepresentation. Hopefully, they'll get their money back and damages.'

'I get that,' said Ross, 'and good for you, but how does all this help the Henshaws?'

Claire was temporarily thrown by the question.

'Well, I'm hoping that now all this other mud is being thrown at Harvey, the police will be less likely to dismiss the Henshaws' complaints. I'm hoping they'll view them as part and parcel of their investigation.'

'They might, but unlike Harvey's customers, they live next door to the man. I'm worried they're going to bear the brunt of all this. It's unlikely Harvey will be remanded on this type of charge, given prison overcrowding. He'll be released on bail, and he's not the type to forgive and forget. He's shrewd and resourceful. He's bound to put two and two together. It will eventually be revealed in disclosure before trial, that is if one of the victims or the police don't let it slip out before then. If he concludes that this all began with the Henshaws instructing us those poor people are going to suffer.'

Claire was crestfallen. Ross was right; she hadn't thought this through.

'What do you suggest?'

'Wearing my policeman's hat, I'd say go ahead and damn the consequences and hope at the end of the day the CPS run the case and get a conviction. But people keep reminding me I'm not a policeman anymore, and in this instance, caution may well be the better part of valour.'

'What do you mean?' asked Claire.

'I mean, the threat of reporting him might prove more potent than the reality. We should go and have a word with Kelvin Harvey. Tell him that if he doesn't pay the money back and stop what he's doing, including terrorising the Henshaws, we'll hand over the evidence we hold, including his client list, to enable the police to add more victims to the charge. We could also threaten to release the information to the media who would love to get their teeth into a story like this. We'll tell him he can forget his fancy website. His name and reputation will be in the mud where it belongs.'

Claire thought about it for a second. 'But aren't we concealing a crime?'

'We're being practical. If the man won't play ball, we go back to plan A and report it to the police. There's poetic justice using threatening behaviour on a man like Harvey, don't you think?'

'He who lives by the sword dies by the sword?' said Claire, as convinced as she'd ever be.

'Or the shovel, in this case. Let's bury the bastard.'

Chapter Twenty-Seven

HMP Fenton

NEVILLE SAVAGE SAT on the bed in his cell, staring at the letter he'd received from a woman called Beth Matthews.

He didn't get much post, not these days, not like when he was first convicted. Back then, he'd been inundated with mail. 'Like a bleeding pop star,' one of the screws had said, with more than a hint of disgust. He'd received bag loads of the stuff, mostly from sad middle-aged women claiming they understood or, in some cases, were in love with him. They'd confess they laid awake at night thinking about him making love to them, how he was their soulmate. The heavily redacted correspondence censured the salacious bits, forcing imagined depravities when the lights went out.

He could tell from reading between the blacked-out text the women often sent photographs, probably titty pics and more explicit poses featuring crotchless knickers and nipple clamps, neither of which was his thing. He assumed the guards confiscated these for their own personal use when they clocked off. He didn't care. Those horny bitches were far too promiscuous for his taste. He had always liked to be the one in charge in the bedroom.

As time passed and his notoriety waned, the letters got less and less and now, other than for a few die-hard groupies who sent him birthday and Christmas cards, his fan base had dwindled to zero.

When the guard had called his name the previous morning, his first thought was that it was bad news, like the time he got the letter from his wife telling him she was petitioning for divorce and wanted him to consent to a change of name for the kids. Imagine his surprise when the letter turned out to be from the daughter of a woman whose mother had disappeared forty years before, asking him if he knew anything about it. He had to admit it was a bold move. If you were a normal, well-rounded individual, writing to a convicted sex offender was risky business. You might end up getting more than you bargained for, especially if there was a chance the prisoner might be released, but he guessed Beth Matthews knew that wasn't on the cards in his case and perhaps her choices were limited.

Her letter, unlike those he'd received in Wakefield, had not been routinely censored. He could sense the desperation in every line. No doubt, she needed answers to move on with her life. The question was, what was in it for him?

His first inclination had been to bin the letter. He didn't need the aggro, but he'd slept on it and now, reading it again, he wondered whether to ignore it would be to miss an opportunity.

He'd spent years trying to get out of Wakefield, the category-A prison where he'd been banged up for the first thirty years of his life sentence. Request after request to be accepted as a volunteer for therapy at HMP Fenton had been turned down by the powers that be.

To be considered, you had to be suffering from something worth their study, an anti-social or psychotic personality. He'd ticked that box no problem, but the place also had a no drugs, no violence and no sex regime, and he had failed again and again because of the addiction he had developed to heroin on the inside, an addiction he had never dreamt of indulging in when he had lived out in the world where he'd needed for so many reasons to keep his wits about him. Boredom had driven him to it on the inside, that and the availability, but it had turned out to be the worst of traps; a prison within a prison and he'd known it would kill him sooner or later. Unless he could get out of the shithole they called Monster Mansions, he'd end up dead one way or another. If not the H, he'd be knifed or battered by some young gun wanting to build himself a reputation or get his name in the papers. It had happened to him before. He had pins in his jaw and a scar across his left cheek to prove it.

He had learnt the hard way. The word NONCE scrawled on the chalkboard outside his cell meant 'Not on Normal Courtyard Exercise' to the screws but something less benign to the rest of the prison population. Prison was about the pecking order. At the top were the career criminals, the armed robbers. Many of them had spent more time inside than out. Next came the gang members who'd stab someone to death for looking at them the wrong way, living in their own tribes, cooking in their cells like it was an Airbnb. Next, the petty thieves and dealers, and last of all, the sex offenders like him regarded as subhuman pond life.

Faced with the prospect of living in abject terror for the rest of his days, he had got clean, and his final application had been taken seriously. Even then, as well as the numerous random drug tests, he'd had to undergo psychological assessments and pass an IQ test to confirm he was intellectually capable of undergoing the Fenton therapy programme. He'd competed with any number of other inmates desperate to get out of Wakefield, most of them kiddie-fiddlers or rapists like him, routinely banged up in their cells for twenty hours a day for their own protection. Marked men whose lives were at risk every day they remained there.

He couldn't deny Fenton had been a culture shock at first. The fact that the screws called him by his Christian name had thrown him for a start, not to mention that during the induction process, all the prisoners, whether violent criminals or sex-offenders, were obliged to mix. They even ate together in the canteen without incident. It had been years since the authorities had thought that was a safe option at Wakefield. The thing that phased him the most, however, had been the therapy itself: the relentless obligation to meet in small groups and talk intimately about your crimes and, worse still, your feelings. This *sharing* was not optional. If you missed more than two sessions, you were in danger of being voted out of the prison by your fellow inmates. What's more, if your group thought you were hiding something or embellishing the truth to suit your needs, they took it as an insult, believing you were treating them like mugs and, once again, they'd throw you out. He had spent years lying and disguising his true feelings, and now he was required to spill his guts twice a week to people way more discerning than any detective he'd ever dealt with.

He had learnt that Fenton was no easy option but had accepted the regime up to the point where he'd divulged enough to keep everyone satisfied and had come to terms with feeling safe again. However, he knew that a problem was looming on the horizon. The average mainstream prison was a hellhole, and requests were coming in thick and fast from inmates wanting to transfer; all of them allegedly desperate to receive treatment and many of them guilty of crimes so heinous even he couldn't imagine. Other prisoners who had been with him since he'd arrived were being told they had progressed sufficiently to return to the mainstream system and if that were to happen to him, he knew with certainty it would be the end one way or another. He needed something to keep the psychiatrists interested, something to help him compete with all those new lab rats who frankly made him look like Micky Mouse. Maybe, just maybe, Beth Matthews had given him the chance to do just that. He picked up a pen and a sheet of cheap paper, not at all like the quality stuff Beth Mathews had used, and began to write.

After several attempts, he had something that captured the right tone. It sounded genuine and sympathetic, and more importantly, it would conjure more information. He read it back one more time before slipping it into the envelope addressed to Eden Gray's office.

Dear Beth

I hope you don't mind me calling you Beth. I would very much like it if you called me Neville. I feel it's only fitting if we are going to correspond. I am sorry to hear about your father. You obviously loved him very much. As you pointed out in your letter, I'm a father myself, but unfortunately, I haven't heard from or had contact with my daughters for many years. I don't even know where they are. I think that's why I found your letter so moving and why I would like to help you.

Through therapy I have learnt that my relationship with women may well have been determined in my childhood as a direct result of the trauma I suffered. Trauma not unlike that suffered by you. You see, like you, I lost my mother at a very early age. Unlike you, I did not have the support of a loving father to get me through it. My father was a violent and abusive man, and my mother and I were his victims. I am not excusing my own actions. I realise that they are inexcusable, but my therapists here have told me my father's treatment of me and the loss of my mother were triggers that led me down the path I took. My treatment here at Fenton has taught me to take ownership of my crimes and my impulses, but it has been a long and painful process. I've had to dig deep to discover events in my past that I have suppressed to the point I have not been aware of them before. I feel that if you were to send me some more information about your mother it might jog one of these buried memories and I might be able to help you. A photograph might help too. We all have our demons. Some can control theirs. Others, like me, cannot. But with your help, I might be able to release the last of mine.

Neville.

He knew that despite the lack of heavy-handed censorship at Fenton, the letter would be read by one or more of the prison personnel and that they would likely notify his therapist, Dr Mason, about this new spate of correspondence. Mason, in turn, would be preening himself, convinced all those years of navel-gazing had done the trick, and he was a reformed character. He'd be wetting his pants thinking there might be a new confession in the offing. Sooner rather than later, he would come calling. In short, his little note to Beth Matthews would place them exactly where he wanted them: in the palm of his hand.

Chapter Twenty-Eight

CLAIRE'S PHONE RANG.

'Claire, it's Beth. Eden's just emailed me a copy of a letter she's received from Savage.'

Claire had no idea why such a chill ran up her spine at the thought of it. They'd been hoping for it, after all. 'That's great news. What does he say?'

'I'll forward it to you, but the gist of it is he doesn't deny any knowledge. He seems quite reasonable but says he needs more information from me to help jog his memory. Would you help me write the next letter? I couldn't have put the last one together without you. It obviously hit the right note.'

'Of course,' replied Claire, imagining how cock-a-hoop Ross would be at the news Savage had taken the bait.

'I feel guilty feeling so excited,' said Beth. 'I really shouldn't because I know what it could mean, but I guess it's because, maybe, I'll get some answers.'

Claire wondered if Beth was mistaking stress for excitement. The symptoms might be the same, but the long-term effect was quite different.

'Once you've sent it through to me, Ross and I will put our thinking caps on. It's great news, Beth. Really, it is. But let's keep our heads, though, and not get too invested. It's still early days.'

'You're right, of course. I'll do my best,' said Beth. 'I'll wait to hear from you.'

'I promise we'll get back to you asap. I do appreciate we need to strike while the iron's hot. He'll be expecting you to get back to him quickly. Our plan was to make you look desperate, and desperate people don't sit around waiting for things to happen.'

Claire already had loads to do on the Harvey case. She needed to get all the statements she'd taken from his clients into a dossier to hand to him so he would be able to see that this was organised and not a haphazard attempt to make him toe the line. Ross probably wouldn't see the point of it. He would want to go in all guns blazing, accusations first, evidence later. It was a fundamental difference between them. His need to keep his opponent on the back foot, hers to lay her case on the table in black and white, ever the lawyer. At least this way, she could be seen to be doing her bit, and if the matter went further and the police or Eden had to take over, they'd have a head start with her file to hand.

She sensed Ross would want to go with her to confront Harvey but also knew with certainty that Savage's response would propel him to request a visit with the man, and it would take priority. That meant she'd have to confess she couldn't go with him. Something she dreaded doing.

Chapter Twenty-Nine

'WHAT DID you think of Savage's response?' asked Claire, looking up at Eden and Beth.

'I think it's *interesting*,' said Eden with less commitment than Claire would have hoped.

Claire had called the meeting so they could discuss their next steps. Eden had told her Luke had retrieved Suzanne Willis's file but that it contained no information about Savage. She also confessed she'd promised, by way of thanks, to keep Luke informed of progress. A detail she had yet to share with Ross.

'I suppose there is always a risk he might just be playing mind games like Ross said he might at the outset?' said Beth.

'I didn't want to get your hopes up, that's all. I'm amazed he's come back so quickly, ' said Ross, determined not to let the woman's concerns crush his enthusiasm.

'It's a long way from a confession, though,' said Eden.

'I worry that he's asking me for more information,' said Beth. 'I don't understand why he'd need more information if he was guilty. I know 1984 was a long time ago, but surely, he'd remember. I thought serial killers revelled in their crimes. Raping and murdering a woman is hardly commonplace.'

Claire didn't want to point out that history showed there were plenty of serial killers whose victims numbered so many they had great difficulty remembering them as individuals. 'I think we need to give him the benefit of the doubt and write again, revealing a little more. Not everything, but enough to reassure him he's calling the tune,' she suggested.

'I'm not sure there is an *everything* to reveal,' said Eden. 'The fact there is no mention of Savage in Suzanne's case file is a mystery. I can't fathom why Brian never shared the guest list with the police if he had his suspicions.'

'Maybe for the same reason he never shared it with me. Part of me wonders if he really wanted to know the truth,' said Beth.

Claire thought about Brian Willis, his days peppered with hope. Once he read about Savage and his terrible crimes and linked his name to the hotel guest list, that hope would have melted like snow, replaced by an unbearable anticipation of the worst news imaginable. Who wouldn't want to put that off? Who wouldn't rather settle for unrealistic wishing in preference to a horrific certainty?

'We could go on forever trying to guess why Brian didn't tell the police about Savage, and we can't go back and ask. It's all very well batting correspondence back and forth, but Savage is the only one who holds the answer, and he could decide to dump us at any time, leaving Beth with a big bill and nothing to show for it,' said Ross, his tone tinged with impatience.

'You're still keen to interview him, aren't you?' said Beth, a tremor in her voice.

'Yes, and the sooner the better,' said Ross.

Beth raked a shaking hand through her hair. 'I need your bathroom.'

'Of course,' said Claire. 'Would you like me to come with you?'

Beth batted her concerns away. 'Just point me in the right direction.'

'First left down the corridor,' said Claire, worried Beth's nerve was waning. 'I need to say something while she's out of the room,' she said once Beth had left. 'I won't be coming with you when you interview Savage.'

'You don't think it's the right thing to do?' scowled Ross.

'It's not that. I agree you need to do it.'

'Then what's the problem?' asked Ross, leaning forward and rubbing his forehead as if he felt a headache coming.

'It's me… I can't face going back inside a prison… not so soon after I've left one,' Claire blurted out, unable to meet his eye.

'I can understand the thought fills you with dread,' sympathised Eden. 'I can't imagine what it was like for you inside. If it was me, I wouldn't be racing back either.'

'I'll admit I'm disappointed. I thought it would be something for us to do together, but I'm fine about going on my own,' Ross soothed.

'Thank you,' said Claire. 'That means a lot to me.'

'I'd tag along, but my diary is stacked at the moment,' said Eden.

'What about Beth? Are you going to risk taking her with you?' said Claire, scanning the corridor for signs of Beth's return.

'Only if Savage insists. You can see the way she reacted just talking about it. I don't think it's a good idea. I want that man to have as little personal contact with her as possible,' said Ross.

Beth walked back into the room as Ross grabbed the bull by the horns.

'We've decided I'm going to see Savage on my own. The fewer distractions, the better. We think you should write him another letter requesting a visit with me. Other than that, the letter should give away as little as possible.'

'Should I give him Mum's name this time?' said Beth, relief flooding her face.

'No, I think maybe you could tell him where she lived. We know he was there; it's just a matter of whether he'll acknowledge that. We'll be able to tell a lot from his reaction to that one little bit of information. It's his time to talk.'

Beth turned to Claire. 'Will you help me?'

'Of course,' said Claire, only too happy to help in any way she could.

Chapter Thirty

HMP Fenton

THE LETTER WAS ADDRESSED *Dear Neville*. He was pleased Beth had taken note. It showed she was serious, as did the fact she had asked if he would be willing to agree to a visit from a man called Ross Trenear, the private detective she'd employed to investigate her mother's disappearance.

He was minded to say yes, confident that he could control the agenda, especially given that, as requested, Beth had provided him with more details about her mother's disappearance.

She still hadn't given him a name but had divulged that her mother had disappeared at night from West Cornwall. He could work with that. He knew the area well. Back in the day, he'd supplied several large independent toy shops in Truro, Falmouth and Penzance. He went through the letter again, this time with a highlighter, picking out the salient points he needed to remember.

He had bittersweet memories of the place. It was before

he started his enterprise in earnest. He had been just another salesman back then. He hadn't been married many years, and his daughter Marney was just four, her sister Gemma a babe in arms.

He had to admit his marriage had already begun to show signs of wear and tear. Working away made it difficult to sustain family life. Lindsay had to manage on her own with two young kids for most of the week and he had to put up with hours and hours of driving and nights on his own in dingy B&Bs. At least in Cornwall, there had always been a decent view out of his bedroom window, and out of season, he could stretch to a hotel room. The tourist industry delivered a steady stream of punters for the pubs and nightclubs, and he often visited one or other of them. He tended to stay in the same places, a couple of nights once a month, more frequently nearer Christmas, and he'd formed friendships with the regulars, enough to go for a drink at the end of the day. Most of the reps he met were looking for something, and if they were honest, they enjoyed being away from home during the week. It relieved the pressure of fatherhood and the monotony of married life. It gave them the opportunity to indulge in vices they would never have dreamt of indulging in nearer to home. Many had, what his father would have called, a 'bit on the side'. What harm did it do? What you don't know doesn't hurt you. Isn't that what they say?

Lindsay certainly never had to worry back then. Their marriage collapsed later when the police knocked on their door and found a young woman's body in their old Frigidaire. He shook the memories from his head, concentrating on the task in hand. He would need to play this carefully. The democratic system at Fenton had its drawbacks. It meant he had a lot more people to convince, and many of them were expert bullshit detectors. If they thought he was trying to steal an advantage, they'd kick back. Every member of his group had power over him. If they didn't believe his story, they could call him out on the lie, and if his explanation didn't impress, they'd call for a vote as to whether he should be thrown out for not showing the proper commitment to the therapy. If he failed that vote, they'd take it to the wing, and if he lost the community vote, it was all but a done deal, and the staff committee would vote the same way. Before he knew it, he'd be ghosted out of the place, back to Monster Mansions or, worse still, somewhere new like Whitemoor or Belmarsh. He couldn't have that. Confinement under rule 43 was a distant memory now and one he had no wish to reconnect with.

He had to convince his group. He had a good chance. He was brighter than most of them, and they generally listened to what he had to say. He'd been a salesman all his working life and damn good at it too. Living on commission instead of a decent basic wage meant you had to be. Hitting your targets meant the difference between a foreign holiday or a trip to Weston. If he could doorstep someone into buying double glazing or convince a shop owner last year's favourite toy was making a comeback, he could convince a motley crew of sensation seekers he had secrets.

The trick was not to be too eager but rather drop crumbs of information, knowing they'd follow them like greedy rooks. They'd all been there long enough to become amateur psychologists. The Fenton system required them to believe in therapy, and over time, they began to talk the lingo. If they thought he was hiding something, it was in their nature to try and winkle it out of him, or in true psychobabble speak, to force him to connect with his inner truth. If he played it right, they'd be all over it.

Boredom accounted for most of their enthusiasm. If you sat in a room with the same egomaniacs week after week while they talked about their crimes and their underlying reason for committing them, even the most colourful renditions became stale. When a new member arrived in the form of a transferred prisoner, they salivated at the prospect of fresh meat to the slaughter.

These men liked to talk and to listen. Many of them had lived secret lives shared only with a small ring of trusted, like-minded perverts. As a father, he detested those creeps, even the ones who had done nothing more than sit for hours staring at their laptop as they downloaded thousands upon thousands of disgusting images that would make a normal man with natural urges throw up. Having to listen to them talk about their childhoods, the routine beatings, and the father who buggered them on a regular basis was the worst thing about the programme. He often wanted to put them through the wall, but he knew he was expected to concentrate on his own journey rather than become obsessed with what others had done, and even a veiled threat of violence towards another inmate would see you voted out.

He knew that if an outsider sat in on one of their group meetings, they would be shocked beyond belief, listening to the gory details of the most heinous of crimes reeled off with about as much emotion as a shopping list. They probably wouldn't get past the introductions.

'Hello, my name is Neville. I'm a convicted murderer and serial rapist who viciously terrorised and raped fifteen women in their own homes without breaking a sweat. They would run screaming from the place. But the group were not so easily shocked. They were the stuff of people's nightmares, the Freddy Kruegers and the Michael Myers. What did they have to fear? Sitting in group, listening to each other's horror stories, was within their comfort zone and a happy alternative to the things they feared, like shit in their cornflakes or the liquid cosh.

He decided the first stage was to accept the visitor's request. That alone would be enough to keep those monitoring his mail interested. Then, in the next group meeting, he'd be uncharacteristically quiet, as if troubled by something... deeply troubled. That, along with the correspondence, would tickle his therapist's fancy. He would tell him about the letters and that he had accepted a request for a visit. He could drop the hint he had something to tell him, something he should have shared a long time ago. Something that had become dislodged since he had entered into correspondence with the daughter of a victim.

He had never lied in therapy. He had never even sugared the pill. He had been clear about the pleasure he got from holding women in a state of fear while he had sex with them. He never embellished his crimes or gave them a television thriller backdrop like some did. He told it like it was. He was glad he had because it meant that they would believe him, and then the fun would start.

Chapter Thirty-One

THE RED-BRICK BUILDING, with its terraced gardens set in the rolling Buckinghamshire countryside, retained much of the character of the stately home it had once been. If not for two rows of high barbed wire fencing, Ross might have reached for his National Trust members' badge as he entered the wrought iron gates.

He had been told that if the weather was good, there was a possibility Savage might request their interview take place in the grounds. Looking up at the lowering clouds, poised to deluge the place at any minute, Ross guessed that option was off the table. He braced himself for the smell of disinfectant and stale sweat he associated with jail.

He was greeted at security by a freckle-faced young man who, after taking his phone, showed him into a room decorated in tasteful pastel tones. The space was light and airy, and unlike any other prison he knew of, the multi-paned windows were bar-free. With its comfortable upholstery and large central coffee table, the place reminded him of a dentist's waiting room. It was a far cry from the tatty windowless interview rooms he'd had at the station with their bolted-down furniture and glitchy strip lighting. He noticed the monitor on the CCTV camera to his left. Guessing he might be filmed, he avoided becoming a sitting duck by skirting the room to inspect the impressive array of artwork adorning the walls which, according to the labels attached, was the work of the inmates.

He paused to study one particularly accomplished drawing of a man's head. The mask-like face had been peeled away in parts to reveal a boy, back against the wall, knees drawn up, head tucked in to make himself so small he might disappear. It reminded Ross of the images used in NSPCC adverts. Powerful stuff.

He started as the door opened behind him.

'I see you're admiring the men's work.'

Ross turned to face a middle-aged man casually dressed in chinos and an open-neck shirt. The lanyard around his neck told him this was a member of staff rather than Savage.

'Doctor Roger Mason,' he said, holding out his hand. 'I'm Neville's therapist.'

Ross reciprocated. 'These are very good,' Ross said, nodding towards the paintings.

'We have a department dedicated to art therapy, headed up by an artist in residence. It helps the men who find verbal expression difficult.

'Excellent,' said Ross, hoping he came across as suitably enlightened.

'I'll be sitting in on the meeting,' said Mason.

Ross realised he must have betrayed his concern with his expression, as the therapist added,

'There is nothing to worry about. Neville is no physical threat to you.'

No, thought Ross, *I'm not a woman.*

'My role is that of mediator. Our therapeutic programme is a process. Neville, like many prisoners here at Fenton, is a lifer. We're not looking to rehabilitate him with a view to introducing him back into society. Rather, we hope to introduce him to himself. Sometimes, it takes years to break down the walls men construct to avoid facing up to who they are and what they have done. You appreciate we cannot allow outsiders to unwittingly jeopardise that progress. If you or Neville feel uncomfortable at any time, I will stop the interview either for a time out or, if I feel that continuing would be detrimental to Neville's therapy, terminate the meeting. I hope that's clear?'

'Okay with me,' said Ross, sensing he had no option other than to agree.

'Good. Now that's settled,' said Mason, rising from his seat, 'I'll fetch Neville.'

Ross had to admit part of him was relieved to have someone else in the room when he met Savage and used the interlude to gather his thoughts. He and Claire had talked through their tactics. The aim was to ascertain how much Savage knew, and only if it was clear there was a reasonable possibility he was involved, reveal Suzanne's name and give him a copy of the missing person flyer released by the police in the months after she disappeared. Ross hoped this interview would lead to something more, but he had to be cautious, not least because he was spending his client's money.

The door opened and Savage sauntered in dressed in a crisp, pale blue shirt and jeans. This was another first for Ross. He was used to prisoners decked out in easy-wash tracksuits, not their own clothes. Savage was clean clean-shaven with none of the grey, doughy complexion of your average sun-starved lifer. His skin had the healthy glow of someone just back from a Mediterranean mini break. Physically fit and wiry, his grey hair was shaved close to his head. His dark brown eyes were clear and focused, giving no hint of drug-taking. He had no visible tattoos or wounds, although Ross noticed there was an old, silvered scar across his cheekbone.

Ross forced a smile. 'Thank you for agreeing to the visit,' he said.

He needed to reassure Savage, the serial rapist, was the one who held the power here and that he, the interviewer, was grateful for any scrap of information he could provide. It was an approach at odds with the mindset of an ex-policeman but necessary.

Savage sat with an ease that suggested he was an old hand at this. He seemed relaxed, his palms resting on his knees. He appeared not to notice the water machine gurgle as Mason poured them each a plastic cup of water. Ross wondered if he was so used to his therapist sitting in on his conversations the man had become a ghost.

Whilst Savage left his water untouched, Ross was grateful for the drink. His face felt unnaturally tight, and his top lip was sticking to his teeth.

'So, ex-inspector Trenear, what would you like to ask me?' said Savage, taking the trouble to emphasise the *ex*.

The man had obviously done his homework. Ross detected a faint hint of West Country burr when Savage said his name, but generally, his voice was as unruffled as his demeanour. Ross was not so composed. He would have felt more at home with a table's width between them and a police file to shuffle. He looked towards Mason for a nod of approval. The therapist sat, legs crossed, scribbling on a pad casually balanced on his lap. Ross had the distinct feeling he was the one under observation in this room. The go-ahead given, he began.

'You'll know from your correspondence with my client Beth Matthews that we are investigating the disappearance of her mother in 1984.'

'Yes, I've told Beth I'm willing to help if I can.'

'I suppose at first instance it would be helpful to know if you stayed in Falmouth that year, or any other for that matter?'

Ross already knew the answer. They had Green Shore's guestbook showing Savage had been a regular guest. The real question was whether he would admit to it.

'Yes, I was there a lot during the early eighties. I supplied several toy shops in the area. One larger retailer in Penryn was one of my best customers. I stayed in a variety of guesthouses over the years and visited a hotel overlooking the water just past the marina. I can't remember its name.'

'The Green Shore?' proffered Ross.

'Yes, that's it,' said Savage.

Ross felt a surge of excitement. 'Beth's mother worked at the hotel during that period.'

'She did?' said Savage, a flicker of curiosity sparking in his dark eyes.

'If I were to show you a photograph, do you think you might remember her?'

'I might,' replied the man.

Still remarkably cool, Ross thought, *if he did have something to do with this.* Ross reached into his inside pocket and retrieved the flyer, which he then carefully unfolded and spread out on the coffee table before pushing it towards Savage.

Savage gazed down at it for a second or two, then slowly... very slowly, he lifted one hand from his lap and, leaning forward, traced the contours of the woman's face with his index finger, lingering on her lips, his eyes never leaving the table.

'Suzanne,' he whispered.

Ross heard Mason shuffle in his seat. He himself could barely breathe.

'Suzanne,' Savage said again. Ross noticed the break in his voice and the tears in his eyes as he asked, 'Can I keep this?'

Ross knew that if he were still a policeman, he would have utilised this chink in the man's armour. He would have banged on the table and badgered his suspect in the hope of prompting a confession, but he wasn't, and he couldn't. All he could do was say, 'Yes'.

Mason rose from his seat, and Savage followed suit, taking the flyer with him.

Ross got up, intent on stopping him from leaving so soon, but Mason intervened and blocked his way. Ross managed to force his card in the therapist's hand, not knowing if he would keep it or bin it after this fiasco.

Fingers on the door handle, Savage turned and said, 'Tell Beth I will be in touch.'

Ross was left alone in the room, frustrated and confused, until the same young man who had greeted him on his arrival returned to hand over his phone and let him out.

What an unmitigated disaster that had been. He had spent less than twenty minutes with Savage, but it had been one of the most intense twenty minutes of his life.

Why on earth had he handed over the flyer so soon? Come to think of it, why had he handed it over at all? Yes, he'd felt shivers down his spine when Savage ran his fingers around Suzanne Willis's face and said her name. Why wouldn't he? It was dramatic, not to mention fucking creepy, but it wasn't a revelation. Suzanne's name was right there in black and white printed on the flyer below the word 'MISSING'. Savage had only to read it. The man had given him nothing, whereas he had given him Suzanne's name and description in a handy foldable format. God only knew what he intended to do with it.

He was glad he hadn't allowed Beth to talk him into letting her come with him to the meeting and that Claire had opted out. Given Savage's reaction to the photo, he could only hazard a guess how he'd react to a real live woman. The man obviously had a screw loose. He didn't know why he should be so surprised at that. From what he'd read, it was a prerequisite for getting into the place. He supposed he'd been thrown because he looked so... well, normal. He wasn't naïve. He knew your average pervert wasn't the guy sitting in the back of the bus with the lascivious grin and dirty raincoat. He'd been a policeman long enough not to judge a book by its cover, but he'd never seen anyone transform so quickly.

It was four o'clock. Had it been earlier, he would have been minded to drive back to Cornwall, but whilst he longed for the comfort of his own bed and Karenza by his side, he was deflated and embarrassed. He'd hoped to return triumphant, having pocketed a confession. What had he been thinking? That lot inside that prison were in a different league. They had endured years of interrogation dressed up as therapy. He was well and truly the provincial rookie. He'd limp home with his tail between his legs tomorrow morning. For now, all he wanted was a shower and a pint. He started up the engine and tapped the address of the pub where he was staying that night into the satnav.

Chapter Thirty-Two

PRIVACY WAS an elusive commodity in Fenton, but following his meeting with Ross Trenear, Neville Savage needed it. Ignoring requests from his therapist for a 'meaningful chat', he retreated to his cell where he lay on his bed facing the wall, Suzanne's photo clasped in his hand.

Seeing her face again after all these years had felt like a punch to the stomach. It had never crossed his mind that Beth Matthews was Suzanne's daughter. It changed everything.

He had been so sure he could manipulate the agenda to his own ends. How wrong he had been. The news brought a confluence of agony and ecstasy he could barely handle, and now, as he looked at Suzanne's lovely face, every detail flooded back. The softness of her hair, the taste of her skin, the pounding pleasure as he entered her. It had been the pivotal moment of his life. It had coloured everything then and since.

He had always stood by his mistakes and learned from them, but he had never been in the dark in this way before.

He'd always believed he knew all there was to know about the shit storm that was his life. He had taken responsibility for his actions and attached blame to those who deserved it, like his drunken, no-mark father and Suzanne. The knowledge that he had been wrong and that the truth had taken him forty years to discover filled him with anger and regret.

His heart was racing. He must be having a panic attack. He'd seen men have them over the years, often with damn good cause, but had no idea it felt like this, as if his chest were in a vice. He felt nauseous and closed his eyes, desperate to stop the room spinning and the ringing in his ears, but she was still there, branded on his retinas, hair falling over her face like a shroud. Judging him. He realised now she had never left him. She inundated every fibre of his being, condemning him for what he had done and the blame he had levelled at her.

He lay like that for hours, feigning illness when the bell rang for the evening meal.

His blankets held all the comfort of the cold earth as he tried to drift off to sleep. He distracted himself by playing back the meeting in his head to distil how much Ross Trenear knew. He wished he hadn't reacted so impulsively when he'd seen Suzanne's face staring at him from the flyer, but he hadn't been able to help himself. It had been such a shock. She had been the catalyst. She was the one. His face wet with tears, he buried his head in his pillow.

He woke early the next morning, sure of one thing. The only way he could regain control of this story was to place himself well and truly in the centre of it. He had to be the narrator, and like all good storytellers, the tale had to begin with 'once upon a time'. He knew exactly where he would find a willing audience, and after breakfast, he headed for Dr Mason's office.

As expected, his therapist was pleased to see him.

'Neville, how are you this morning? I heard you were unwell yesterday evening?' he said, his face a picture a contrived concern.

'Not so good to tell you the truth.'

Mason pushed aside the file he had been working on. 'And is this to do with your meeting yesterday?' he asked, leaning forward, hands steepled in front of him on his desk.

'Yes,' said Savage, looking down at his own fidgety fingers. A manifestation of angst he was sure Mason would pick up on.

'Do you want to talk about it?'

'I think I need to get something off my chest,' Savage replied, meeting the therapist's eye for the first time.

'And is this something to do with Suzanne Willis?'

'Yes.'

Mason leaned back in his chair, a smug look on his face. 'I know the woman's name was on the piece of paper Trenear gave you, but from your reaction, I'm guessing you knew Suzanne.'

'I did,' said Savage calmly, despite the knife in his gut every time the man mentioned her name.

'How?' said Mason, clearly pleased he'd guessed correctly.

'I met her at the hotel where she worked.'

'And?' said Mason, a begrudged smile failing to conceal his impatience.

'I took a fancy to her.'

'When you say *took a fancy*, are you saying that you—'

Savage didn't let him finish. 'Yes.'

'Let's be clear here, Neville. Are you telling me Suzanne was one of your victims?'

'I'm telling you Suzanne was the one who started it all.'

Mason rocked back in his seat, head tilting backwards, eyes fixed on the ceiling.

Savage held his breath, not knowing what to expect. Then, as if he had just watched his favourite team score a goal at a football match, the therapist gave a whoop and banged both hands down hard on the table.

'Neville, this is a meteoric breakthrough. This could be the key for you.'

Savage said nothing. Mason was doing a very good job of filling in the gaps without his help.

'When do you want to go to group with this?' asked the therapist. His face flushed with anticipation.

Savage shrugged. 'I think I should tell Beth Matthews first and the police, of course.'

Mason was on his feet now, hands on his hips, pacing.

'I suppose so,' he said, raising one hand to rub the back of his neck, 'but once they get hold of this, they'll lose sight of your needs, Neville. It will be all about the victim.'

Savage stiffened. As far as he was concerned, it *was* all about the victim.

Mason continued. 'Here at Fenton, our primary concern is you and what this means for the therapy programme. You coming clean to your group could help all those other men with their journeys.'

Savage didn't give a fish's tit about those other men's journeys. Neither did Mason. He could read this man like a book. Mason was wondering how he could buy sufficient time to gather enough material for a scientific paper in some psychology journal before he shopped him to the police. He'd want to add the group's reactions to that report. Without the final pieces of the jigsaw, his paper would fall short on the benefits of group therapy.

'How about we call group right now?' Mason said excitedly.

'There's a session booked for tomorrow. They'll be involved in activities today,' said Savage, feeling he needed more time to prepare.

'True, but with the governor's permission, I can override that. These are exceptional circumstances,' he said, licking his lips.

'Okay, but I insist on one thing. You ring Ross Trenear and invite him to sit in on the session.'

'He may well have gone back to Cornwall, and in any case, do you think that's wise after what I've just said?' parried Mason.

'I don't care if it's wise or not. It's what I want, and don't try and trick me with excuses that he's not around. I don't care if he's gone back to Cornwall or Timbuktu for that matter. I want him here. No Trenear, no session.'

Mason moved behind Neville and squeezed him on the shoulder.

'Very well, leave it to me. This is an amazing thing you are about to do. It shows that all your hard work in therapy has paid dividends,' he said, patting Savage on the back as he steered him towards the door.

Chapter Thirty-Three

BY MID-DAY, Neville Savage was sitting in a therapy session orchestrated by Mason. Present were the other members of his group, Mason and, by special demand, Ross.

Ross guessed that, unlike him, the men sitting patiently in a circle had an inkling of what was about to go down because as he scanned the room, he noticed all eyes were on Savage. He had woken that morning expecting to have breakfast in the bar, where he'd spent most of the previous evening drowning his sorrows, and then head back to Cornwall. Instead, he had received an urgent text from Mason saying it was vital to his ongoing investigation that he return to Fenton later that morning. He had immediately rang Karenza to tell her he'd be home later than expected.

'Why do they want you back?' she'd asked, a silent *what have you done now?* implied by her tone.

'No idea, but it'd better be good whatever it is. That place gives me the creeps and I've got no wish to go back.'

MASON GREETED him at reception but was careful not to divulge anything other than he had called an emergency therapy session and that everything would become clear there. The man was buoyed up with anticipation and it made Ross nervous, but he'd promised himself he'd keep his head this time.

Mason opened the session. 'Group, this is Ross. He is an ex-detective inspector, but let's not hold that against him. He is now a private investigator. He will be sitting in on the session today, which has been called because Neville wishes to share something with you. I appreciate some of you have given up your free time and missed out on hobbies or classes, but rest assured, you will have time allocated to catch up, and I am certain you will find this a valuable experience.'

Ross noticed a few grumbles but not what he would call mass dissension from the gathering.

'Before we begin, I feel that introductions are appropriate. Ross has already met Neville, so I think we should start with you, Ian,' Mason said, nodding to a man to the left of Savage, sitting legs splayed.

'My name is Ian. I'm a convicted paedophile serving consecutive sentences for the rape of my ex-girlfriend's daughters aged twelve and nine.'

For a moment, Ross wondered whether he was the butt of a sick joke, until the man next to Ian, a burly brute with full sleeve and neck tattoos, which from a distance looked to Ross like a navy-blue rash-vest under his T-shirt, joined in.

'My name is Jason, serving life for the rape and murder of my seventy-year-old next-door neighbour.'

A toxic cocktail of emotions spiked through Ross. Horror, revulsion, loathing, to name but a few, but the overwhelming one was fear. He had an irresistible urge to run.

Being locked in a room with these men with no boundaries, no moral compass, was something you couldn't prepare for. He braced himself but could not steady the involuntary jiggle of his left leg or quell the beginnings of a nauseous headache. As the next man spoke, his stomach fell like a stone.

'Alan,' he said, in a heavy Brummie accent. 'I'm a serial stalker, serving time for the kidnap and torture of a thirty-two-year-old mother and her two kids.'

One by one, the group laid out their litany of evil as if disclosing their hobbies in a speed dating session. They hailed from every region of the country. An exclusive club of the worst miscreants

gathered under one roof. Ross wondered what the people who lived close to Fenton felt about that.

He tried to drown out the men's voices as images of his own family swamped his thoughts. He imagined the lives these men had destroyed. Parents, children, husbands. Young women who would never trust another man. All those lives and for what? To satisfy their sick sexual quirks.

He'd had colleagues who had served in vice or child protection and wondered how they coped. How did they go home every evening to the wife and kids and not think about this stuff? He had the luxury of knowing these men were behind bars. God only knew how he would feel if he was trying to lock one of the bastards away. He guessed the only way was to detach, to immerse himself in thoughts of the mundane. The drive home, what Karenza might cook for dinner.

He was catapulted back into the room by Mason's voice.

'So, there we have it. I dare say Ross has tried his best to assimilate the information you've provided. Now it's down to you, Neville. This meeting has been called because you have something to share with the group.'

Ross wasn't sure he wanted to hear any more of this. He'd been disappointed yesterday when he'd come away with nothing, but what could be worse than delving into the souls of demons? He had no idea what Savage was going to say or how it might impact Beth.

He wondered what purpose these men served in a world already stacked high with misery. He had never been an advocate for capital punishment, but as he looked around the room with its pale blue carpet and pristine paint work, he wondered how much money this freak show was costing and how it would be better spent trying to rebuild the lives these monsters had ruined. If he had a choice, he'd exit this hellhole now before Savage opened his mouth, but he couldn't. He owed it to Beth to stay and listen to whatever he had to say.

'I know that some of you are pissed off about being called to this meeting on a recreation day and that you'd like me to cut to the chase so that you can get back to what you were doing,' Savage began. 'But, if we believe any of this therapy shit, we have to believe each of us has a story worth telling that goes beyond the atrocities we have committed. If we are nothing more than our crimes, what the fuck are we doing here? They might as well string us up here and now.'

My sentiments exactly, thought Ross.

'Trust me, my story is worth your time. It doesn't start with my abused childhood or my drug addiction. My story starts with a woman called Suzanne Willis. I'm going to tell you that story on the condition you don't interrupt me. I know we all have equal standing here, and I accept you have the right to interrogate me, but please... please, wait 'til I've finished.'

There was a rumble of agreement around the room.

'That goes for you too,' he said, looking at Ross. 'And you, Mason.'

'We agree,' said Mason, speaking for both.

'You're all familiar with my crimes. What's more, I know because of your own histories that you, unlike them outside, understand what I got from it beyond the sex. The psychologists here say rape is all about power. And they're right up to a point, but us lot know what it's really about. It's about women, or in my case, one woman. We fool ourselves we're in control, but it's them who have the real power.'

Ross listened, thinking *here we go again. Tired old rhetoric by tired old misogynists, peddled these days to a whole new generation of isolated youths listening to podcasts by creeps like this who the law hadn't caught up with yet.*

Savage continued. 'It's not that women *do* anything or ask for it. That's a sorry excuse. What I did to those women I did because I could, and it made me feel good. For one precious moment, I could recapture the feeling I had with Suzanne.'

Some of the men were shuffling in their seats as if they wanted to say something. Ross guessed Savage sensed this too as he cut to the chase.

'We all have different reasons why we rape and kill. My reason was Suzanne Willis. Every woman I raped became her in my mind. Every throat I squeezed was Suzanne's throat.'

Ross sat bolt upright in his seat, listening intently. The man was admitting he'd had contact with Suzanne. He noticed the wistful look on Savage's face every time he said her name. Ross reminded himself it meant nothing. The man was a fiend, incapable of real emotions.

'I first met her when I was a guest at the hotel in Falmouth where she worked. She was hard to ignore. No disrespect to my wife, Lindsay. She was a good wife and a great mum. Pretty too, in her way, but she was never what you'd call a stunner. Not like Suzanne. Suzanne lit up a room. A knockout figure and long dark hair and those eyes… the type that keep laughing even when the smile has faded. She was kind and friendly and there was chemistry right from the start. You know what I mean: flirtatious banter, stolen looks. We connected. Nothing was ever too much trouble for her. She made me feel special. On the days she was on duty, I left that place each morning feeling like I could sell anything. I started thinking about her more and more in between visits and looked forward to the Cornish trips. Eventually, I plucked up the courage and asked one of the waitresses who worked at the hotel where she lived. She told me she was married, had a kid and lived in Flushing, the village directly across the water from the hotel. After that, I spent every night looking out of my window, wondering which house was hers. I arranged my trips to Falmouth to coincide with the days she usually worked. When she was there, I felt totally happy in a way I'd never felt happy before. Not as a kid… not ever. If she wasn't there for some reason, because she'd changed her shifts or had taken a day off, I'd get anxious, wondering why she was avoiding me. I knew I was becoming infatuated, but I couldn't help it. I was smitten.'

Ross noted a couple of the men nodding along as Savage spoke. He himself was transfixed.

'One morning, I met her in the corridor. She stumbled and dropped the menus. I helped her pick them up and our hands touched. It was like a bolt of lightning. That's when I sensed the danger. I told myself we were both married, and this could come to nothing. I tried to put her out of my mind, even going to the extent of swapping my sales area with a colleague so I didn't have to go to Falmouth. But ultimately, I needed the commission, so I started up again, avoiding the hotel. Then, by chance that September, I saw her in one of the shops I supplied. A big old toy shop in Penryn on the outskirts of Falmouth that stocked everything. She was with her daughter. I was in the back office with the owner and watched her from the doorway. The way she kept the little girl close to her, like something precious, never taking her eyes off her as the kid walked along the shelves, pointing out the toys she'd like for her birthday. "You can make a list," Suzanne said, "but remember, you can only have one thing. You'll have to wait for Christmas for the others, so make sure you put your favourite at the top." I remember thinking as I looked at Suzanne, *you're at the top of my list.*'

Savage's romantic prelude sickened Ross. The rapist could polish the turd all he liked, but in the end, it was still a turd. He now knew the reason he was here and the ending to this story.

'I followed her home that day,' continued the dreamy-eyed Savage. 'I took the ferry across to Flushing. She didn't see me. The boat was full, and I kept my back to her. I watched her go into the house and the lights go on. I saw her sitting in the living room with her daughter, her arms around her, watching telly. It looked so natural... so cosy, like something off the top of a biscuit tin. I wanted to be there with them, to be part of their life. That night, back in the hotel, I tried to think up a way of meeting her again, and I thought about the little girl. I knew about kids, especially girls. I had two of my own. I knew what they liked and remembered what the child had been looking at that day and how Suzanne had directed her away as if she knew she couldn't afford it. If I could help her to give her little girl the thing she wanted, she would know I wasn't an ordinary sort of man; that I was special. The kind who, if she were to make a life with me, would give her and her daughter everything they deserved. I didn't think about my own wife. I didn't think about my kids. In my mind, they were my past. All I wanted was Suzanne, and the child was the way to her heart.'

Ross was certain Beth would be devastated to know that, in one way or another, she had played a part in Savage's plans for her mother.

The man unfolded his fixation as the group sat in silence. Ross scanned the faces for signs of the disgust curdling in his gut but could see none. This warped fairytale was familiar to these men. Many of them had lived it; others wished they had. He imagined the mention of a kid had raised the excitement level for some in the room, and his skin crawled.

'The next morning, I booked out of my B&B and into the hotel, hoping she would be there, and I was lucky. I told her I'd seen her in the toy shop with her little girl and that I'd noticed she liked the Care Bears. She said she liked a lot of things and couldn't have them all. I told her I could get her the bear. It would be a sample, and she could have it free of charge. It was the first time I used that lure, but you all know, not the last.'

Ross noticed a look of mutual understanding pass around the group as Savage referred to the stalking tactic employed to target his later victims.

'When she said she couldn't take it for free and must

give me something for it, I said maybe she would have a drink in the bar with me after work one evening. I could see she wasn't sure, so I mentioned Lindsay and how I missed her and the girls when I was away, and that seemed to reassure her that I wasn't on the make, that I was trustworthy. I didn't push it, but the next time I was in Falmouth, I asked again, and she agreed but said not at the hotel. I must admit that gave me hope. It meant she wanted privacy.'

Although Ross appreciated why he was there and what was to be expected, given the man's history, he did not relish what was coming. He had heard confessions of violence towards women many times before. The capacity of some men to violate and abuse in the most brutal of ways the people they claimed to love had always left him bewildered and fearful for the women in his life. It was one of the things he had hoped to leave behind with the job. Yet, here he was, sitting in a room of such men, hoping for a confession. He felt a swell of self-reproof, bile rising sour and bitter in the back of his throat at his hypocrisy.

'I took her to a bar and gave her the toy I'd promised. She was thrilled. She called her little girl Byrdie, and I said it was a cute name for a cute kid. I told her the Christmas brochures and samples of all the newest toys would be arriving from the manufacturers soon if she wanted something special for her. She was delighted and so grateful. She had one drink and left, but I knew it was the start of something. I felt it in every bone of my body, and from then on, every waking moment was taken up with how I could change my life to be with her. I thought of going to a solicitor about a divorce, thinking if I told Suzanne how I felt and I intended to leave Lindsay for her, she'd understand how much she meant to me.'

Deluded stalker logic, thought Ross.

'Other times, I'd worry that if I divorced, I'd have no money, and Suzanne wouldn't want a man who couldn't support her and her child. To be honest, I even thought of ways to get rid of Lindsay. Faking an accident or suicide, but then I thought of my girls. I was a mess. Finally, I worked it out. Plenty of men lead double lives, so why not me? I could shelve the decision for a time. Let it work itself out and in the meantime, have Lindsay and the girls in Taunton and Suzanne in Cornwall.'

Ross had no idea where this was going, but despite himself, he was intrigued. This was not what he had expected.

'I was due to visit in early October and decided not to book the hotel or the B&B. Instead, I rented a ground-floor flat on the other side of town. Once I'd unpacked, I headed up to the Green Shore. Suzanne was on the front desk. I think she was relieved I wasn't staying at the hotel when I told her about the flat. Fraternising with the guests, although it went on, was frowned upon by her manager, and I guessed she was finding it hard to hide her feelings for me from those around her.'

Dream on, thought Ross.

'I asked her if she was having a party for her little girl's birthday. She said she was and couldn't wait to see her face when she unwrapped the Care Bear. I said I had that Christmas brochure I'd told her about if she was still interested. She asked if she could borrow it, but I said it was the only one I had, and the manufacturers took a dim view of information getting out about their products before launch. Bullshit of course, but she fell for it. I said I was out and about selling the following morning but could meet her early afternoon, and she agreed. I didn't like lying to her, but I knew if I rushed in, revealed my plans for her, she might be scared off.'

No shit, thought Ross, glancing at Mason, hoping to see a half-normal reaction, but the man sat blank-faced, chewing his biro.

'We met for a drink in a pub Suzanne suggested called the Cutty Sark.'

Ross knew the old Georgian pub overlooking the harbour. Back in the eighties, it would have been frequented by locals, whereas these days, like many others, it had been revamped and now operated like a small hotel. It had been a strange choice for Suzanne if she wanted somewhere private. She would have been known there. Maybe it was an indication she had not trusted Savage as much as he'd thought she had.

'We had a couple of drinks. She asked about Lindsay and the kids. The jukebox was playing, and we talked about the music we liked and what we enjoyed doing in our spare time. Things were going well, I thought, until she suddenly said she needed to get home and asked to look at the brochure I'd promised to show her. I'd half hoped she'd forgotten about it. I said I'd left it back at the flat and that we could go back together to fetch it, but she wouldn't, no matter what I said to try and persuade her. She said she had to go and thought it was best if we left separately. I guess it was because she knew too many people there. She'd said hello to a couple when we came in and the barmaid knew what she drank. I was pissed off. I couldn't understand why she'd chosen the place and led me on if all she wanted was the damn brochure. I had splashed out on the flat. I had a bunch of flowers and a bottle of wine cooling in the fridge, and there she was, ditching me without giving me a chance to tell her my plans for us, but what choice did I have? I let her go.'

Savage sat back in his seat, head bowed.

'I ran back to the flat, got the brochure and took the next ferry to Flushing. When I knocked on the door, she was surprised I knew where she lived.'

I bet she was, thought Ross.

'I held up the brochure and she invited me in. There was none of the tension like in the pub when there were other people around. She picked out the toy she wanted. Teddy Ruxpur, the talking teddy bear. It would be one of our best sellers the following year. She apologised for running out earlier, and while she made a cup of tea, I made a note of the number from the telephone in the hall. I thought when she sat down, I'd open the discussion about my plans, but some old biddy called. She didn't answer the door, and the woman left, but Suzanne's mood changed, and she insisted I went out the back way in case she was still hanging around. As it turned out, that was the best bit about that day because as we said goodbye, I took my chance and went with my instincts, knowing I couldn't let the moment pass. I grabbed her around the waist and kissed her, and I could tell she enjoyed it, even though she acted all coy. You can imagine I was on cloud nine. I knew sooner or later we'd be together. We'd have to be careful. We wouldn't be able to meet at the hotel or that pub she'd taken me to. I decided next time I'd book the flat again. At least there, we'd have privacy. I longed to make love to her. I fantasised about it all the time. How we'd undress each other, then sip champagne in the bath. You know, like in the films. I bought candles and silk sheets. You must understand, this was a love affair, not just sex.'

Ross wondered if the other men in the room believed

that or whether, like him, they were imagining Suzanne wiping her mouth in disgust as soon as the man left her doorstep.

'I didn't see her for a few weeks after that, and it was hell. I was busy with this and that, and me and the family had a holiday booked in the Canaries over half-term. I couldn't wait to get back to Cornwall to see her. I tried ringing but didn't get through, and sent her a postcard but wasn't sure she got it. I was careful what I said. I didn't want her husband to cotton on to us.'

Mason interrupted. 'This might be a good time to take a short break, don't you think, Neville?'

The therapist sounded uncharacteristically anxious.

Savage's face reddened, eyes glaring. 'I fucking said I wanted no interruptions, didn't I?' he snapped. 'We agreed as a group and when we agree as a group, we stick to it. Isn't that what you're always telling us, Mason, or is that rule just for the likes of us and not for you?'

Mason, who had risen from his seat, abruptly sat back down.

No one else said a word, and Ross guessed they had just seen the other side of Savage. A side those in the room knew well and feared. The one his victims had seen.

'I apologise, Neville. Please continue,' said Mason.

'That evening, my first night back in Cornwall, I'd worked out that her husband was on nights and waited for him to leave for work, before moving my car to the lane at the back of the house. I knew Suzanne would want me to be discreet. I clocked movement behind the blind in the kitchen, someone at the sink. I guessed it was her and that she was alone apart from the kid, who I knew slept in the back and whose curtains were pulled. My guts were churning, but I managed to paste on a smile before I knocked on the door. She answered right away. She was in a jumper and jeans. I'd only ever seen her dressed up until then... you know, made-up, hair done, but she looked even more beautiful with none of it. My mouth was as dry as sandpaper. I could hardly spit out the words. "I would have rung ahead." I said, "but you haven't been answering my calls." "No," she said. Nothing else, just that... no explanation, no nothing. "Can I come in?" I said, feeling a right numpty, standing there in the rain. I couldn't work it out. What was wrong with her? Why was she being so standoffish? Our kiss in that very spot had been the start of something. I felt it then and still felt it. So, I couldn't understand why she was treating me like a stranger. Then it suddenly struck me. She was probably mad at me for going off on holiday with the wife. Sending her that postcard had been like rubbing salt in the wound. She was miffed, and her attitude was down to jealousy. "What are you doing here?" she said, all tense and tight-lipped.

'I didn't know what to say. I thought it was obvious. I wanted to see her, and I'd expected she'd want to see me too. It crossed my mind that I was coming empty-handed. I should have bought her some perfume at the duty-free, but surely she understood that Lindsay would have spotted it. "I've brought the present you wanted, and I've got a boot full of other stuff you might be interested in for Christmas presents," I blurted out. She seemed to relax a bit then. She smiled and said, "That's good of you." "I don't mean to be funny," I said, "but it's brass monkeys out here." She seemed to wake up then, and I thought everything was going to be alright after all. I can tell you I was getting a bit pissed off by this time. "I need to get my coat," she said, heading away from me towards the hall. I realised she meant to come and have a look in the boot. It was like she was already trying to get rid of me. I'd imagined we'd fall into each other's arms and kiss like before, but here she was, giving me the cold shoulder. As soon as her back was turned, I locked the back door behind us.'

Ross felt a wave of revulsion as he began to glue the pieces together.

'I followed her into the hall as she pulled her coat from the hook and began to slip it on. "Will a cheque be okay if I see anything I like?" she asked. That hurt... that really hurt. I didn't want her bloody money. She knew that. "What's the hurry?" I said, moving in closer and reaching to tuck a piece of her hair behind her ear. She flinched and backed away, and that shocked me I can tell you. She was making a show of herself, trembling and making excuses, but funnily enough, it only made me want her even more. I grabbed her and pulled her in real close. I was hard, and she was struggling, but the more she fought, the more aroused I became.'

Ross noticed several of the men in the group lean forward, their eyes firmly fixed on Savage as if they knew he was finally getting to the juicy stuff as far as they were concerned. Ross felt the opposite.

"My daughter's upstairs. She might hear us," she said. As if I didn't know she had a daughter. "We don't want to wake Byrdie, do we?" I said. "Let's stop this nonsense and go upstairs. I'll be quiet as a mouse, I promise."

Ross imagined the mounting terror Suzanne felt with the mention of her daughter's name and the awful realisation of the man's intentions.

'I slipped her coat from her shoulders and led her towards the stairs. She stumbled on the first step, and I had to steady her. I had no idea why she was so reluctant. I half wondered if she and her husband didn't do it anymore, and

I'd caught her on the hop. I know women like to prepare, you know, shower and shave their legs. I didn't care about any of that, not with her. I loved her, no matter what. I couldn't understand why she would think anything different.'

Ross could feel a tightness growing in his chest. He wanted to get up and punch Savage's lights out just to relieve the tension.

'In the bedroom, I told her to undress. She was so slow... taking ages to take off her top and her jeans, then her bra and pants and all the time looking at the door, as if she was expecting someone to come in.'

More likely looking to see how she could escape, thought Ross.

'I noticed she was trembling and wouldn't look me in the eye as I slipped off my clothes. It was endearing how nervous she was. Anyone would have thought it was her first time.'

Ross clenched his fist.

'I took her in my arms and started kissing her. Her neck, her breasts. She was so beautiful. It wasn't ideal, you can imagine. It would have been so much easier had she come to my flat. She was tense. I could feel it as I reached between her legs. I think she was worried the girl would hear us. I pushed her down onto the bed. "Please, wait," she said. "I want you to wear protection." That's the kind of woman she was, always thinking of others. She knew it would only make things harder for both of us if she got pregnant. Lindsay would have hit the roof. I was a bit ashamed I hadn't thought about it too and brought something with me, but I'd assumed she was on the pill like Lindsay. "Have you got something?" I asked. She reached into the bedside drawer and pulled out a condom.'

232

Ross imagined her terror and the thought of falling pregnant by the man intent on raping her.

"You put it on," I said. 'To tell you the truth, I was a bit rusty. It was years since I'd used one, and didn't want to cock it up, so to speak. Mind you, her hands were shaking too when she slipped it on. You can imagine I was fit to burst by then.'

Ross couldn't bear the way the men smirked at Savage's pun. The way they seemed to revel in what they must know was Suzanne Willis's rape.

'I'm not going to go into the ins and outs of how we did it or what it was like. Gentlemen don't tell. Suffice to say it has never been bettered. Afterwards, I ran a bath for her and bathed her. I could tell she was as stunned as me about the whole thing and what it meant for us, how we had sealed our future. It was like a dream come true for me. I could have stayed there like that with her forever, but the phone rang, and the spell was broken. She told me I had to leave. She said her husband that he sometimes rang in his break, and if she didn't answer, he'd know something was wrong. So, I did as she said and left.'

Savage fell silent, and it took a good minute or more for the room to sense he had finished his story. It was safe to speak without incurring the sharp end of his tongue.

As expected, it was Mason who took the plunge. 'Thank you, Neville. Most enlightening. I am sure that Ross and the group are grateful for your sincerity and courage in sharing this. I am not sure whether there is time for questions, unfortunately. I imagine Ross is on a tight schedule and will want to get back to Cornwall this evening. The rest of us can pick this up tomorrow at our next session.'

Ross had no wish to leave at the expense of being able to cross-examine Savage. The M5 wasn't going anywhere.

He was relieved when the inmate who had introduced himself as Alan, piped up.

'I think we'd rather discuss this now, eh, boys?'

The room reverberated with the group's agreement, and Mason waved a limp-handed gesture of dispensation. Ross was itching to speak but, feeling the weight of the peer pressure in the room decided to hold fire until the men had butchered their pound of flesh.

'Let's cut the bullshit, Nev. All that lovey-dovey stuff is window dressing. Don't get me wrong, we all do it. I'm a master of it, for fuck's sake. I stalked my victims, thinking we had something going on, but it was fantasy. Therapy has shown me that. All I'm saying is it's disingenuous of you to dress this up when you've had a go at me in the past for doing the same thing.'

'That was different. You hadn't even spoken to your victims. You followed them from a distance. Any relationship you had with them was in your head,' countered Savage.

'They knew I was there. They enjoyed the game as much as me.'

Ross felt deeply uncomfortable.

'They enjoyed the game so much they reported you to the police for stalking, you dumb bastard. The fact the plod didn't take them seriously wasn't an indication the women liked it,' gloated Savage.

There was a ripple of accord from the group, and Alan's face dropped. It was clear to Ross that Savage was treated with a good deal of deference. His opinion counted here. It made questioning him in front of the group even more problematic, but he had to agree with Alan. Savage had raped Suzanne whether he realised it or not. It was abundantly clear he misread the signs as much as Alan had with the women he stalked. Suzanne, like all of Savage's subsequent victims had complied only because she feared for the safety of her and her child. She had not consented to sex with the man. The fact he knew her was neither here nor there. It was rape. The real question was what happened afterwards? Were they supposed to believe that he left her as he said? That he never saw her again? If that was true, his investigation was far from over. Where was Suzanne? He had to say something.

'Thank you, Neville, for being so forthcoming. I have only one question and it stems directly from your account of the relationship you had with Suzanne. You say you left Suzanne there in the house. Is that the last time you saw her?'

Savage looked him in the eye. 'Yes.'

'You see, that's where I'm struggling. If you had the kind of relationship you say you had with Suzanne, surely you would have contacted her the next day to check she was okay?'

'I didn't think it was appropriate.'

'That didn't seem to worry you before. You'd taken her for drinks, sent her postcards, phoned her at home. You'd planned liaisons in a flat you'd hired specifically for the purpose of sleeping with her. You'd followed her home on at least two occasions. You'd even thought of ways to get rid of your wife so you could be with her. You were a married man. She was a married woman. None of this was *appropriate*, was it, Neville? So why suddenly, after you'd slept with her, did contact seem *inappropriate*?'

Savage said nothing.

'He's got a point, Nev,' piped up the scouser whose

name Ross had forgotten but whose crime was indelibly fixed in his mind.

'I thought she'd need time to process things,' said Savage.

'What things?' said Ross.

'Us… where we were going from there.'

'How long did you imagine she'd need for that?' questioned Ross, determined not to let the man off the hook.

'I don't know, a couple of days… a week maybe?'

'So why didn't you ring her after that?'

'I don't know. I just didn't.'

'It's because you knew,' said Alan, emboldened by Ross's interrogation. 'Her behaving strangely was her not consenting. You knew you'd raped her, and if you pushed your luck, she'd call the police.'

'You're talking out your ass,' sniped Savage.

'Can we please remain civil?' said Mason from the sidelines.

'I've had enough of this,' muttered Savage, his lip curled in disdain.

'Thank you everyone,' said Mason abruptly.

Ross knew he had to nail this now. He might not get another chance.

'Did you really leave her, Neville, or did you take her with you? Did you misread the signs, and the whole thing went wrong like with Melanie Rowse?'

Savage's eyes narrowed to slits. 'Alright. I can see with hindsight, now I know the legal test that this could technically be categorised as rape. But I can tell you straight, it didn't feel like the ones that came after and, like I fucking told you, I left her there in the bath.'

Ross could see Mason out of the corner of his eye,

casting a warning scowl in his direction. He took the hint and backed off.

The others in the room did the same.

And that was it. They were dismissed.

Chapter Thirty-Four

'I WONDER if you could spare me a moment before you leave?' said Mason as they exited the room.

Ross's blood had run cold during Savage's revelation and during the so-called group session following it. He wanted to get out of this mad house, get to his phone and call Luke. He knew there was no danger to the public, but nevertheless, there had to be justice. Savage had confessed to rape in the presence of witnesses. He didn't need a psychological analysis by the men in white coats to know that much. Reluctantly, he followed Mason along the corridor to his office.

The large room had a traditional vibe completely at odds with the modernity of the place they'd just left. Mason positioned himself behind a highly polished mahogany desk and gestured for Ross to sit opposite. To the doctor's left was a floor-to-ceiling bookcase stacked with volumes on criminal psychology, biographies of various serial killers and leather-bound legal volumes, whilst to his right was a Victorian fireplace hung with framed certificates and photographs of Mason shaking hands with various dignitaries, including government ministers and at least one director of public prosecutions Ross recognised. Clearly, modesty was not one of Mason's virtues.

'I imagine that wasn't quite what you expected?' Mason said.

'I'm not sure what I expected, to be honest,' Ross replied.

'I thought we should debrief,' said Mason.

Who the hell does this prick think he is? thought Ross.

'I didn't want you to leave here with the wrong impression.'

'I'm sorry?' said Ross. 'I don't follow. Are you saying Savage was lying in there?'

'Not lying... well, not intentionally. I'm certain that much of what he said was true. However, you must understand Neville's condition renders him prone to hyperbole.'

Ross felt like saying *what condition are we talking about here: rapist or murdering bastard?*

'Neville is a fantasist and much of what he told us has the hallmarks of erotomania. He was likely reading stuff into things that weren't there. Interpreting every small gesture of kindness as a secret communication meant only for him.'

'What bits were delusional?' said Ross.

'His perceived romantic relationship with Suzanne Willis, for one. It is likely he was imagining emotional ties that didn't exist.'

'Let's get this straight,' said Ross. 'Are you saying you don't believe he raped and potentially killed her?'

Mason rocked back in his expensive leather chair, his

finger pressed to his lip. Every action contrived. 'Yes... and no,' he drawled, in a cut glass accent Ross couldn't decide was genuine or for effect. 'I think, on balance he raped her and, with careful therapy, may admit to more. That's why I need your reassurance you will be discreet with the information he divulged.'

'Discreet?' asked Ross, unable to hide his confusion.

'It's important we follow certain protocols.'

'What protocols?'

'My job is to protect the integrity of this institution and the programmes we run here. You were invited as a guest. You are no longer a policeman, and therefore, you did not attend in a formal capacity. You have no corroborative evidence to support Neville's confession. What's more, it was not made under caution, and real or not, it is inadmissible in a court of law.'

Ross looked at the law books on the shelf and felt a wave of disgust.

'Hang on a minute,' said Ross. 'I don't care what bullshit label you choose to fasten to this place, be it therapeutic community or hospital for the criminally confused for that fucking matter, the sign outside says HMP Fenton. This is a prison, and your job is to keep the lunatics from taking over the asylum. I'd suggest that includes shopping them when they admit to committing a crime.'

'A rather simplistic view,' said Mason, batting Ross's arguments away. 'I need to consult the board and the Home Office. Until then, I require your reassurance that you will allow me time to do just that before you tell your client. We don't want the press getting hold of this until we have all our ducks in a row, and I'm sure you appreciate that Savage's rather romanticised interpretation of his relationship with Suzanne Willis muddies the waters somewhat for the authorities. Surely *your job* is to protect Suzanne Willis's family from allegations that she might have in some way encouraged Neville's attentions or worse still, consented to sex with him, and this was a sex act that got out of hand.'

Mason was right, of course. The press would vilify Suzanne just as they had Savage's wife. Suzanne's murder, if Savage ever chose to admit to it, would become a crime of passion. All of this would have been collateral damage if he'd still been in the force. But now, first and foremost, his duty was to his client.

'You're not saying you expect me to forget about his confession and let him get away with this?' said Ross.

'No, of course not. Neville has confessed to the rape of Suzanne Willis. That's not something easily ignored. I am merely asking you to withhold the information about his relationship with the woman. That information is of little importance to the authorities but of great importance to my research and the long-term viability of this institution.'

'Even if I agree, how are you going to stop the other inmates from telling?'

'Leave that to me. We have a code here built on trust. If broken there are consequences. Every one of those men is aware of that, as is Neville. There will be no further confessions from him for the time being without my approval. The police will have to rely on what you have to build their case.'

'But they will insist on re-interviewing him. The woman disappeared the night he raped her. The two incidents must be linked. The inference is he killed her, and there is a very real chance that if questioned by the authorities, he'll admit to it the way he did with his previous victim. If he talks about Suzanne in his statement, the way he did today, it's bound to leak to the media.'

'By then, I will have put that element into context. I would have given my report and written my paper and diagnosed Neville's erotomania as something he needed to justify his future crimes. It will be of enormous interest to my fellow practitioners and of course, give credibility to this institution. We will be seen to have delved to the bottom of the man's psyche through therapy rather than punishment. In doing that, we will help hundreds of other institutions around the world understand the motivations of men such as Neville. Do you not think that is more important than you relaying what is a questionable truth to the daughter of that poor woman? Do you think it'll serve any purpose for her to know her mother was the catalyst to the pain and suffering of all those victims who came after her?'

Ross didn't know what to say. He detested this man almost as much as he detested the inmates he treated, but he couldn't fault his logic even if his motives were self-serving. He felt he had no alternative but to acquiesce. He would not tell Beth about Savage's romantic delusions about her mother. What's more, he wouldn't tell Luke, Claire or Eden. He would keep that part of the story to himself. If he didn't, he was afraid the whole confession would melt away before his eyes. Mason would spin this to suit his needs, and there was not a damn thing he could do about it.

HIS LEGS WERE wobbly on the walk back to the car. Savage had raped Suzanne, but what had happened to her afterwards? He was stewing with rage and frustration as he drove out of the gates.

He waited until he was well clear of the prison before he pulled over for the postmortem.

He could not get the images Savage had imprinted out of his mind. Suzanne had silently endured her ordeal in order to protect her child. He imagined her naked and broken as he walked her to the bathroom to suffer yet further humiliation, her sitting in the water, petrified as he washed away the evidence under the pretext of tenderness. Savage had repaid every shred of kindness she'd shown him with brutality dressed up as love.

He had been careful not to betray his inner thoughts to Mason, but there was another explanation for Suzanne's disappearance other than her murder. Suzanne could have taken her own life. The scenario had never been looked at because no one knew of her rape, but it was possible. She was not to blame, but that may not have been how things were perceived by the police and the community back in 1984. She had known Savage and invited him in. She would have been disbelieved by many and bad-mouthed by some in the small community she called home. If the Crown Prosecution Service chose to charge her attacker and it was a big *if,* she'd have suffered the horror of facing Savage in court and humiliation in the witness box. Infamy and shame would have infected her life and the lives of those she loved.

Was it beyond the realms of belief that someone brave and selfless like Suzanne Willis would sacrifice herself to save her husband and child from that? She had lived by the sea all her life. She would know the channels and tides, where to go and how not to be found. Ross knew about suicide. His best friend, John Taylor, had taken his life when desperation propelled him to a place where he felt there was no other option. He had chosen the sea as his final resting place, and Ross knew if he was ever driven to that point, he'd do the same.

He felt the sting of tears as his heart caught in his throat before escaping in a string of body-racking sobs he could not seem to stop. The amassed horrors of the day hit him all at once, and there was no escape from his feelings. Pity for Suzanne, loathing for the men inside those walls, and shame for occupying a world where they existed.

Chapter Thirty-Five

'FIRSTLY NEVILLE, may I commend you on the extreme candour you have shown thus far in confessing to the rape of the woman you say was your first victim?' Mason had summoned his patient to his office the minute he was satisfied Ross Trenear was clear of the building.

'It's not what I say. It's the truth,' said Savage, his tone truculent.

'Yes, yes, I'm sure. You were brave confronting what must have been a painful realisation, given you seem to have convinced yourself you were in a romantic relationship with this woman.'

'Suzanne,' Neville said. 'Her name was Suzanne.'

'Suzanne, yes, of course,' said Mason, noting Savage's use of the past tense with a frisson of excitement he hid well.

'So, what happens now?' asked Savage. 'I suppose you'll have to alert the authorities, and they'll charge me. I'm assuming, as I'm confessing, there will be no need for a trial. I'll be sentenced in my absence, and I imagine you'll need to have some one-to-ones with me, but other than that, nothing will change. I'll serve any additional sentence here at Fenton.'

'Ah well, not necessarily,' said Mason.

'What do you mean?'

'That may not be possible. I'm sure you and your fellow residents are aware there is increasing demand for places here at Fenton. Times have changed. Crimes that were once rare are now commonplace. It may be that they are reported more readily by victims who feel they will be treated sensitively by the police or that, generally, society has become increasingly violent. At the risk of sounding crass, rapes are two-a-penny and less compelling than they once were in the face of allegations of organised child abuse by the church or celebrities. Then there are the acts of terrorism committed by seemingly integrated individuals influenced by the ideology of radical religious or political groups. All these people need to be studied. Society demands we find solutions and how are we going to do that by locking these criminals up in the mainstream system? The answer is we are not. The government is turning to places like Fenton and professionals like me to give insight into what makes an otherwise normal individual raised in the west leave home one morning to commit jihad.'

'Are you telling me that despite my confession, there's a possibility I might be transferred?'

'I'm afraid it's more than a possibility; it is highly likely. Not to worry, though, most cater for some form of therapy these days, so you will not be without help of sorts, albeit of a sporadic and rather pedestrian nature. There is little to be done, I'm afraid. Had you confessed to Suzanne Willis's murder, it might have been a different story.'

'What are you saying?' said Savage.

'Isn't it obvious? You've already been convicted of one murder, and we once believed there was a high probability with the appropriate therapy, you might be triggered into remembering more. A confession of murder would be seen as a breakthrough. You'd be a potential serial killer, and we all know they warrant priority. Serial killers are the criminal crème de la crème. You'd rise to the top of the pile.'

Savage shuffled in his seat. 'You're saying that if I confess to killing Suzanne, I could stay here indefinitely?'

'Now, Neville, please let's not put words in my mouth. We are talking hypothetically here. You did not kill Suzanne, so the question doesn't arise. You had nothing to do with her disappearance.'

'But I did,' mumbled Savage.

'I'm sorry?'

'I did. I didn't leave her in the bath. I killed her.'

'How do I know you're not just saying this in the hope of securing your place here?'

'I'm telling you I killed her, goddamn it. I strangled her and put her in the boot of my car.'

'I'm afraid the authorities will need a little more than that, as will I if I'm to recommend you stay here indefinitely.'

'Alright, alright,' Savage stuttered. 'I'll tell you everything.'

Savage's whole body trembled as he rubbed his hand over his closely shaven head and looked Mason in the eye. 'I killed Suzanne. What's more, I can show the police where her body is buried.'

Chapter Thirty-Six

ROSS RECEIVED the call from Mason the next day.

'I have news.'

Ross braced himself for the worst that Savage had retracted everything he had said the day before.

'I have met privately with Neville, and after some gentle persuasion on my part, he has authorised me to say he is willing to endorse in writing the statement he made to you in the group session. The information about his personal relationship with Suzanne will be excluded, as I previously advised. Is that understood?'

'You're saying he's willing to confess to raping Suzanne?'

Mason hesitated. 'I am, and there is more. He has confessed to her murder and offered to assist with the recovery of her body.'

Ross could hardly believe his ears. He had driven home to Cornwall with a creeping certainty that Savage had been telling the truth about leaving Suzanne following the rape.

'Where is she?'

'Bodmin Moor. He thinks he will be able to guide the police to the place where he buried her.'

'Fuck.'

'Quite,' said Mason.

'Have the authorities sanctioned it?'

'I've spoken to the Home Office, and they have confirmed that provided adequate security is in place and the area to be searched is sectioned off from the public, they agree. The press will have no access, and there can only be limited contact with Neville, who must always be accompanied by at least two security guards.'

'Have they notified the local police?'

'You mean your ex-colleagues? Not as yet. I thought you might like to do that. I assumed it would give you a good deal of satisfaction. If that's not the case, I'm happy to go through the usual official channels from the outset.'

Ross resented the man trying to psychoanalyse him but had to admit he was right. It would be deeply satisfying to break the news to Luke.

'I would suggest everything is organised quickly given the time of year. The weather conditions on the moor could prove problematic once we enter the winter months. I'm sure Suzanne's family will not want to wait until next year. Also, I would like to restart intensive therapy with Neville as soon as possible. I wouldn't want that to be delayed by future unscheduled interruptions.'

Only Mason could describe a police search for a body as an unscheduled interruption. Nevertheless, Ross had to accept he was relying on the therapist's goodwill.

'Okay, I'll make contact. Should they approach you directly after that?'

'I think so, don't you? Much as they might appreciate

your input, I don't anticipate them seeing you taking a major role from here on in.'

Ross had no intention of giving Mason the satisfaction by rising to the bait despite his putdown hitting home. He finished the conversation and immediately rang Luke. He told Luke about the interview with Savage, his confession, and his latest conversation with Mason before finally revealing the bombshell that he had agreed to lead them to Suzanne's grave.

'You have been a busy boy,' said Luke.

'To be honest, it's a relief to tell you. It would have been beyond my pay grade when I was on the force, let alone as a civilian. I'm happy to hand this over. I only have one request.'

'Go on then,' said Luke.

'I want to attend the search, and I'd like the agency to get a mention when this is released to the press. Claire and I could do with the publicity.'

'I think the chief constable will agree to the first, especially if I can sell it on the basis you're accompanying the victim's daughter. I'll appoint Denise as the family liaison officer. He'll insist we have one of ours on the inside, but you two can work together, I'm sure. I've got no control over the latter, but I'm hardly going to deny your involvement, and I'm sure the press will be delighted to run the story. Retired detective turns amateur sleuth and solves major crime. It'll give them an opportunity to have a pop at us and re-run Savage's story. We haven't had an old-style serial killer on the front pages for a while. With that in mind, you are sure Savage is genuine, and he's not doing this for a day out?'

'I think he's happy where he is, to be honest. It's not like any prison I've ever known. The grounds look like something from the Eden Project. I don't think the prospect of a trip to a fog-bound moor would hack it.'

'But you're sure the evidence stacks up?'

Ross knew he needed to be careful here. It wouldn't do to unwittingly reveal snippets of Savage's romantic fantasy on the basis it added credence to his connection to Suzanne. He had all but convinced himself Suzanne had taken her own life.

'I'll hand over the evidence we have. He stayed at the hotel where she worked and had contact with the victim. He delivered plenty of first-hand evidence about her, her home, and her family setup, and a lot of those details couldn't have been accessed elsewhere. She disappeared at the same time, and we have his past crimes to go by. His record shows what he's capable of. He already has one murder on his record. It's not too much of a stretch to assume there was another. I have no idea why he's chosen to admit to it now. I don't think he's found God or has had a crisis of conscience. I can only assume it was down to Beth's letter. I think it's linked to the therapy regime at the prison. Like it or not, it might just work. The whole process freaked me out. If you had to subject yourself to that sort of scrutiny day in day out, it may well change your perspective. His reaction to seeing Suzanne's face is something I'll always remember.'

Ross came off the phone just as Karenza walked into the room.

'Are you alright? You're looking a bit peaky.'

Ross told her the story as she poured him a whisky from the bar.

'Is Luke going to search the moor?'

'How could he not? There's a woman there, and who knows... there may be more.'

'When are you going to tell Beth?'

'When I've finished this,' Ross said, lifting his glass. 'It's better coming from me and Claire than the police. She is our client. She set out to find the truth and now she's got it.' As he said the words, he knew he wouldn't be sure that was the case until they found Suzanne's body.

'If I was her, I'd wish I never started this,' Karenza said, taking the empty glass from him and walking to the sink.

'The truth will out. Isn't that what your old man always says?'

'He's also fond of "don't poke the bear",' said Karenza, looking at Ross in a way he always found challenging, a mix of reproach and concern.

Chapter Thirty-Seven

SAVAGE WAS due to arrive at noon. Luke called Eden that morning to tell her that he and Denise, along with a van load of uniformed police and the forensic team, would be there before the prison van arrived in order to section off the area of moorland earmarked for the search.

'Thank god he's narrowed it down. It would take weeks otherwise.'

'How sure is he?' asked Eden, trying to shake the grainy images clogging her mind of Moors Murderer Ian Brady dragging the police around Saddleworth Moor on a wild goose chase.

'He's pretty sure where he left the main road and parked his car, and we can assume he wouldn't have been able to carry her far on his own. The terrain is too rough to drag a corpse, and it was dark.'

Eden squirmed.

'Look Eden, are you sure it's a good idea to bring Beth? It's bound to be a long day, no matter what. If we find a body, I doubt very much they will get it out of the ground there and then. The CSIs will want to preserve the scene and photograph everything as they go.'

'She's determined to come, but Ross and I are travelling separately, and I'm bringing Beth. If it gets too much for her, I'll drive her home. No doubt Ross will want to stay until the bitter end.'

'You're right,' said Luke, 'and who am I to argue? We wouldn't be here if Savage hadn't opened up to him. I can hardly begrudge him his share of the glory.'

'I suppose not,' said Eden. 'But it all seems a bit macabre.'

'I know what you mean, but the man's confessed. We can hardy ignore it and leave Suzanne Willis on the moor.'

Eden hesitated. 'Do you think there will be anything left of her after all this time?'

'Skeletal remains, if we're lucky and wildlife hasn't interfered with the body. Apparently, twelve years is the average timescale to get to that state if you're buried straight into the ground. It's been too long for much else. Hopefully, we'll be able to get DNA or use dental records from what's there. They're not bringing the cadaver dogs. They reckon it's beyond that, and what with the wild ponies and other animals, there are likely to be loads of remains in various states of decay that will confuse the matter. We are relying almost totally on Savage's ability to pinpoint the burial place.'

'Has he given you any landmarks?'

'He said she's near a lake, so we're assuming Dozmary Pool. It stacks up. It was before the bypass was built in the nineties, so it was just off the A30. He wouldn't have had to deviate much from his route home. Also, the ground is softer there. Much of the moor is granite. He wouldn't have been able to dig everywhere, not quickly in any event.'

Eden had visited the moor many times as a child with her parents, who were fascinated by its ancient landscape, with its Bronze Age fort and standing stones. The granite tors were a feature, the hard grey rock forming the backbone of the county, from the moor to Land's End.

Eden had camped there as a teenager as part of her Duke of Edinburgh award and had thought it a desolate place prone to mist and drilling rain.

'Got to go, my landline's ringing. We'll catch up later,' said Luke.

'Of course,' Eden said, not at all sure she relished the day ahead as much as Luke and Ross seemed to.

Chapter Thirty-Eight

BETH HAD NEVER SET foot on Bodmin Moor, although she had driven past it many times. They turned off at a place called Bolventor, where they were immediately stopped by a police cordon. Eden spoke to the young police officer who waved them through, directing them to where a line of police vehicles was parked in the narrow lane.

'I'll go and have a quick chat,' said Eden, leaving Beth in the car and striding off with purpose towards a tall, dark-haired man wearing a Barbour and wellies. Eden had informed her this was DCI Luke Parish, the detective heading the Devon and Cornwall Police team.

Beth sat for ten minutes, not knowing whether she should follow or not, until deciding this was as much her show as anyone's and she got out of the car to stretch her legs. Though thankfully dry, it was cold, and the bitter wind whipped her hair in all directions as she struggled to gather it under the hat she'd pulled down over her ears.

The moor stretched out before her, the bracken stitching the hills with a rolling tapestry of orange and tawny brown beneath the ever-shifting clouds. Occasionally, the sun poked through, gilding a patch of yellow gorse and deepening the shadows in the clefts and gullies of the rocks piled and wedged together like rickety shelving. It was a bleak and lonely place in winter, a wilderness scarred by millennia of wind and rain. The few trees she could see were thin and bent like arthritic old men and would give little shelter, and she wondered how the wild ponies who lived there survived.

She walked slowly towards Eden and DCI Parish. The pair had been joined by Ross and a young woman who, she could see from her lanyard as she approached, was another detective, DS Denise Charlton. Eden introduced her.

'How are you holding up?' asked Ross warmly.

'Oh, you know, nervous… apprehensive.'

'There's nothing much happening until Savage arrives,' said Luke. 'Eden and I were wondering whether it would be best for you to go into the village and wait. You can get a coffee and at least you'll be warm.'

Beth looked at Eden for guidance.

'Entirely up to you,' said Eden. 'But it sounds better than waiting in the car.'

'So long as you promise to call me as soon as he gets here,' said Beth.

'Of course I will,' reassured Ross.

Beth had no idea why it was so important for her to see Savage in the flesh. She imagined most people in her situation would shy away from the idea. It was more than curiosity. The idea of him being this side of a prison wall freaked her out. Since finding his name in her father's briefcase, the man had taken on Titanic proportions, crashing through her life like a marauding ogre. She needed to cut him down to size. She needed to see the old man behind the myth, shackled and helpless.

They headed back to the car.

'Jamaica Inn for coffee it is then,' said Eden.

As soon as Eden and Beth had driven off, Luke, Ross and Denise made a beeline for the lake. Dozmary Pool was said to be bottomless. Legend had it King Arthur threw his sword Excalibur into its black waters to be held in the withered hand of the lady of the lake until his return. It was a lonely, mysterious place steeped in local myth and superstition. The usually still, mirrored surface was ruffled by wind today as the three of them walked the perimeter. Ross scanned the bank for indications of disturbance even though he knew it was fruitless. Any tell-tale signs of Suzanne Willis's grave would have, over time, earthed over and tufted with grass. He'd spoken earlier to one of the geophysicists unloading the ground-penetrating radar contraption the forensic team aimed to use. But for Savage's impending arrival, this whole enterprise felt more like an archaeological dig than a murder investigation.

'This place gives me the creeps,' shivered Denise.

'It's beautiful in the summer,' defended Luke.

Ross pulled up his collar. 'Give me the coast any day.'

'How do people manage to live up here?' asked Denise, betraying her city-girl sensibilities.

'Roadkill,' Ross answered, straightfaced.

'What?' laughed Luke.

'I'm deadly serious,' said Ross. 'I watched a documentary once about this bloke who lived on the moor. He had a freezer full of it. Badgers, squirrels, flattened hedgehogs. He was writing a cookery book.'

'Jesus,' Denise snorted, holding her hand over her mouth.

'You're a sick bastard,' grinned Luke, suddenly aware how much he missed Ross's gallows sense of humour.

Ross checked his phone. He needed to call Claire. He had no signal. He wanted to make sure she did not do anything rash, like contact Kelvin Harvey without him being there. He didn't know why he thought she might. She had promised him she wouldn't, but there had been something in her demeanour when he told her about the expedition to the moor on the back of Savage's confession. It was as if she felt she was missing out, which she was, in his view. He guessed she'd felt uncomfortable because of her reluctance to accompany him to Fenton to interview the man. She should have known he hadn't held that against her, and she'd done her bit. The insightful help she'd given to Beth when constructing her letters to Savage had opened the door to a bigger conversation. A conversation that had led to this place. He had told her as much and asked if she had wanted to come today, but she'd declined the offer. The last thing he wanted was Claire going off on a foray of her own to prove herself. Neville Savage was an evil piece of work in handcuffs. Kelvin Harvey was free as a bird. He hoped to god Claire understood the difference.

'Much as I'm enjoying this little stroll, I need to go back up to the main road,' he said, waving his phone by way of explanation.

Luke looked at his watch. Savage was due in fifteen minutes. 'We might as well get back too,' he said.

'Fine by me,' said Denise, glad of the reprieve.

Chapter Thirty-Nine

DESPITE THE DEFINITE theme park vibe, Jamaica Inn still managed to cling to much of the brooding menace attributed to it in the famous novel of the same name. Its cobbled courtyard and slate facade conjured images of highwaymen and smugglers creeping amongst the picnic tables.

Eden and Beth were almost blown off their feet as they headed for the entrance, passing on the way a notice inviting tourists to have their photo taken trapped in the village stocks.

'I bet that's caused a few sleepless nights for the paying guests?' said Eden, wincing at the metallic creak of the sign depicting a pirate complete with eye patch and parrot swinging above their heads.

Inside, the place was cosy with plenty of olde-worlde charm. Whitewashed walls hung with maritime memorabilia and horse brasses and pewter tankers criss-crossing the blackened beams. Du Maurier's novel had put the place on the world map if the vast array of foreign banknotes pinned on the lintel above the bar was anything to go by.

The pub had its own smugglers museum and a farm shop, but neither Beth nor Eden was in the mood to visit. Whilst the plastic mannequin variety of villain might seem more desirable right now, it was hard to shake the thought that they were killing time waiting for a real killer.

They plonked themselves down at a table close to the log fire and grabbed a menu. Neither felt hungry and settled for a pot of tea and a couple of rounds of toast.

'It's lovely and warm here,' said Beth.

'Let's not get too comfy,' Eden warned. 'It won't be long until he arrives.'

The chat behind the bar was all about Savage and the search for Suzanne's body.

'Are you part of the police team?' asked the barman as he took Eden's order. She was pleased she could answer honestly in the negative. She guessed they'd had a good few of the local force in that morning. She imagined the full English went down a treat.

She'd thought of suggesting Beth might like to stay there if she intended to attend the search every day. It was close by, and the rooms looked charming, but having delved deeper on the website and read the place was haunted by, among others, a seventeenth-century smuggler found murdered on the moor, she decided Beth had more than enough drama to deal with without adding the paranormal to the list.

'Ross will call, won't he?' asked Beth.

'Of course.'

'I'm sorry. I didn't mean to sound like I doubted him. It's just he might think I'm not up to seeing Savage face-to-face.'

'He may do, but he won't break his word. He's a good man to have in your corner.'

'He's very good-looking,' said Beth, smiling. 'Although he doesn't seem vain about it.'

'No, he isn't,' agreed Eden. 'I think he takes it for granted.'

'I'm not sure I'd like to be his wife. I'd always be looking over my shoulder.'

'He knows when he's onto a good thing. He and Karenza are a match made in heaven. They're a very special couple.'

'The other one, DCI Parish. Is he a friend of yours too?'

'Yes,' said Eden. 'He used to be in a relationship with my sister. They split up but have a child together.'

'I thought you seemed close,' said Beth.

Eden blushed.

'I'm pleased you know each other well,' reassured Beth, worried Eden may have thought she disapproved. 'It means he'll keep us in the picture. I know sometimes the police can't talk about cases in the middle of an investigation.'

'Usually that's true, but this is different from the norm. You and Ross were instrumental in getting Savage's confession.'

'That's a relief. I wonder if he'll be on time?' Beth said, looking at her watch for the third time since they'd arrived. 'If they find her, will they let me see her?' she said quietly, looking into her teacup.

'I doubt it. Until your mum is formally identified, there's a chance the body could be another victim. I don't think they've ruled that out yet. The forensics team will want to secure the site from contamination, and of course, the police won't want the press jumping to conclusions either.'

Eden's phone rang. It was Ross.

'He's here,' she said.

Chapter Forty

CLAIRE WATCHED the live feed from Bodmin Moor on the midday news. The country was transfixed by the prospect of Savage leading the police to the grave of his first victim. The bird's eye view delivered by the network's drone lent a Nordic noir feel to what was already a dramatically charged scene.

Ross, Luke and Denise stood in a huddle by the roadside as a prison van, flanked by four police cars pulled up, and a handcuffed Savage was bundled out onto the moor. The solemn blow-by-blow observations had an edge-of-your-seat tone. She imagined Luke cursing the distracting drones and tv stations who had sent them. She guessed he would be doubly irate if he knew the viral effect the ghastly expedition was having on the social media platforms, where any number of so-called experts were giving a running commentary. Add to that the sycophantic babblings of Savage's weird and wonderful fanbase, who seemed to regard him with a mix of awe and bonhomie, and the thing had all the trappings of a circus with Savage as ringmaster. It was voyeurism at its worst and deeply disturbing.

Beth loitered some way off with Eden, who, with her long auburn hair swishing about her face, resembled a heroine in a gothic novel. Claire felt guilty about not supporting Beth through what must be for her, one of the most difficult days of her life. Ross had phoned earlier to tell her of the state of play and to warn her yet again not to challenge Harvey without him being present. He had a real bee in his bonnet about it, and it was beginning to annoy her. Part of her resentment stemmed from the implication that she wasn't up to the job, an assumption she disputed. She knew her own frailties only too well. They had prevented her from accompanying Ross to HMP Fenton to interview Savage, which in turn had meant she did not feel she had earned the right to tag along today. However, her fear had stemmed from her memories of incarceration, not a fear of Savage. She had been a criminal lawyer for twenty years before her life disintegrated and had appeared in court with men who could eat Harvey for breakfast. She was no coward and saw no reason why Ross should think she needed him as her wing man to present her folio of evidence to Harvey.

It had been bad enough worrying people would vilify her on discharge from prison. For Ross to regard her as an emotional invalid was unbearable.

As she watched Eden and Ross on the moor, she felt decidedly left out, but there was nothing she could do about it now. She could however, do something about Harvey. She had interviewed the victims and planned his entrapment. On the back of that, she had prepared the evidence against him, so saw no reason why she shouldn't be the one to go to his office and challenge him. It would at least show Ross she didn't need to be treated as if she would shatter at the slightest hint of conflict. If that was truly the case, she had no right being his partner. She knew no amount of talk would convince him, not once he'd made his mind up, but if she got the job done in his absence, it would dispel these ridiculous concerns once and for all, and he would see her as his equal again.

She wouldn't forewarn Harvey. She'd turn up at his office and, if necessary, wait for his return. After all, she was a private detective now and it wouldn't be the last time she'd be sitting in a car waiting for something to happen. She might as well get used to it. It was now or never.

She picked up the file from her desk and headed for the door. Rummaging in her bag for her car keys she did not notice Harvey's van pull up until it was too late, and Kelvin Harvey had jumped out and was walking up the path.

'I thought I'd drop by with the samples we spoke about the other day, but I see you're on your way out,' Harvey yelled, flashing the sycophantic leer Claire had come to expect from him.

Claire had psyched herself up to take the battle to him. Faced with the enemy literally at the door, she felt ill-prepared and nervous. She clutched the file to her chest, knowing Harvey's name was emblazoned across the front cover. Given the pace of her heart and the pep talk Ross had given her only an hour before, she knew the sensible response would be to say indeed she was and to ask him to leave the samples with her to look over. The man wouldn't be in the least bit suspicious, and she could revert to the original plan once Ross had finished his exploits on Bodmin Moor. She discarded the thought almost as soon as it came into her head. She needed to get this over with. If she let Harvey leave now, sooner or later, he would get wind of what she'd been up to and regain the upper hand. He could try and intimidate his victims into retracting their statements, and all her hard work would have been for nothing. She would have rattled his cage and, in doing so, caused aggravation for everyone concerned. Furthermore, she would have done nothing to help the Henshaws.

Her stomach churned with a familiar feeling of indignation and an overwhelming urge to deliver justice. Scattering reason to the wind, she answered, 'I can run my errands later, come in.'

She directed Harvey through to the sitting room, pausing to tuck her file into her bag on the way. She needed to put him at ease before proceeding to tell him she had decided not to go ahead with her garden project after all. Then when he asked why, lay down her ultimatum.

Harvey sat on the settee and began taking his samples from the box, lining the inch-thick squares of cut stone in a neat line across the top of the coffee table.

'Quite a selection,' said Claire, feigning interest in the tiny slabs of marble and granite.

'Any you particularly like the look of?' Harvey asked, trailing his finger along the line from left to right, loitering over the most expensive. 'Or would you rather wait for your aunt to help you choose. Where is she by the way?'

There was something in the look he shot her that made the hair bristle on the back of Claire's neck, and for a second, she was completely stumped for an answer. Then, remembering Harvey's visit had been impromptu, pulled herself together, reckoning any excuse would appear plausible.

'She's staying with relatives for a couple of days. A family function.'

'And you're not invited?' Harvey said. 'What a shame... when did she leave?'

His questions were quick-fired and loaded. Did he know something and wasn't letting on?

'I was invited but have other plans,' Claire said, ignoring the second part of his question.

She felt hot and clammy and realised she still had her jacket on. She hoped Harvey didn't notice her hands trembling as she fumbled with the buttons.

'I imagine it's nice for you to have a break from her. Old people can be wearing when you have to put up with them day in day out, and your aunt sounds a bit of a liability to me. Fancy her deleting that email. The elderly and technology; what a nightmare.'

Claire felt nauseous. He knew.

'Perhaps the old dear didn't tell you? Darci, my secretary, said she was in a state about it. Apparently, she deleted the first email with the names of the few clients I'd arranged for you to call for references, then talked Darci into sending a new list of all my customers. Pages and pages of them. Your printer must have been red hot.'

'Oh really? I didn't know. I must have been out when she called,' said Claire as nonchalantly as she could manage.

'But it was you who contacted the clients, wasn't it?' said Harvey, fixing Claire with a cold, penetrating stare.

Claire knew she had two choices. She could deny all knowledge, blaming everything on her fictitious relative, or she could fess up and confront Harvey, tell him exactly what she'd found out about his motley enterprise. Her mind was racing, but even in her anxious state, she was in no mood for running away. The first option was futile. From his attitude, he probably knew the truth in any event.

'Yes, it was. I rang around for references just like I said I would and to be honest, I was not impressed. In fact, I've compiled a dossier.' Claire said, extracting her file.

'A *dossier*... well, there's posh, and what do you intend to do with this *dossier?*'

'That depends. I'm sure the police would be very interested to know you are in the habit of extorting money from elderly, vulnerable people.'

'What the hell are you talking about?' said Harvey, jumping to his feet.

Claire reached for her bag and pulled out her file. 'I suggest you sit back down and listen to what I have to say.' She could hear her voice, stern and strident as a headmistress, but had no idea where this show of confidence was coming from. Her legs felt like jelly about to melt from beneath her.

Harvey, to her surprise, obeyed. He looked younger and less impressive as he slumped back into his seat.

'I have numerous statements from customers who you have tricked into paying you for the removal of toxic waste from their gardens.'

'Would they prefer I left it and reported them to the environmental health?' said Harvey, in a show of cockiness.

'But you'd never do that, would you, because the asbestos and the mine shafts were never there in the first place? You invented them so you could fleece them of their cash.'

'Prove it,' said Harvey, eyes wide with panic despite his bravado.

'I don't need to prove it, you idiot. This is not a court of law, but make no mistake, the statements I have in this file, along with the financial evidence showing the money paid into your account, would be sufficient for the police to arrest you. Once the results of the independent surveys are in, showing no evidence of these hazards having ever been present in those gardens, they'll charge you. They could put you away for several years. Plus, you would be hit with a confiscation order in respect of the money you stole and possibly a civil claim for damages for distress.'

'What makes you the legal expert?'

'I was a lawyer for over twenty years. Trust me, I know what I'm talking about.'

'Who the fuck are you?'

'I'm a private detective engaged to look into the way you operate.'

That was, of course, not strictly true. The discovery of Harvey's nefarious business activities had been a spin-off from her initial conversations with the Henshaws, but she had no intention of letting the man know her instructions came from them.

As if on cue, Harvey asked the question, 'Who asked you to investigate me?'

He was clearly rattled. Every word levied with a punch.

'It could be the people you've cheated and bullied or someone who's been watching you from the sidelines. It could be a charity interested in helping the aged. A concerned neighbour or relative. You'll never know unless you go to court where of course, all will be revealed.'

'So, what do you want?' Harvey shrieked.

'I want you to pay every penny back, and I want you to write a letter of apology to all the people you've cheated. Then I want you to pack up and leave the county.'

'But I've got the business and the house here.'

'Sell it. It'll help you pay back those you owe.'

'It would be my word against theirs. Half of the old duffers don't know whether they're coming or going. I can just see them trying to give evidence in court. Some of them might be dead by the time it comes to trial.'

'Are you stupid enough to think that would matter? I don't reckon you'd have much of a business left either way once the story hits the press. Who is going to employ a gardener who rips off the elderly. Who is going to trust the remains of their much-loved pet to a conman? This way, you can take your business elsewhere. But understand this much. The people who instructed me will be watching your every move. Any more stunts like this, and the file goes to the police.' Claire felt emboldened now, sensing she had him on the back foot. 'You've got a month to put your property on the market.'

'I could report you to the police for threatening me,' snivelled Harvey, his bottom lip quivering as if he might at any minute burst into tears.

'Be my guest. Better still, I'll dial the number for you. Ask to speak to DCI Parish. He's a friend of mine.'

Harvey sloped from his seat and darted towards the hallway.

'Don't forget your rock collection,' shouted Claire after him.

He didn't hear. He was already out the door.

Chapter Forty-One

THE NERVOUS CHATTER pervading the scene all morning came to an abrupt halt the minute Savage's entourage drew into the carpark. Ross was certain the tension he was feeling, like an overwound violin string ready to ping, was felt by everyone there. He cast a sideways glance in Beth's direction. She was standing back a little with Eden, cold hands pocketed. He could only imagine the turmoil Beth was in. She was subjecting herself to all this because of her ravenous need to know the truth. It was risky. She might leave here damaged by the experience, but none the wiser.

He was the only one there who knew what to expect having seen Savage recently. The rest, including those watching from the comfort of their settees, didn't know what toll the years of incarceration had levied. They had no idea whether Savage was still strong enough to slip his guards and run amock or whether they were dealing with an old man, a spent force to be jeered at rather than feared. Ross knew the reality rested somewhere in between.

Savage, tight-faced and bundled up in a woolly hat,

thick overcoat and heavy boots, was helped out of the back of the van as the country held its breath.

Luke was keen for Ross to shadow Savage during the search on the basis Ross knew the terrain and the man had developed some kind of rapport with him. It made sense to Ross. This was a massive operation, and Luke was in charge of the whole show. He had to make sure security remained tight and that protocols were maintained. He was working with CSIs who had to be managed alongside his own team and all the time keep the chief constable informed of his every move.

Ross was happy to take on the role of good cop. He had played it many times in his career. So what if he wasn't carrying a warrant card? Bar Luke he had years more experience under his belt than anyone else there.

Denise Charlton had been assigned to go with him. Ross had an inkling Luke hadn't been happy to delegate the role to Denise. He was no sexist, and Denise was as good as any man on his team, but working closely with someone like Savage for any woman knowing his history would be difficult. She'd need support and as it couldn't be him, he'd told Ross he was the next best thing. He and Luke hadn't always seen eye to eye, but Ross knew he could trust Luke Parish with his life. He was flattered Luke felt the same way about him.

Luke had set up a centre of operations in a police surveillance van in the car park. Everyone was relying on their radios as mobile reception was poor. There was a link to a TV screen feeding back from a camera team onsite. Once he was sure everything was running smoothly, Luke planned to join them on the moor. In the meantime, Ross was to get as much intel as he could from Savage. They hadn't ruled out there were other victims' bodies out there, and they didn't know if they'd ever get another chance to talk to him without Mason and his cronies breathing down their necks.

Denise was to stay close by to corroborate anything that was said. They would play this by the book.

Ross watched Luke approach and speak briefly to the man's guards before cautioning Savage and then beckoning half a dozen of his own constables over. The conversation was brief, stripped bare by the knowledge of the task in hand and the need to get on with it. Ross looked on, his critical gaze scrutinising every step. They needed to chivvy Savage along. At this time of year, daylight lost its grip early. By four, the light would fade and by five, without any artificial light, it would be cinder dark and they'd be forced to abandon the moor to the night.

The prison authorities had arranged for Savage to be put up in Exeter prison that night so they could make an early start the next morning if they made no headway today. According to Luke, Savage had already been given access to maps, photos, and video footage of the moor, and this had enabled him to narrow down the area to be searched.

Ross couldn't wait to get out there. He knew once they'd walked the man closer, he'd get the nod from Denise to join her. In the meantime, he decided to place himself between Beth and Savage as he passed. He knew she was safe enough. Savage was handcuffed, and half of the Devon and Cornwall forces were present. It was not so much the risk of harm but rather the risk of a scene or some form of contact that might upset her. He had suffered sleepless nights since visiting Fenton. Breathing the same air as the likes of Savage had left him feeling tainted. He didn't want that for Beth.

Ross overheard Savage asking for gloves. The handcuffs would have to come off to accommodate them. Ross knew Luke wouldn't contemplate that until they were away from the throng by the cars. Savage looked none too happy about being turned down. If the man thought this was bad, wait until he'd spent a night in Exeter nick. Then again, it could have been worse. It would have been Dartmoor had they not shut the prison down that year because of a Radon gas scare. The thought of Savage in that Victorian hellhole raised a smile.

The prisoner acknowledged him as he passed. For Beth's sake, he remained rigid and straight-faced. If Savage thought he was going to dance to his tune, he was sorely mistaken.

Ross heard a sharp intake of breath from behind him, which he assumed came from Beth. It was only when he noticed her scarf, whipped up by the wind, floating past him and landing at Savage's feet he realised why.

The man bent to pick it up. It took him two attempts with his hands shackled. Ross expected one of the guards to take it from him. When they didn't, he stepped forward and retrieved it. Savage was staring past him, his preying eyes burrowing into Beth as he let the silk scarf slither into Ross's palm. He mumbled a single word quietly enough for it to be lost in the wind, but Ross heard it plainly enough.

'Byrdie.'

It was as if an icy tongue had licked the back of Ross's neck.

'Best keep moving, Neville,' said one of the guards in the patient tone Ross had got used to hearing from the Fenton staff.

Savage turned his back on them and carried on towards the gateway to the moor.

Ross walked towards Beth. She looked startled.

'I don't want it,' she stammered as Ross tried to hand her the scarf. 'Throw it away. Or better still, burn it. I want nothing that man has touched with his filthy hands. It would remind me of him every time I wore it,' she said, blotting her tears.

Ross was relieved she had not heard Savage call her by the name her mother used.

'I'm not sure I can do this,' Beth said. 'I thought I could, but now it comes to it... I can't. I just can't. The thought of her being thrown into the ground and her being alone out here for all these years...'

Eden put her arm around her. 'I'll take you home. You've seen him. He's an old man. He can't harm you anymore.'

Ross watched Eden walk Beth back to her car. It was a good decision.

Denise was waiting for him to join her at the gate.

Ross wasn't sure Savage knew where he was going despite what he'd said. In his book, whenever someone behaved oddly, you had to examine it to see if you could make sense of it. If you couldn't, they needed to be regarded as suspect. Savage's offer to reveal Suzanne's last resting place fell into that category as far as he was concerned. Mason was a clever manipulator. He wielded power like a scalpel. He hardly knew Ross, but he'd still felt comfortable threatening him against mentioning Savage's belief in a romantic connection between him and Suzanne, and he'd gone along with it. The man exercised even more control over Fenton's inmates, who seemed to perform to order.

'She looks like Suzanne,' said Savage as he joined the search party.

'She does,' agreed Ross, who had noticed the striking resemblance between Beth and her mother the minute he'd seen Beth's mother on the missing person flyer.

'Taller, and her hair's not as dark, but she has the same eyes. I'm sorry if I upset her back there. I was only trying to help.'

Ross bit his lip. He didn't trust this bastard as far as he could throw him, which in this wind wasn't far.

'She's gone home.'

'That's a shame,' said Savage. 'Where is home?'

Ross didn't answer. There was no way he was going to divulge anything about Beth to her mother's murderer.

They walked down the pathway, Ross on one side of Savage, Denise on the other. The two guards assigned from Fenton in front and six uniformed police behind.

'Do you recognise anything yet?' asked Denise.

Savage, who had previously been looking down at his feet the way men tended to do when their hands were tied, and they could not save themselves if they stumbled, looked up.

'This path wasn't here. It was just a muddy track back then. I remember I ruined a decent pair of Chelsea boots.'

'How did you carry her?' asked Ross.

'Over my shoulder. Suzanne was dainty. She weighed practically nothing.'

It was plausible. Suzanne Willis was five foot three and weighed just over seven stone. Savage was a big man, young and fit at the time.

'Did you wrap the body the way you did Melanie Rowse?'

Rowse had been wrapped in rolls and rolls of thick polythene. The forensic pathologists examining her had to wait until she defrosted before they could remove them. The meticulous wrapping, along with the freezing, had preserved the body.

Luke had been told that if Suzanne had been wrapped in the same airtight way, it would have slowed down the decomposition. That, and the combination of being buried in boggy ground, might mean the body had become mummified. It was a terrible thought.

'No, I didn't have time, and I could hardly bear to cover her lovely face with the sheet.'

'You used a sheet from the house?'

'No, from the flat. A pale blue silk sheet,' said Savage, looking off into the distance as if remembering.

'You took Suzanne back to the flat?'

Denise glanced at Ross, eyes wide and questioning. She knew nothing about any flat. It was one of the things Ross had omitted when retelling Savage's story as part of the deal he'd struck with Mason. He had steered away from anything that pointed to Savage having a relationship with Suzanne. Notwithstanding, she had never stepped foot in the place, Mason was right. The flat had the makings of a love nest.

'She was in the boot of the car. I had to call in to collect my things. I'd bought the sheets, so I took them with me. She deserved something soft and expensive. Something I had chosen just for her.'

Ross imagined that if the press were aware of the information Savage had just divulged, they'd be waiting for that eureka moment when the CSIs lifted a perfect piece of pale blue silk from the earth. Ross knew better. The sheet would have long since turned to powder. They were looking for bones.

Denise looked confused.

Ross knew he had to tread carefully from here on in.

She was astute. She'd herd clues like sheep and inspect them later.

They had reached the bottom of the pathway at the point where it curved in a loop around the lake. The wind ruffled the dark water, leaving nicotine-coloured spume trembling where it lapped against the tufts of Marram grass. Off the pathway, the ground was uneven underfoot. Savage had been given walking boots, but with his hands tied, he would make slow progress. He had been tagged when he left the prison, and Luke had agreed that once they were away from the roadway, his guards could release his hands.

Ross and Denise stood back as they did so and then handed the man some much-needed leather gloves.

Savage rubbed his wrists and then slipped them on.

'I think I went that way,' he said. 'I remember those buildings. I carried her in the opposite direction, worried somebody might see me.'

Ross looked to his left at the huddle of stone farm buildings fringing the horizon. They looked as if they might be occupied now, but he had no idea whether that was the case in the eighties. They could well have been derelict back then.

'Why didn't you dispose of her body in the lake? You could have weighted her down.'

'I could never have done that,' said Savage with a shiver. 'The thought of her in the cold water, being eaten by the fishes. Oh no, I couldn't have that.'

Denise looked up as another drone began to hover above their heads. She waited for it to move away so she could use her radio and call Luke without its infernal buzz drowning her out.

'We're here by the pool. We're taking the right-hand

route around the lake, slightly inland. The prisoner recognises the area.'

Though Savage had indicated he knew where Suzanne's body was and could lead them to it, Ross was sceptical. Part of him doubted the prisoner remembered anything about the terrain if this was his first victim. The cold, collected individual he was to become was in its infancy. He would have been panicky, finding it hard to make rational decisions, and if he truly cared for this woman, he would have felt distraught. It's not easy to dig a grave, not one that isn't going to be found. If you're serious about it, you need all your faculties about you, and you need to come prepared. Ross hadn't quizzed Savage yet about what he used to dig the grave or why he picked the moor. He intended to. They were in a county surrounded by water on every coast. Suzanne had lived in a village on the shore of one of the deepest harbours in the world. Why hadn't Savage simply weighted down her body and dropped her in the ocean or thrown her off a cliff edge. Why risk putting her in his car boot and driving for miles in the dark to dispose of her here?

'Lead the way, Neville,' he said, banishing his doubts to the back of his mind for the time being.

The weather was changing with every step they took. Everything was suddenly shrouded in grey mizzle that was slowly drenching them. Ross pulled up his hood. It was already impossible to see beyond a few metres across the lake. If this got worse, they'd have to abandon the search.

Underfoot was difficult too. Rocky in places, spongy with moss and lichen in others. Everyone was concentrating on where they put their feet. At one point Denise stumbled, and Savage put out his hand to help her. Ross smiled as she batted him away. She might well have done the same if it had been him. She was fiery and independent, but Savage looked wounded by the rebuff.

The man clearly didn't understand how normal people felt about him. Ross guessed that years of being closeted and coddled by psychiatrists inside Fenton with others just like him had queered his understanding of the real world. He may think that by showing willing, he was redeeming himself in the eyes of the public. In truth, he was irredeemable. No amount of penitence could wash him clean. Finding Suzanne's body would only confirm what they'd always known about him. He was a killer.

Ross intermittently asked Savage if he recognised any landmarks. Invariably, his answer was a non-committal 'maybe' or 'perhaps', their conversation ending in a series of cul-de-sacs. They were getting nowhere fast, and Ross could feel frustration rising like steam from the search team. He imagined those back at the car park were equally dissatisfied with Savage's performance.

It was difficult to keep track of where they'd been, and Ross had the distinct feeling they could be going around in circles as his coat caught on the prickles of a bilberry bush for the second time.

'Fuck,' he muttered, tugging his arm free and ripping his sleeve in the process.

The sky was darkening, slowly inking them in, and still Savage offered nothing concrete. Exhaustion was hitting him like a tsunami. He was not a young man. After two hours of searching, Ross didn't think he had much left in him. He pulled Denise aside for a quiet word.

'This is hopeless. It's the blind leading the blind. He hasn't got a clue. The camera's been rolling the entire time. I think we should stop and playback the footage. At least then we'll know whether we're covering old or new ground.'

'I'll run it past the boss,' she said, walking away to radio Luke.

Ross knew Luke would be under pressure. Huge amounts of valuable police resources had been lavished on the search from a budget that barely covered the costs of everyday policing in the county. Bad news spread like COVID. If they drew a blank, questions would be asked, and fingers would be pointing at him.

Denise came back with the news Luke wanted them to keep searching for one more hour. 'He said the weather forecast isn't looking any better for tomorrow, so we need to make the most of every minute. The camera team can go back now and plot the places we've covered so we don't duplicate those areas tomorrow.'

Ross could see from the expressions of the men around him that the news had gone down like a lead balloon.

'Okay, one hour, everyone. Neville, we need you to make the most of the time. You need to pause and cast your eye around. I know it's a long time ago, and it was dark, but is there anything... anything at all that looks familiar to you?'

'Maybe that way,' said Savage. 'I remember there was a boulder like that one very nearby.'

They trudged on. Conversation took a back seat, the silence only punctuated by Savage's rasping laryngitic cough that sounded like he smoked forty a day. Ross doubted that was the case. Mason, being Mason, was bound to have a no-smoking policy.

They rounded the boulder and were faced with a wide expanse of unspoilt ground, but none of them were in the mood for rhapsodising about the view. Ross had no idea if Savage was using his salesman's skills to string them along like a tub of plastic monkeys. If he was, he was certainly thick-skinned. He must be able to feel the doubt growing.

Denise's eyes were drilling into his like those of a mutinous child every time he looked her way. If Savage was dredging his memory, he was coming up short.

Ross felt as if the wind was flaying the skin from his face. He had started the expedition buoyed up with the thrill of the search. Now with dusk rolling in and the rain pounding his back, he was counting down the minutes until someone called it a day.

Chapter Forty-Two

BACK IN THE CAR PARK, they were met with a disgruntled forensic team who, from the look on their faces, blamed them for their lack of an outing.

Savage, still breathless, looked grey with fatigue as his guards refastened his handcuffs and led him back to the armoured vehicle that would take him to Exeter. Denise followed them to supervise the prisoner's departure from the moor.

Ross headed for Luke's van. 'What a waste of time that was,' he announced as he opened the door.

'Watch the mud,' scolded Luke, looking down at Ross's filthy boots.

'I've been watching bloody mud and not much else all afternoon,' answered Ross, scraping off the worst of the offending clods on the metal step.

'Have you checked the footage. Is it as bad as I thought?'

'You weren't going around in circles, it's just it all looks the same in this weather.'

'That's something, but it was still a disaster. Savage has no sense of direction, and his memory is sketchy as fuck.'

'It's to be expected, I suppose,' said Luke. 'It was decades ago.'

'But he studied the maps and the video footage. He said he knew where he buried her. Now when it comes down to it, he's suddenly developed amnesia. What's to say he isn't just toying with us?'

'Or he genuinely underestimated how much the moor could change over time. Cattle and tourists, the weather, they all erode the landscape. Plus, it was dark, and it wasn't as if he knew the place beforehand. I'm not even sure he'd ever been there before that night. The alternative doesn't bear thinking about. If we've been hoodwinked and it's cost a small fortune in the process, there will be uproar. I'm not saying you haven't got skin in the game. I know this is important to you, but I'm the one who will be called to account, and I'm not prepared to throw in the towel just yet.'

'I'm sorry,' said Ross. 'I'm tired, and it's so damn frustrating. The man I met in Fenton was cocksure of himself. I thought when he confessed and said he knew where the body was, he'd be just as confident leading us to Suzanne, but it was a different bloke I saw out there today. He was hesitant and confused, like a doddery old man.'

'He is old... well, oldish, and by the look of him none too fit.'

'It's that place. They play mind games all the time. Can we really trust him, that's the question?'

'Don't tell me you think he's lying about the whole thing because if that's what you're saying, they will find a body on that moor, alright? It'll be yours, and they'll be dragging me off to the cells on a charge of murder.'

Ross smiled despite his mood. 'No, don't get me wrong. There's the reaction that day when I showed him her photo. His whole story, and the fact he met her and stayed at the hotel. He had motive and opportunity. That's what we look for, isn't it?'

'Yes it is, but a little corroborative evidence in the form of a body would be a bonus.'

'What if she's not here at all? What if that's the bit he's lying about? There are a hundred and one places more obvious in Cornwall. We would never have contemplated mounting a search of those. If he'd told us he'd thrown her in the sea, he'd know we'd have no chance of finding her after all these years. I can't get it out of my head he's show-boating for his own ends.'

The door opened and Denise came in.

Luke looked exasperated and Ross knew he needed to shut up. The DCI wouldn't want him airing his misgivings in front of anyone else on his team.

'What's the plan for tomorrow?' Luke asked.

'Back bright and early. Savage's guards said they'll get him here by ten o'clock,' replied Denise.

'Good,' said Luke. 'Let's call it a day.'

Chapter Forty-Three

DAMP AND DEJECTED, the drive from Bodmin to St. Ives had seemed longer than usual as Ross rewound the day's events, trying to make sense of it all. Knowing he'd have to go through the same thing again the next day didn't help.

Karenza was waiting for him in the cottage when he arrived home. He was glad she had taken the evening off. He needed some reassurance from someone on the outside. Once he'd slipped off his clothes and showered the day's dirt away, he joined her downstairs.

'How did it go?' she asked, handing him a beer from the fridge.

'Not good. What did it look like on the telly?'

'Grim. Savage's arrival this morning has been shown umpteen times. I spotted you in the car park with Beth and Eden. The weather looked awful. I imagine that's why there was very little footage of you actually on the moor.'

'Awful is putting it mildly. It was blowing a gale, and there were times you could barely see your hand in front of your face.'

'What was Savage like?'

'Oh, you know, your average neighbourhood serial killer,' Ross replied facetiously.

'Fine. Don't talk about it,' huffed Karenza, sliding from the chair next to him.

Ross grabbed her by the hand and pulled her down onto his lap.

'Sorry love. It was naive of me to think he'd be able to lead us straight to her.'

'Nothing wrong with looking on the bright side, so long as you've got a torch in your backpack for when it turns dark.'

'You sound more like your father every day.'

Karenza gave him a playful punch in the arm.

'It's this niggling feeling Mason is behind all this,' Ross continued glumly.

'Look. It's no good you trying to second guess those men. It is what it is. You're no longer in the force. You've got no control over Mason or Savage. It's time you took that on board and came to terms with it.'

She was right, of course. He squeezed her and kissed her on her neck.

'I assume you're there again tomorrow?'

'Yes, unfortunately.'

'Will Eden and Beth be there?'

'No, Eden took Beth home. It was too much for her.'

'It's hardly surprising,' said Karenza.

'I suppose I could call Claire and ask if she'd like to come instead?'

'Oh… that reminds me, Claire called. She said she'd been trying to reach you but couldn't get through. She said the strangest thing. She told me to tell you that you could have your mother's ashes back. What did she mean by that?'

Ross jumped up, dislodging Karenza from his lap in the process and ran to the hall. Pausing for a second to examine the tear in his sleeve, he pulled his mobile from his jacket pocket and called Claire.

'Ross, how did it go?'

'Never mind that. Did you go ahead and see Harvey on your own after I specifically advised against it?'

'Yes, and I'm glad I did. It went well. What's the problem?'

'The problem is anything could have happened. You had no idea how he'd react.'

'He reacted just as I thought he would. All bluff and bluster until faced with the evidence and the prospect of the police getting involved, at which point he blubbed like a baby.'

'He didn't threaten you?'

'No, like I said, it was me doing the threatening.'

Ross calmed down a little. 'Did he agree to leave the Henshaws alone?'

'I didn't mention the Henshaws. I didn't even have to tell him which of his customers had given statements. All I had to do was plant the seeds of paranoia and convince him someone powerful was on to him. I told him he has to pay back his victims, and to do that, he'll need to sell up. I anticipate a 'for sale' sign going up outside number fifteen any day now.'

Ross could hear the sense of achievement brimming over in Claire's voice. If only he'd come back from the moor with a bit of that.

'I'm a big girl. I can fight my own battles and even win them occasionally.'

'I know. I'm sorry if I've come across as the heavy-handed big brother, but I feel protective after all you've been through.'

'And I appreciate it, but if we're going to be partners, I need to know you feel you can rely on me. This has to be a two-way street.'

'I can... I know I can.'

'Good,' said Claire, the tension melting away. 'So, I told Karenza, you can have your mother's ashes back.'

'I'm not sure she's even noticed they're missing.'

'I've got one thing to say to you that might make you think again about that.'

'What?'

'Crème de Menthe.'

Ross had been grounded for weeks after pilfering a bottle of the sickly stuff from his mother's drinks cabinet when he was fifteen. He thought he'd got away with that too, at first.

'Message understood. If you don't see me for a while, you know she's locked me in my bedroom and confiscated my CD player,' he laughed.

He was about to put down the phone when he remembered he'd meant to ask her a question. 'Hey, no pressure, but do you want to come to the moor tomorrow? I'd be glad of your company. It's an early start mind. We've got to be there by nine.'

There was a pause at the other end of the line.

'Yes... yes, I'd like that. Pick me up on your way through. I'll be ready.'

Chapter Forty-Four

ROSS AWOKE the next morning with a new approach in mind. He'd decided to follow Karenza's advice and go with the flow. She was right. He had little influence over Savage or Mason. Whatever game they were playing was their business. He had a limited agenda to helping Beth Matthews find her mum. If he could do that, all well and good. If not, he'd make sure he'd given it his best shot.

Despite the gloomy forecast, the skies were clear this morning. The predicted storms had blown through the county overnight. It was still windy and cold, but hopefully, they were rid of the relentless mist that had fogged their senses the day before.

He picked Claire up as planned. He was pleased to see she'd had the sense to dress warmly. He'd promised himself not to quiz her further about Harvey for the time being. He'd let her enjoy her victory.

'Luke won't mind me being there, will he?'

'I called him yesterday after I spoke to you to okay it. He was fine about it but said we might have to leave if they find anything. The forensics boys will take a headcount if we reach that point.'

'That suits me,' said Claire.

The traffic was unexpectedly heavy, and the team was assembled by the time they arrived. Luke and Denise walked across to greet them. Ross noticed Luke looked crestfallen.

'Is he on his way?' he asked.

'He isn't coming. He's gone down with a chest infection. They bussed him back to Fenton last night.'

'You're fucking kidding me?' said Ross.

'I wish I was. Apparently, he took a turn for the worse on the way to Exeter, and Mason called a halt.'

'That bloody man,' said Ross, gritting his teeth.

'So, what now?' asked Claire.

'We carry on the search without him,' said Denise.

'Have you told the chief constable?' asked Ross.

Luke nodded.

'You're a braver man than me. I guess he didn't take it well?'

'Like the true professional he is,' said Luke without trying to hide the sarcasm.

'I suppose it'll be less of a performance without Savage,' encouraged Ross, remembering his wife's words of wisdom and reconciling himself to the situation. 'We'll probably cover more ground without him.'

'And to be fair, he looked like death warmed up when he left here yesterday evening,' chipped in Denise.

'We'll use the information he provided. The GPR team are chomping at the bit to get their equipment onto the moor, so we're giving them free rein.'

'That's a positive move,' said Ross. 'Yesterday's efforts weren't exactly scientific.'

'They have a geologist on board who has pinpointed the areas where burial is impossible, and they've got some whiz kid using AI. Apparently, they have taken the info Savage initially provided: timings, time of year, weather and where he parked up, etcetera, and the stuff he shared with you and Denise yesterday about carrying Suzanne on his shoulder, her weight, his age and even his footwear, and fed it into a laptop. With the geologists' input, they've narrowed the possibilities down to four locations, all within two hundred metres of the pathway.'

'Are you sure you need us at all?' said Ross flippantly. 'The geeks have everything sewn up.'

'Sign of the times,' smiled Luke. 'You and I are dinosaurs, my friend. This is the dawn of a brave new world where the best we can hope for is to be allowed to carry the shovels.'

'Talking of which,' said Ross, 'did Savage happen to give you any information on how he buried her? I meant to ask him yesterday but never got around to it. You and I know it's not easy to dig a grave deep enough not to be discovered.'

'But we don't know it was deep, do we?' countered Luke. 'It could have been a shallow grave that has been disrupted. Trampled by cattle or ponies. Parts of the body might have been lifted by buzzards or dragged off by foxes.'

It was a grotesque image and Claire shuddered.

'He took the trouble to wrap her in a silk sheet. That smacks of effort. I can't see him just dumping her if he bothered to do that.'

'I get your point,' said Luke. 'Let's hope you're right.'

'Perhaps he used stones to cover her?' said Claire. 'There are plenty on the ground. It's unlikely passers-by would notice the grave if he'd covered it with stones, then bracken or gorse.'

'Especially if he chose the spot carefully. Maybe he had the presence of mind to fold the body. If his timings are right, rigour mortis wouldn't have set in, so he could have wedged her between a crevice. He wouldn't have had to dig so deep, and it would take up less space,' said Denise.

'Who needs AI when we've got this pair?' smiled Ross.

The tension of the previous day had dissipated now Savage was not onsite. Security, though still evident, was limited to excluding the public and the press. Luke had decided he would delegate police operations and accompany the search team today. He'd had enough of the steamy, claustrophobic van and there was the added bonus he would be incommunicado, out of reach of the chief constable.

The ground was sopping wet, but at least the rain and gale-force wind had abated.

Denise carried the map, pinpointing the four locations chosen by AI, and they made their way to the first of these, following behind the geoforensic team.

'Looks like we're in for another long day,' said Ross.

'I've come prepared,' said Claire. 'I've filled a flask, and I've got a bar of Kendal Mint Cake in my rucksack.'

Luke began to laugh.

'What's so funny?' asked Claire.

'Nothing, it's just I'm sure I can get a constable to run down the road for a McDonald's if we are in dire need of sustenance. We're hardly in the back of beyond.'

'I like to be prepared for every occasion,' said Claire.

'Talking of which, you looked as if you were having a good time at the party the other night,' said Luke.

'I was, thanks.'

'I'm glad. It's good to see you out and about again. I'm not sure about your new partnership with this one though,' Luke said, pointing to Ross. 'I hope you know what you're letting yourself in for.'

Claire smiled. 'I think I do. In fact, I think we make a great team.'

'Nice to know someone appreciates my worth,' said Ross.

'I always knew what you were worth,' retorted Luke. 'I just wasn't sure I could afford you.'

Ross took the backhanded compliment.

The forensics team had begun to set up their kit. As they approached, they could hear them planning their day.

'We'll mark out a grid, then start from the left, working towards the track. If we get a bounce, we'll log it and return if it looks significant. We're only going to investigate further if it's possible remains. Anything else we ignore. Agreed?'

There was a rumble of consensus amongst the three men manning the GPR equipment.

'What do they mean, bounce?' asked Claire.

'It works by sending radio signals into the ground. They bounce off anything they hit, giving a reading. The reading determines what the material is likely to be,' said Denise authoritatively.

'I see, so they'll ignore anything not likely to be human remains?'

'Given the timescale, they're looking for voids or cavities because we're looking for skeletal remains. If they are recent or the body is wrapped in plastic or heavy-duty material, the reading is magnified. We know that's not the case here,' said Luke.

'How can you measure a void?' asked Claire.

'Differences in density. During decomposition, the rib

cage collapses, leaving a cavity. If the skeletal remains are well preserved, they yield a decent reflection, and the reading will record a contrast between bone and the air pocket left,' offered Denise.

'Very good,' said a lanky member of the forensics team who had overheard her. 'Nice to know some of you lot listen when we give those lectures.'

Denise blushed.

'Swot,' teased Ross.

'There are other issues here,' the man continued. 'The site may well have been penetrated by groundwater over time. Plus, we haven't been able to de-turf the ground. That makes the GPR potentially less effective.'

'Why can't we take the turf off?' said Ross.

'Bodmin Moor isn't like Dartmoor. It's not a national park. Most of it is common land, but other bits are privately owned, and we've had to seek permission to even touch it. It's been a bloody nightmare to tell you the truth,' said Luke.

'At least using radar, we won't have the Moorland Trust after us. They prefer this to random digging, which could destroy the delicate eco structure,' said Denise.

'But we'll have to dig if we come up trumps.'

'We will, but this way, we tighten the search beforehand and preserve the integrity of the crime scene.'

Chapter Forty-Five

WHILST THE TECHNOLOGY WAS FASCINATING, the process was tedious, and after an hour or so of watching the GPR team map their grid and painstakingly scan, Claire's feet were numb, and her brain wasn't far behind.

'I'm going to stretch my legs around the lake,' she whispered to Ross.

'I'll come with you. There's nothing much to see here. This lot have everything under control.'

'Do you think they'll get their magic bounce?' Claire asked as they set off on the main track.

'Who knows.'

'Archaeologists believe bodies have been buried on the moor since the Bronze Age, you know. Digs are going on all the time near the henges and stone circles.'

'Well, let's hope the team don't discover anything ancient. That would close us down.'

'Not all the digs are successful. I remember a few years back, a schoolgirl found a sword in the lake at low tide.

Everyone thought it might be Arthur's sword… you know, Excalibur. It turned out to be a leftover film prop.'

'I thought the lake was deep?'

'Another myth promoted by a local legend of a farmer who was said to have sold his soul to the devil whose penance was to empty the lake with a limpet shell. During droughts, it's barely waist-high.'

'Bang goes another theory. I've been wondering why Savage didn't weigh Suzanne's body down and throw her in the lake. He gave me some cock and bull story about not being able to bear her being in the water. Perhaps he knew it was only feet deep?'

'To be honest, I can't understand why he chose the moor at all,' said Claire.

'Exactly my thoughts, but Luke's committed to it now,' said Ross, still not willing to give voice to his concerns about the integrity of Savage's confession. Ross couldn't help wondering if Savage had sold his soul to the devil, too. His version might wear a white coat and have letters after his name, but he was just as manipulative, and if yesterday's fiasco was anything to go by, the penance just as exhausting.

'Do you think Savage will be coming back?'

'I doubt it. Mason didn't waste any time whisking him away to Fenton. Mind you, it wasn't as if we were even close to finding her. If the tech boys are correct with their predictions, we were definitely off the pace.'

'Don't beat yourself up about it. Let's face it, even with all that technology, the chances of finding anything are pretty slim, and cynically speaking, this is a PR exercise for the police.'

'How so?'

'They have to be seen to be doing something. They are

playing catch-up. It was you who encouraged Beth to write to Savage and you who extracted the confession. It's only a feather in their cap if they find the body. If they don't, they come across as inept. They could have asked Savage years ago whether he knew anything about Suzanne's disappearance if they were minded to, without any prompting. I would have thought they should have done that with any missing women once they knew about Melanie Rowse. As things stand, it'll be you who's making the headlines, not them.'

'You mean us,' said Ross. 'I told you the publicity would be good for business.'

'I've had more than enough media coverage for one lifetime, but I do think all in all, we can be proud of what we've done so far. We've managed to get results in at least three of our cases. Savage, the Henshaws and the restaurant scam, although strictly speaking, we have Beth to thank for putting us on the right track with that one.'

'Oh, and I forgot to tell you. The client with the wayward son. She rang me to say she'd found out what he's been up to.'

'Go on, enlighten me,' said Claire.

'Samba classes.'

'Really?'

'Yeah, she caught him practising his Botafogos in his bedroom. Strictly has got a lot to answer for.'

'So, we don't get our fee?'

'No, but three out of four isn't bad.'

Claire smiled. She was enjoying herself despite where they were and why. It was good to have this chat with Ross, and she was pleased she'd signed up to be his partner. There was something deeply satisfying about helping people with their problems without the regulatory constraints they'd suffered in their previous jobs. They were accountable only to the client and each other.

'Will we be coming again tomorrow if they don't have any luck today?' she asked.

'Luke says they are here for the whole week, but I don't think we need be. Yesterday, there was some sense in having me around because of the so-called rapport I've established with Savage and because we owed it to Beth to support her. Now Savage isn't here, and Beth has chosen to stay away, there's little point unless Luke specifically requests our presence. I think we can probably call it quits this afternoon. Like you said, we've done our bit.'

They had walked one-third of the way around the lake. Ross had read it was about a mile in circumference. Luke and the forensics team had remained in clear sight throughout.

'We've missed the coffee break,' said Ross.

'No worries. I've brought refreshments, remember,' said Claire, shrugging off her rucksack to retrieve her flask and pour Ross a cup of steaming tea.

'God, that's a blast from the past. Can't remember the last time I had tea from a flask.'

'Nothing like it,' said Claire, offering him a piece of Kendal Mint Cake.

'No thanks, I'd like to keep my teeth if possible,' he smiled, sharing the gravy brown tea with her.

'Better get back,' she said, shaking the dregs onto the grass. 'Looks like something could be happening. The CSI team are coming down the track.'

Ross and Claire retraced their steps, picking up the pace as they got nearer, arriving back at the site breathless. The CSIs had joined the geophysics team in the far left-hand corner of the grid, close to an outcrop of rocks. Both groups of scientists, along with Denise, were huddled over the equipment.

'Have they found something?' Ross asked Luke.

'Maybe,' said Luke, watching intently.

Denise walked back to join them. 'They say there's a definite cavity about half a metre to the north of those boulders.'

'Maybe we were right,' said Claire. 'Perhaps he did tuck her between the rocks.'

'Let's not get ahead of ourselves,' said Luke, a muscle twitching in his jaw despite every effort to keep things calm.

One of the tech team sauntered over. He was smiling, and Ross couldn't help but think the man probably lived for moments like this. He knew he shouldn't be critical. He had been excited at the prospect of finding Suzanne yesterday. Today, he'd all but convinced himself she wasn't here, or if she was, they wouldn't find her.

'I think we have enough to warrant further investigation. We'll lift the turf and dig a trench in the direction we think the body is lying. It'll be a good day's work if we find her in the first place we've scanned,' he said, rubbing his hands together in anticipation. 'We've got plenty of daylight to get a tent up and a cordon around it. We might even be able to lift her today if the remains are intact.'

Ross had attended the recovery of many bodies in his career, mostly traffic accidents, suicides or lonely old folks discovered weeks after they died in their sleep. He had also been present at numerous postmortems. It never got any easier, and they never ceased to affect him. It was the disconnect between the person they had been when alive and the shell that remained. It was all the more poignant when the individual had been murdered.

Luke gave the go-ahead for the CSI team to lift the first sods of turf.

Once the team had cleared an area of approximately two metres square, they began to scrape away the topsoil to get to the compacted earth underneath. The whole scene felt like an episode of *Time Team* with the grid, the geophys and the slow scrape, scrape, scrape of the trowels that set Ross's teeth on edge. He wondered how long it would take to uncover enough to be sure that these were modern remains and that they were female. He knew the test for ascertaining sex was the width of the pelvis, but even if that part of the skeleton was intact, the remains would still need to be DNA tested before they could be identified as Suzanne's.

Luke was standing by the trench with Denise. Ross decided to edge closer. He noticed Claire hanging back. He wasn't sure whether it was because he'd warned her they might be asked to leave if the team got this far or because of her natural reluctance to witness the remains uncovered. Ross took her arm and walked her forward.

The men crouched by the ditch were removing a gritty layer of soil peppered with small stones and shingle.

'The bones are scattered,' said one, looking up at Luke. 'They've been disturbed probably by animal activity.'

Ross stole a sideways glance at Claire, who looked pale. The men nibbled away the dirt until one revealed something greyish-white and shiny. His movements were measured and careful as he scratched away the debris around the surface until it was almost free. There was silence. Everyone was holding their breath as they watched him gently wriggle the bone free.

'It's a femur, but I'm sorry to say I don't think it's human.'

'How can you tell?' asked Ross, who thought from the look of the long straight bone it could be.

'Much denser than a human femur and shorter than I'd expect for an adult and, can you see here, the linea aspera?' he said, pointing to a rough ridge running along the middle third of the bone, 'It isn't singular like it would be in a human.'

'Can we dig some more, just to be sure?' said Luke, frustration seeping into his tone.

'Of course.' The man rose from his haunches and grabbed a shovel. He had soon sifted free several more bones.

'See here, the fibula and tibia are fused. They'd be separate in a human. I believe we have a sheep or goat, maybe. If you're still not convinced, I can go on and see if we can find the skull, but we'd be wasting time.'

The disappointment was palpable. The group, so buoyant before, had deflated. Only Claire looked relieved.

'I don't think my heart could stand another one of those,' she said. 'I was so certain they'd found her.'

Ross noticed she was shaking. 'Shall we go?' he said. 'I don't think we need to be here any longer.'

'Are you sure? I don't want you to feel you have to leave for my sake.'

'No, I want to leave.'

They said their goodbyes to Denise. Whilst she still looked upbeat, Luke looked despondent.

'We're off,' said Ross. 'One of those perks of not being in the force anymore you were talking about the other night. Good luck, mate.'

'It's a no win situation as far as I'm concerned,' said Luke. 'I'm going to be disappointed if we fail, but I'll get no pleasure in succeeding.'

'I know how you feel,' said Ross, patting his old boss on the back. 'Ring us if you find anything, won't you? I would want to let Beth know before it went on general release.'

'I will, but don't hold your breath.'

Claire and Ross made their way back to the car. They said nothing for the first couple of miles. It was as if they needed silence to digest the day's events. It was Ross who spoke first.

'If I tell you something, will you promise to keep it to yourself?'

'It depends what it's about.'

'It's about Savage and what he said at that group session Mason set up.'

'Go on.'

'He said he was in a relationship with Suzanne Willis.'

'Did you believe him?'

'No. Mason called it an erotomanic delusion. He told me not to say anything about it.'

'Why?'

'He said it could muddy the waters. That some might believe Savage and it would cast doubt on the rape charge.'

'But he confessed to her rape, didn't he?'

'Eventually, but he was reluctant to see it like that in the session. He confessed to date rape... you know, like it was a technicality, and afterwards, Mason went to great lengths to remind me the session wasn't an official interview, that I wasn't a policeman, and that Savage hadn't been cautioned. It was as if he was lining me up for a retraction.'

'So why do you think it didn't play out that way Why do you think it ended up with Savage admitting to Suzanne's murder as well as her rape?'

'I've no idea. Don't get me wrong. I think he's capable of it... well, we know he is, but it all seemed a little convenient, and then when he offered to lead us to the body, it rang even less true.'

'But what's in it for him, or Mason for that matter?'

'For Savage… notoriety, I suppose. You and I have met his type before. As for Mason, well, he was thrilled to hear Neville confess to something new. He was going on about writing a paper about the erotomania thing, and the fact that Suzanne was the trigger for Neville's future crimes. I can't help thinking by adding murder into the equation and by getting the extra publicity surrounding the search of the moor for Suzanne's body, it's played to his personal agenda. It's proof the therapy works.'

'So, do you think Savage killed her or not?'

'To be honest, I don't know. I know with certainty he raped her, no matter what he believes in his warped little mind, but he never even touched on murder in the session, and I can't get it out of my head that Suzanne might have killed herself.'

'You mean right after he raped her?'

'Yes. The whole thing was so horrendous. Trauma, shame. People have been driven to it for less.'

'Well, as someone who's tried…'

'Oh god, I'm sorry, Claire. I totally forgot… I shouldn't have said anything.'

'It's fine, really. I thought I was dying from cancer. I didn't want to suffer a long and painful death. I'd had enough of chemo and hospitals and other people's pity. I saw no future and wanted to die on my own terms.'

'I think Suzanne could have felt like that after what happened. I think because she knew him and let him into her life, she thought she wouldn't be believed. You know what it was like back then. We now know thousands never reported their rapes and how many of those that did, weren't believed by the police or had their cases thrown out of court. It was a different time with different attitudes, and remember, Savage was unknown then. He was a well-liked, respectable family man. Who would have believed him capable?'

'I suppose unless they find her body, we will never know for sure. At least Beth will never have to fret about it. Even if they don't find Suzanne, the official line will be that Savage raped and murdered her mother. I suppose it's better than not knowing?'

'I'm not so sure about that,' said Ross.

Chapter Forty-Six

IT FELL to Eden to break the news to Beth. After four days of fruitless enterprise, the search had been called off and Savage's inability to cement his recollections into solid directions meant it was unlikely to be reconvened for the foreseeable future. The moor was too vast and the budget too small.

Beth didn't seem surprised. Neither was Eden. Without Savage onsite, the media had lost interest, and by the end of the week, they had moved on to bigger things. The chancellor was due to deliver her first autumn budget, and it looked like Trump would be back in the White House in November. A forty-year-old cold case didn't cut it. Once the spotlight was off them, the Devon and Cornwall police force could withdraw without fanfare and get back to their day job.

Eden wondered if, in the long term, not finding Suzanne's body was a blessing in disguise.

'You did all you could,' she comforted Beth. 'Whilst we didn't find her, you at least have the certainty of knowing what happened to her. If you hadn't pursued this, Savage wouldn't have confessed, and you would have been none the wiser.'

'Deep down, I think I knew as soon as I saw his name on that hotel register,' said Beth.

'No regrets then?' said Eden, seeking reassurance. She couldn't help feeling she was somewhat to blame. If on day one she had sat on her suspicions, she could have saved Beth a lot of heartache. She could have told her there wasn't enough to go on and not made the call to Ross, igniting his appetite for a challenge. Beth would not have written her letter to Savage and would have returned to London satisfied.

'None at all,' smiled Beth. 'Once I opened Dad's case, I knew I couldn't walk away. He never stopped looking for Mum, and once he'd gone, who else was there to carry on the mission?'

'I suppose,' said Eden, relieved but still uncertain the man she'd met, who had talked so fondly about his only child, would have left the briefcase if he'd thought for one second it would cause her such grief. 'I can see why it sold so quickly. It's in a lovely spot. Will you be sad to let it go?' said Eden, changing the subject.

'Not really. It was never a happy house. Not after Mum was…' she hesitated, 'left us.'

Eden guessed Beth still could not bring herself to say murdered.

'I'm glad all this didn't affect the sale. I suppose the moor drew attention away from here,' she said, covering Beth's discomfort.

'That, and the fact no one in the village would talk to the press. They're a close-knit lot who protect their own. To them, I'm still little Beth Willis who lost her mum. They cosseted me all my life from gossip. No one ever mentioned Mum to me. They did it back then for Dad's sake, and they've done it again for me now,' Beth said, flicking away a stray tear.

Eden had brought Brian Willis's briefcase with her. In the face of Savage's confession, the police had not been remotely interested in retaining its contents. She'd toyed with the idea of keeping it just in case they changed their minds but had, in the end, decided against it. The information it contained had been a gift from a father to his daughter from beyond the grave. It may have been an unwanted inheritance, but it was Beth's to do with as she wished.

Beth took it from her, and after a brief conversation about the logistics of paying Freda on completion day, Eden left. She sensed Beth needed to move on, and dwelling on the tragedy of the last few weeks wouldn't help her with that. She seemed happy to be turning her back on the house in Flushing. Pretty as it was, it held too many bad memories for her.

Eden knew only too well how she felt. She had suffered not the slightest pang of regret closing the door on her former matrimonial home in London. She wondered now how she ever imagined she could live in the city. She had gone along with Andrew's plans without question. She had allowed him to dictate every aspect of their home, from the colour of the front door to the bedding they slept in, only to have him ditch her and the thousand-thread-count pillowcases for another woman with a queen-size four-poster and a bank balance to match. How she had changed since was as much a surprise to her as to those around her. It had been a struggle at first to rediscover her identity, but she was finally her own person. Moving back to Cornwall and renovating the beach house had been a large part of the process. It was so much more than a house to her. It was a testimony to her ability to make decisions for herself, and she was pleased she had been able to imprint her own unique mark on the place.

The road had been all but deserted on the drive home. The next few weeks would change that. November was nearly upon them, and soon, the shops would begin heralding the coming of Christmas. Their rallying cry seemed to start earlier each year.

Eden's mind drifted back to the horrors of that fateful November night the year before when she and Luke had witnessed a murder outside her office during the Festival of Lights. She shook the hideous image of the man in flames from her mind.

Flora would be arriving later for her sleepover.

She'd stopped at the supermarket on the way to Beth's for popcorn and a giant pack of Haribo. She had been worried that Luke might cancel again after all that had been going on. The search on the moor and the constant press intrusion had taken its toll, but he'd rang that morning to say he'd given his final interview on the matter and that it would feature on the tv news that evening. She decided to record it. He and Flora were due to arrive at six. Both her and Luke wanted to keep Flora free from the demons they dealt with for as long as possible. It was difficult. She was bright and knew what they both did for a living. Soon, social media and playground gossip would kick in and innocence would turn to curiosity. For now, they were resolved to let her shelter in a world of unicorns and princesses. Tonight, they'd ride on a sugar-fuelled high of show tunes and dance routines. There was no room for gloom.

She'd lit a fire before she left, and the beach house felt cosy as she hung up her coat.

The forecast for the weekend was for yet more rain, but this evening, it was dry, with only a light mist drifting across a sea the colour of molten lead. The ebb and flow provided the soundtrack to her life here on the cliff edge. She was never lonely. In summer, the place was teeming with life. She would surf, walk the cliffs, or head for the beach, where she'd be sure to find someone to talk to. Other times, she'd take a chair outside and watch the turn of the tides as the gulls swooped above her head.

This evening, a wintery sky tinged with purple and apricot, had lifted her spirits. Maybe someday she'd find someone to share this place with, but if not, she wouldn't beat herself up about it. Flora might turn out to be the closest thing to a child of her own she'd ever have. If so, it was enough for her.

She put the brown paper bag of popcorn in the microwave, listening to it pop and crackle as the kitchen filled with the delicious sugary scent of caramel. She heard the front door open and close and looked up at the clock. Luke was early.

'I'm in the kitchen,' she shouted, toppling the popcorn into a large plastic bowl.

'Popcorn coming through,' she said, stopping in her tracks as she entered the sitting room and saw Tristan standing by the fire, holding a bottle of champagne.

'Salty or sweet?' he asked.

Eden almost dropped the bowl. 'What are you doing here?'

'I thought I'd surprise you,' he said, his mouth twitching with the approximation of a smile.

She carefully placed the bowl on the table and took a

deep breath. 'I thought I made myself clear. We're not a good fit.'

Tristan placed the bottle of Moët on the table next to the bowl. 'But we could be. We got off to a bad start, that's all. You can't end what we have because of one drunken mistake.'

'I can do what I like,' said Eden, unwilling to pander to his ego.

'It's unfair,' he snarled, his mouth set, his tone vicious.

'Don't they say all's fair in love and war?'

'Surely you can do better than resort to tired cliches,' he goaded. 'Put your arguments forward if you want to defend your case.'

'I have no need to defend myself. I am not on trial. I'm sorry you think I'm your intellectual inferior. No… actually, I take that back. I'm not sorry. It illustrates my point perfectly. We are very different people. I was once married to someone who criticised every move I made. My taste, my clothes, the books I read, and I won't let it happen again. Move on, Tristan. Find someone you can share your life with without the burden of having to bring them up to your standard. The only reason you're still interested in me is because you can't have me. You're used to getting what you want. Put this whole episode down to good fortune on your part. You have had a lucky escape.'

Tristan's face was puce with rage. 'Don't tell me what I should or shouldn't do. If I say I want you, I mean it.'

The front door opened. It was Luke, Flora by his side, loaded down with her backpack and clutching her favourite cuddly monkey. Luke's face dropped as he saw Tristan.

'Are we interrupting something?' he said.

Eden could tell from his expression he sensed the tension in the room.

'No… no, you're not. Tristan was just leaving.'

'I didn't see your car parked outside?' said Luke, fixing a steady stare on Tristan.

'I parked in the village.'

Luke helped Flora out of her coat. She ran to Eden, who gathered her up into her arms.

'Where are you staying?' Luke asked.

'I haven't booked anywhere,' Tristan replied, with frozen-faced sullenness.

Eden guessed he had wrongly assumed he would wheedle his way back into her affections and stay there the night.

'Well, if you set off now, you'll be over the border in no time and in Bristol in a couple of hours. You'll have a better choice there,' Luke said, crossing the room to join Eden and his daughter.

Tristan glared at the pair of them. Then, lifting his discarded jacket from the arm of the chair, he headed for the door.

'I'll give you a lift to the village if you like?' offered Luke.

'I'll walk,' snarled Tristan.

'Don't forget this,' Luke shouted after him, lifting the bottle of champagne.

'Keep it,' said Tristan.

'No thanks,' said Luke, following him to the door and thrusting the bottle into his hand. 'The stuff gives me wind.'

Eden watched the door slam. She had a feeling she wouldn't be seeing Tristan Villiers again.

Heart pounding, she retreated to the kitchen. Her hand was shaking as she grabbed a glass and turned on the tap. Luke came up behind her, took the glass from her, and filled it.

'Here,' he said, handing it to her.

She was trying not to cry as she took a sip but felt a treacherous tear trickle down her cheek.

'Did you know he was coming?' asked Luke, his voice gentle and concerned.

'No. I left the door unlocked for you and Flora. When I saw him… I could have…' The floodgates opened.

Luke took the glass from her and drew her to him, holding her for a long time with her face buried in his chest as she sobbed.

'You're okay,' he soothed, resting his chin on the top of her head.

Luke's shirt was wet when she finally pulled away.

'I'm sorry,' she said.

'Don't worry,' he grinned. 'Didn't you know snotty tops are all the rage?'

Eden laughed.

'Come on,' Luke said, taking her by the hand, 'let's get this party started.'

Flora was sitting cross-legged on the floor and colouring. Sweeping her up onto the settee next to him, Luke grabbed a handful of popcorn. Eden settled next to her niece, who immediately snuggled into her.

'God, I love a good musical,' said Luke, raising his eyebrows at Eden.

She imagined he was lying. Then again, maybe not. Maybe Flora had inherited her love of show tunes from her dad? After all, he was full of surprises.

———

LATER THAT EVENING, once Luke had left and Flora had gone to bed, Eden watched the recording of Luke's press conference. He had seemed happy and relaxed with her and Flora. He'd had the sense not to question her more about Tristan, and she had felt vindicated.

The figure he cut on the television screen was a different creature altogether: tense and dejected, like a battle-weary soldier, wounded but still standing.

'It is the policy of this force to always respond to credible evidence in a missing person case such as this. We had direct testimony from the man who confessed to the murder of Suzanne Willis, and it was our duty to investigate. Unfortunately, despite an extensive and gruelling search with the benefit of all the manpower we could muster and the assistance of modern technology, we have not found human remains on Bodmin Moor. However, I must stress this does not mean the matter is over. We will strive to gather more information from the perpetrator of this terrible crime in our endeavour to return Suzanne Willis to her family. This has been a stressful and upsetting time for them, and I hope that the media will now allow them time to come to terms with their loss and to grieve in private. Thank you.'

Eden switched off the television and made her way upstairs to bed, wondering if Beth had watched the interview. The woman deserved some peace. She, like Luke, hoped to god she would get it.

Chapter Forty-Seven

One week later

BETH WAS SURPRISED to see Freda waiting for her on the doorstep, her spare frame hunched against the cold. On spotting Beth, an expression of relief flooded across her aunt's face. Beth wondered what on earth she wanted. Eden had confirmed she'd told her the sale of the property was going through and had asked for her bank details. Everything was settled as far as Beth was concerned.

Beth still hadn't quite forgiven Freda for the callous way she had broken the news of her dad's death or for not attending his funeral. It had niggled for weeks like grit in her eye, but given everything that had happened since finding Dad's briefcase and Savage's surprise confession, it now seemed insignificant. This might be the last time she sees Freda. Once the house was sold, she had no reason to come back to Cornwall. In fact, she had every reason to stay away. She decided to remain magnanimous no matter what.

She had no wish to part with the taste of an argument in her mouth.

'I've been to the shops. I wasn't expecting you,' she said, managing to crack a thin smile.

'No, I'm sorry. I should have rang,' said Freda.

'Let's not talk on the doorstep. You look cold… come in.'

Beth led the way through to the kitchen. Most of the house, including the sitting room, had been cleared, but the buyers had wanted the pine kitchen table and chairs because they matched the units. Beth was glad of them now. At least they could talk sitting down.

Freda did not remove her coat, and Beth wondered if seeing the house empty was too much for her and she'd decided she wasn't stopping.

'Can I get you a cup of tea?' Beth asked.

'If it's not too much trouble.'

'I hope you weren't waiting long?'

'No, not long,' said Freda, but the way she cradled the warm cup between her hands suggested otherwise.

Beth sat opposite and noticed for the first time how pleated with wrinkles her aunt's face was and how her eyes were red-rimmed and puffy as if she'd been crying.

'I wanted to thank you for the money from the house,' Freda said.

Beth felt embarrassed. 'Fingers crossed, everything will go through smoothly. We exchange contracts next week and complete a couple of weeks later. The money will go straight into your account.'

'It will make such a difference,' Freda said, her bottom lip wobbling.

Beth had never seen Freda so emotional, and it felt a little uncomfortable, given the circumstances.

'Please don't upset yourself,' she comforted. 'It's no more than you deserve for taking care of Dad and me for all those years.'

'I should have been kinder to you both,' Freda said, pausing to blow her nose. 'I feel so awful now I know what happened to your mother. I can't stop thinking about the way that man killed her and dumped her body like she was a piece of rubbish.'

'Look, Freda, I know it's hard, but no one could have known Savage was involved.'

'But I know your dad suspected something. I saw him taking cuttings from the paper after that man was caught when what he'd done to those other women came out. I think your dad suspected he might have something to do with it. He might have gone back to the police if I hadn't persuaded him not to because... well, because I was so sure Suzanne had gone off with the other chap.'

Beth put down her cup. 'What other chap?'

'The one she was seeing.'

Beth remembered her conversation with Jean about Freda's allegations... about the hotel and the girls having relations with the commercial travellers who stayed there. If Freda had come there just to spread more lies and rumours about her mum, she had a good mind to follow Jean's advice and let her whistle for her money.

'Will you never give up on this?' she snapped. 'This nonsense you've got into your head about mum being... what do you call it... a floozy? Mum was never involved with another man. I spoke to Jean about it. Some of the other single girls at the hotel might have had flings with the men who stayed there, but not Mum.'

'But I saw her with my own eyes,' said Freda, twisting a handkerchief between dishpan hands.

Beth's temple began to throb. 'What do you mean, you saw her?'

'I saw the man with your mum.'

'Who was he… what was his name?'

'I don't know, I never got a proper look at him, tall, shortish dark hair.'

'It could have been anyone, a colleague from work. There's nothing to say there was anything untoward going on,' argued Beth.

Freda grasped the handle of her cup tightly as if it was the only thing keeping her grounded.

'They were kissing,' she stuttered.

The words came like a blow. 'When was this?'

'A month or so before she disappeared. I called around with some scraps for the dog. I knew your mum was home because her car was parked outside. I tried the door, but it was locked. It was never locked when people were home.'

Beth knew Freda was right. Back then, she doubted if anyone in the village had locked their doors during daylight hours.

'I thought she'd popped around to the shop or something. The container didn't have a lid, and I didn't want to leave the scraps on the front step in case the seagulls got them, so I went round the back thinking I'd leave them by the back door with a stone on the top… that's when I saw them. They were down the bottom of the garden by the door, and they were hugging and then … they kissed. I was at the top of the garden. They were too wrapped up in each other to notice me hiding behind the shed.'

The back garden, like all of those in the street, rose steeply in a series of terraces up to a lane that ran along the back of the houses.

'He left that way,' continued Freda. 'Walked straight past me to his car, which was parked in the lane.'

'But you still didn't recognise him?'

'He had his collar up, and I only saw him for a second. I had my head down. I was so worried he'd see me,' she said, her voice cracking.

Beth's heart was in her mouth. 'Did you confront Mum?'

'To be honest, I didn't know what to do. I was so shocked. I left with the scraps still in my hand.'

'Did you tell Dad?'

'To my shame, I didn't.'

'Didn't you tell anyone... the police... anyone?' said Beth.

'I told Ron. I knew Jean would snap my head off if I told her, but I'd known Ron for years since he and your dad were kids together. So I told him, knowing he'd tell Jean, and she'd have a sisterly word with Suzanne, make her see sense before too much harm was done. I thought if she did that, there would be no need for your dad to ever know.'

The picture Freda was painting was so at odds with the one drawn by Jean that Beth didn't know what to think or what to believe.

'And did she... have a word with Mum?'

'You'd best ask Jean.'

'You never checked?'

'No, when your mum left, I assumed Jean had failed to persuade her to stay.'

'But why didn't you tell the police?'

'I know how bad it sounds... but how could I admit I'd seen them together? Your dad would have blamed me for not telling him, thinking if I had, he might have been able to stop her. I thought it best to say nothing and to let the police do their job and find her. That way, they would be the ones to break the news to your dad and I need not be involved. But they never found her, did they, and now we know why.'

'And Jean, she decided to keep quiet too?'

'I suppose she must have because the police never came back to me with any questions about what I'd seen.'

'Did you not wonder why Mum hadn't taken me with her?' cried Beth, her heart wrenching.

'I thought she might send for you later when she was settled. As time went on, I just thought she was selfish… that she'd met someone she thought was better than your dad… better than all of us. That she didn't care… but she did… she did.'

Freda slumped in her seat, her body rocking back and forth.

BETH WASN'T sure what to do with the grenade Freda had lobbed at her. Was it so hard to believe her mother was having an affair in the weeks or even months before she died? She wasn't the first married woman to be unfaithful, and given what had happened to her, no one could begrudge her anything.

Beth had no idea who her mum was, if she was honest. Parents kept secrets they didn't share with their children. She knew that much from her own experience. When she and Liam were in the throes of splitting up, they routinely put on a brave face for Grace's benefit, even on days when they could have happily killed each other.

If she was honest, it wasn't her mother's infidelity she found difficult to swallow, but rather the fact Jean had chosen to deny it, albeit in a roundabout way, by dismissing Freda's accusations as spiteful nonsense. She had given her every opportunity to tell the truth. She'd specifically asked her about her mother's private life, and she'd chosen to lie about something that could have been relevant.

As far as she was aware, Jean had known nothing about her dad's obsession with Savage, yet her reaction had nevertheless been to dissuade her from digging further concerning her mum's disappearance. Had this been the reason why? Had she wanted to keep her sister's reputation intact? Beth appreciated her concern, but there had been no need to react in the way she had, especially her attack on Freda.

At least Freda had the temerity to come clean after Savage's admission. Jean, on the other hand, had remained resolutely silent. There was nothing for it; she'd have to ask her aunt why.

Ron and Jean had invited her over for Sunday lunch. She'd raise the subject then. She wouldn't make a big deal about it, but it needed to be out in the open. If she was going to draw a line in the sand, she needed to do it once and for all. Her past would be where it belonged, behind her, but it needed to be a past with integrity.

Her mother was a living, breathing human being like the rest of them. The fact that she had been murdered by Savage did not make her a saint any more than it made Savage the devil or the voice she had heard in her head on the night of her mother's disappearance that of an Angel. She was determined to mourn her mum as the woman she really was and not some after-the-event concoction to make her look good. There had been enough brushing of things under the carpet.

Chapter Forty-Eight

BETH ARRIVED at Jean's at twelve-thirty. She'd been warned that her cousin Ruby and her ten-year-old twin boys were joining them for lunch, and there was to be no talk of Savage in front of them. Beth had no wish to raise the subject of her mum's infidelity while they were there either. She needed to say what she had to say after they'd left.

Jean greeted her with a hug, as always, before ushering her into the kitchen, where she was putting the finishing touches to a roast dinner that looked as if it would serve double the number coming.

'There's a bottle of white chilling in the fridge,' she said. 'You're not driving, are you?'

'No, I came across on the ferry,' replied Beth.

'Good, then pour us both a glass. I think after what we've been through over the last couple of months, we deserve one, don't you?'

Beth wanted to say *we're not out of the woods yet* but bit her tongue as she retrieved the Sauvignon Blanc and poured two glasses.

'Ruby's driving and Ron's got a beer on the go. Dave's not coming. He's got a rugby match in Camborne this afternoon, so we've got the bottle to ourselves,' Jean continued, opening the oven and pulling out a tray of golden-brown roast potatoes.

'Would you be a love and give that gravy a stir while I go and call Ron to carve the beef?'

Beth took a large gulp of wine. She needed Dutch courage to get through today. She listened to Jean shout up to Ron from the bottom of the stairs, then heard the heavy clatter of the man as he descended.

'What were you doing up there? This meat won't carve itself. Ruby and the boys will be here in a minute,' Jean chided.

Beth looked at her watch. She was longing for time to fly this afternoon.

Lunch was a raucous affair, and the meal seemed to go on forever. Ruby was her usual ebullient self and, after lunch, seemed reluctant to leave. Given the way the kids were running riot in the garden, Beth guessed she was glad for an opportunity to share the load rather than take them home without Dave there to keep them occupied. By the time she gathered them up and Jean packed her off with the leftovers for Dave, it was nearly four o'clock.

Once Ruby had gone, Beth helped Jean load the last of the dishes into the dishwasher while Ron cleared the lawn of the kid's detritus. Beth chose the moment to open the conversation she'd been itching to have all afternoon.

'Freda came to see me yesterday,' she said.

Jean was at the sink scrubbing the roasting dish.

'Really? What did *holier than thou* want?'

Beth ignored the jibe. 'To thank me for the money from the sale of the house. Not that she's got it yet, but we exchange and complete within the month, so I suppose she knows it's only a matter of time.'

'I hope she was suitably grateful.'

Beth noticed the edge to her aunt's voice. 'She was. I don't think I've ever seen her so emotional. We talked a bit about Mum.'

Jean said nothing, but Beth could tell she was biting her lip as she wiped the sink clean and began polishing the tap so hard Beth thought she might dislodge a washer.

'Jean, can we sit down for a minute to talk?'

Jean turned, the dishcloth hovering in her hand.

'Of course,' she said, her eyes searching as she plonked herself down at the kitchen table next to Beth.

Beth shared the last of the wine between their empty glasses and took a deep breath.

'She told me about Mum's affair.'

Jean's eyes narrowed. 'I've told you before that woman's obsessed,' she ranted. 'My sister was raped, and god knows what else before that maniac strangled her and buried her heaven knows where, but that's not enough for Saint bloody Freda. She won't be satisfied until she's dragged Suzy's battered remains through the mud. I'm telling you Beth, that woman, for all her praying and piety, is evil... pure bloody evil.'

Beth was determined not to be put off by Jean's outburst. She believed Freda, and if that was the case, Jean's attack was a well-rehearsed diversion tactic she wasn't going to swallow for a second time. She continued in a measured tone.

'She told me everything. About seeing Mum in the back garden with a man in the weeks before her disappearance and about telling Ron.'

Jeans jaw dropped. 'Ron?'

Beth drained her glass and then slowly relayed Freda's story.

Jean, pale and dumbstruck throughout, twisted in her seat as if tied to the chair but longing to escape. When Beth got to the part where Freda divulged everything to Ron expecting him to tell his wife to have a word with her sister, her face screwed into an expression bordering on agony. Her voice was little more than a whisper as she said:

'He never said a thing.'

Beth's stomach roiled. 'You're saying he never relayed the message?'

Jean, peering into her empty glass, shook her head.

Beth jumped as the kitchen door opened. Ron stood there, ruddy-cheeked and puffing from the exertion of clearing up after his grandsons.

'All done,' he said cheerily. 'That pair are a two-man demolition crew,' he grinned.

Beth watched his gaze settle on his wife, and the smile slip from his face.

'Is everything alright in here?' he frowned.

Jean hastily wiped a tear away with the back of her hand before casting Beth a look that told her niece in no uncertain terms to keep stum.

'We're fine,' Jean said, 'you go through to watch the football. I'll bring you a cup of tea in a bit. We're just finishing our wine and having a bit of a girl talk. We got a bit nostalgic that's all, didn't we, Beth?'

Beth nodded. 'Yes, that's it… drinking in the after-noon… never a good idea.'

Ron's smile returned. 'I'll let you get on with it then,' he said.

Jean shut the door after him and turned to Beth. 'You need to let me have this out with him on my own.'

'Can't we just ask him now and get it over and done with?'

'No, we can't,' said Jean, struggling to keep her voice down. 'You've just told me my husband has kept something from me for years... something that might have helped the police find my sister when she went missing. Do you not see how devastating that is... to be told that the person you share everything with has kept something that important from you?' she said, rising from her seat and turning her back on Beth.

'You need to leave,' she said.

'But...' Beth stuttered.

'Now!' shouted Jean, head bent, knuckles white, as she clung to the edge of the worktop.

Beth grabbed her coat from the back of the chair and left.

———

THICK PURPLE CLOUDS bundled as she queued to board the last ferry back to Flushing. It had just gone five, but it seemed as if dusk had already fallen. The waterfront cafés were tallying up their takings and closing their doors for the day, the threat of yet another biblical downpour scuppering any chance of a last rush. Across the water, her neighbours had their lights on. She imagined their warm, cosy interiors so unlike the hollow house devoid of comforts she was heading for. As the engine started, she pulled up her hood, hoping she'd make it back before the heavens opened.

She was confused by Jean's reaction, not to mention angry with herself. Why had she felt so compelled to relay her conversation with Freda? She regretted it bitterly now. It had caused yet more trouble after they'd already had a gut full of that over the last few months. What purpose did it serve when Savage had admitted to everything? Was she really so needy she needed everyone to acknowledge that despite having an affair, her mum had not abandoned her. Was that what this was all about? If so, she was a hypocrite on top of everything else. She might not have left her own daughter for another man, but she'd all but abandoned Grace since her dad's death to solve the mystery of her mum's disappearance, and even now, after the mystery had been solved, it wasn't enough for her. She had to know everything, every sordid detail of her mother's life before she could lay her ghost to rest and make sense of it all. Did that mean she had to disregard everyone else's feelings… ruin the trust between her aunt and uncle? Was she, just as Freda said back when Dad died, a drama queen?

Chapter Forty-Nine

BETH WAS SOAKING and chilled to the bone by the time she got back to the house. The rain had well and truly set in. She hadn't intended to switch the heating on during her stay. The boiler had been serviced just before her dad died, but she hadn't wanted to tempt fate and risk it going on the blink before the sale went through. Nevertheless, she needed to dry her clothes. She flicked the switch and hoped for the best. Either way, she'd be lighting a fire in the sitting room later. She intended to burn the contents of her dad's briefcase. She didn't want to take any of it home with her, and in the absence of a shredder, she wasn't happy to bin the documents.

She looked at her watch. It was six o'clock. She decided to pack now and set the alarm for an early start. She didn't have the stomach to stay any longer. If Jean rang that evening, all well and good, but she wasn't going to hang around waiting for her to finish arguing with Ron. She had all the answers she needed. She had no doubt in her mind that Freda had told the truth but that Jean had not known a thing about it because Ron had chosen not to tell her. She was relieved that her Auntie Jean had kept nothing from her.

Showered and packed, she made herself a sandwich from the last of the loaf she bought the day before. She decided to make an extra one to take in the car with her for the journey home. It would save stopping at a service station and paying their exorbitant prices. She'd double up on coffees when she stopped for petrol in Truro.

She hadn't realised until today how much she wanted to get home to Grace. She never thought she'd admit to missing the antics of a hormonal thirteen-year-old, but absence made the heart grow fonder and the senses more forgiving. She longed to hear her daughter's bedroom door slam and the 'It's so unfair', and the 'nobody else's mum minds them staying out past ten o'clock!'

She knew from now on, she'd have to avoid firing off the obvious retort; 'Nobody else's mum has crossed paths with a serial killer.'

She'd never use it, of course. She did not want her mother's disappearance to define Grace. Her dad had done the best he could to protect her, and now she would protect her own daughter in the same way. She didn't want her to grow up suspicious and fearful, seeing danger around every corner. She had raised Grace to be a feminist, but that didn't mean she had to be afraid of men. Liam, like her own dad, was a gentle, loving, sensitive man. Men like Savage should not be allowed to hijack an entire gender. Beth was no psychologist, but it stood to reason, if you encouraged young women to vilify young men, those men would become introverted and resentful and some, inflamed with anger. You would create a self-fulfilling prophecy.

She decided to phone her daughter on the landline so she could let Liam know her plans for collecting Grace the next day.

'Hiya, how's it going?' asked Liam cheerfully.

'Well, the packing's all done, and I've managed to bury the hatchet with Freda. I'll tell you the rest when I see you. How's Grace been?'

'Fine. I hardly see her to tell you the truth. She seems to live a sub-aquatic life in the bathroom. I spend most of my time running around the house picking up wet towels. What's all that about? How can one small person use four towels every time they have a bath?'

'Welcome to my world.'

'Do you want to speak to her?'

'In a second. I wanted to let you know I'll be home to pick her up from school tomorrow. If you make sure she takes her holdall with her, that would be great.'

'Why don't I bring that over tomorrow evening? You know she'll kick off if I ask her to drag it onto the bus. She brought enough for a month... in any event, I'd like to see you. That's if you haven't got plans?'

'Only ones that involve a large bottle of wine and a comfy mattress.'

'Good, then I'll be round after work. I'll bring a take-away. Save you cooking after a long drive.'

She heard Grace's voice in the background.

'Is that Mum?'

'I'll hand you over... see you tomorrow, Beth.'

Grace came to the phone. 'Hi Mum, when are you home?'

'I'll be there to pick you up from school tomorrow.'

'Buzzing... can we go into town next week? Sophie's got these cool new trainers, and mine are really cringe, and it's nearly my birthday, and Dad said he'd throw in some money, and I'll do lots of work at home… jobs and things around the house… and—'

Beth laughed. 'Okay, okay… I surrender,' she said, relieved normality had been restored.

'Dad said he'll bring your bag over later, so no need to take it to school with you. He's bringing a takeaway too, so tell him what you fancy.'

'Wicked… I'm vegetarian now, just in case you didn't know.'

'You won't be wanting a bacon sandwich later then,' Liam shouted in the background.

'Lame…' retorted Grace.

Liam took the phone. 'Bye, Beth, see you tomorrow.'

Beth's heart lifted as she put the phone down, relieved all this would soon be over. She had one more thing to do. She walked to the hallway and opened the understairs cupboard where she had stashed the briefcase Eden had dropped back to her the day before. She carried it through to the sitting room before returning to the kitchen for the box of matches and firelighters she'd bought in the village shop, especially for the occasion.

The doorbell rang. Ron and Jean stood on the threshold, a pair of bedraggled strays. They slipped in without speaking. Beth turned her back on them, remaining poker-faced, as she gestured toward the kitchen table, glad they wouldn't be sitting like cub scouts cross-legged on the floor. Beth sensed this would be no jamboree.

Ron looked like a man on the brink. Beth imagined he'd endured a grilling from his wife.

'We've had a chat,' said Jean, 'and we want to talk to you about the house. You said you haven't exchanged contracts yet?'

'Look, if this is about Freda, I've told you before, my mind is made up.'

'It's not about Freda,' snapped Jean. 'Everything isn't about bloody Freda.'

Ron rose from his seat and walked to the window. It was pitch-black outside, and Beth had no idea what he was searching for in the darkness other than an escape route.

'Ron and I have discussed things, and we'd like to buy this house.'

Beth hadn't been expecting this. She'd anticipated an explanation as to why Ron had not confided in Jean about her mother's affair.

'Why would you want to do that?' asked Beth, confused.

'We'd like to move back to Flushing. It's where Ron grew up after all. It holds so many memories, and this place is the right size for us now we're getting on a bit.'

'But what about your house?'

'Ruby and the kids need more space, and we've got plenty of that and a big garden. You saw yourself what the boys are like. They need room to run wild. Their place is pokey, and they've only got a small backyard. We've decided to let them buy ours for the same price as they can sell for.'

'And you can afford to do that?' said Beth, sceptically.

'Ron got a decent lump sum when he was made redundant from the dockyard which we invested carefully. We've got no debt, and we're both on good pensions. Ron does a bit of work now and then for a few regulars, so yes... we're comfortable, and you can't take it with you.'

'Why didn't you say anything earlier, before I put the place on the market?' Beth said, thinking about the estate agent's fee she'd incurred.

'I suppose until you told me today that everything was

going through, we hadn't really thought about it, but now we realise it's just what we need.'

Beth noticed Ron hadn't said a word.

'What do you think about all this?' she asked him.

'It's what your aunt wants. Like she said, our place is too big for us.'

He didn't sound convinced. Neither was she. She couldn't get her head around why they would want to do this. This place needed all sorts of work done to it; new windows and the kitchen units were on their last legs. Ron had transformed their place into a little palace over the years. It was only last year that they converted their fourth bedroom into an en-suite. Neither Ron nor Jean had ever mentioned moving before or that they found their place too big.

Beth scrutinised Jean, looking for clues. 'What's really going on here?' she said.

'I don't know what you mean. I've told you we'd like to buy it. We'll pay the same price... more if you think you'll be out of pocket because of withdrawing from the other sale. You can still pay Freda the way you said. I don't know why you're making so much of this?' Jean stammered, her voice rising to a near-hysterical pitch.

'Because there's something not right here. You're not telling me something.'

'Our money isn't good enough for you, is that it?' screamed Jean.

'For god's sake woman, tell her,' barked Ron, stirring from his apathy. 'She deserves to know.'

Jean looked up at her husband, her eyes pleading.

'Tell me what?' said Beth, trying to keep her voice even as she trawled their expressions for answers.

Ron turned to face them, his huge workingman's hands hanging by his sides like shovels.

'Jean, get the girl a glass of water.'

Why did he insist on calling her a girl and talking to her as if she were a child?

'I don't need a glass of water,' said Beth, beginning to lose her patience. 'What the hell is going on?'

'Freda told you the truth,' said Ron. 'She told me about your mum, but I didn't tell Jean like she asked. It took me a while to decide not to. It wasn't an easy decision.'

Beth looked at Jean. Her face was blank.

'Why did you decide not to tell her?'

'Because I chose to tell your dad instead.'

Beth's stomach squirmed like a barrel of eels. 'Dad knew?'

'He was my best friend. How could I not tell him? He wouldn't have kept something like that from me. If Jean was playing away, he'd have told me. He'd stood as best man at our wedding, and I returned the favour when he married your mum. I thought the four of us would grow old together, but Suzy seemed intent on ruining it for all of us.'

Silence descended as Beth tried to process what Ron was saying. Her throat tightened. Her words were little more than a whisper. 'How did he react?'

'What does it matter, all these years later? You know what happened to her.'

Jean straightened in her seat. 'How dare you,' she spat, shooting a viperous glare at Ron. 'You just told me to tell the truth, well now it's out there, I'll be damned if I let you rein it in when it suits you.'

'Jean, we agreed,' said Ron, his face creased with anxiety.

'She was my sister... my best friend. You protected

Brian but didn't give me the chance to protect her,' she screamed, jaw set, eyes blazing.

Beth had no idea what they were talking about. It was a shock knowing her dad had known about the affair, but why was it relevant to them wanting to buy the house?

Ron sighed. 'Alright, have it your way, but on your head be it.'

'She's not stupid, Ron. She's her mother's daughter.'

'What did he say when you told him?' said Beth, imagining her dad's anguish. He adored her mum.

'He laughed it off at first. He said Freda was a jealous cow and that she'd never liked Suzy because of the way she looked and how she fooled around all the time. He said his sister thought fun was a dirty word and would have preferred him to marry a meek-mannered virgin from the Kingdom Hall. Someone she could bully. He hadn't even bothered to ask Suzy about it. He thought relations between the two of them were bad enough and that if Suzy knew Freda had been stirring the pot, she'd hit the roof. He didn't like his sister much, but he was all she had.

'Bitch,' muttered Jean under her breath.

Beth heaved a sigh of relief, but the reprieve was short-lived, and her heart sank as Ron continued.

'I knew there was more to it, and the clues hadn't been difficult to spot once the idea was in my head. There was the time Jean came home saying Suzy was having problems with her phone. She'd had two wrong numbers while she was around at hers having coffee and had, on the third call, taken it off the hook. You don't have to be a genius to put two and two together there. Then there was the evening your dad and me went for a drink in the Cutty Sark after work. I'd gone to the bar to get the first round in, and the landlady let slip that Suzy had been in that afternoon. I asked if Jean had been there too, but she said no, Suzy had been with a man. Something to do with the hotel. Why would Suzy meet someone trying to sell to the hotel in a pub when the hotel had plenty of places to talk and the drinks were free? I decided there and then to watch her like a hawk. My suspicions were confirmed when I called round to go fishing with your dad one Saturday morning and picked up the post on the way in. I wouldn't ordinarily read another man's mail, but the post-card caught my eye. Playa del Ingles, Gran Canaria. Palm trees and winter sun. Curiosity got the better of me, and I flipped it over, wondering if the lucky sod who sent it was someone I knew. It read *Wish you were here. xx*. I didn't think anything of it until I handed it to your mum, who, hearing Brian on the stairs, ripped it in two and chucked it in the bin.'

'You told Dad your suspicions?'

'If you could have seen his face. I hadn't seen your dad cry since we were kids. It's a terrible thing to see a man like your dad go to pieces. After that, he sort of turned in on himself. When he didn't mention it again, I thought he'd sorted it. I didn't think bringing it up would be a good idea. Once I'd told him I stopped watching Suzy, they seemed fine. But that night, he told me he hadn't said anything yet… that he'd wanted to find out who the hell this man was before he'd confronted her. He'd been to the hotel and photocopied the guest list in the office behind reception when your mum was fetching her coat after her shift. I asked him for the bloke's name, but he said he'd rather keep it to himself.'

'You make him sound like a bloody martyr,' spat Jean.

'When you say *that night*. What night are we talking about here?' said Beth.

'Go on, tell her,' Jean yelled, her lips twisted with contempt.

'Think about the girl, Jeanie. She doesn't need to know this. That man has admitted to killing Suzy. It's over.'

'It's not over just because you want it to be. You can't change things to suit you... so you feel better. Not now... not ever,' Jean raved, jumping up and rushing at him, fists clenched.

Ron grabbed her by her wrists and pulled her into him. Jean's legs buckled as her husband gathered her in his arms and buried her sobs.

Beth's head was swimming with thoughts she was struggling to process. Her dad and the contents of the briefcase. A thick, murky, foul-smelling miasma of information which wouldn't clear.

'I'm so sorry, Beth,' said Ron, beads of sweat trickling down his temple.

'I helped him after, that's all.'

Jean pulled herself free of her husband, wiping the tears away with her sleeve.

'That's all...' she scoffed, slumping back into her chair like a rag doll, the stuffing knocked out of her.

Ron joined them at the table. 'I gave Brian an alibi for the night she disappeared,' he said, exhaling loudly. 'We were both meant to be working at the dockyard that night. He came to me and asked if I'd cover for him. He said he needed to go home and have it out with your mum. He had a wildness in his eyes. He seemed almost excited. I warned him not to do anything stupid. "I won't need to", he said. "I'm going to tell her a few home truths about that fella, that's all."

'Home truths?' said Beth.

'He told me he'd done some digging, and he was a

married man with kids. "I bet the cheating bastard's not told Suzy that", he said. I knew there was nothing I could say to stop him. I knew if I didn't cover for him, he could lose his job, and that was the last thing he needed on top of everything else. I punched his card in, and I punched it out again when I left the next morning.'

'And you stuck to the story when the police checked his alibi?' said Beth.

Ron nodded. 'I was in too deep by then, and he swore to me he'd had nothing to do with your mum's disappearance. He said when he got home, she was already gone, and I believed him at first.'

'What changed your mind?'

'Something Jean mentioned,' he said, reaching across the table and taking his wife's hands between his. 'She was worried because your mum left with nothing, no clothes... just what she was wearing. She hadn't taken her purse, and her car was still outside. It didn't sound like her, and it began to niggle, but it was when she didn't contact you. She would never have left you.'

'Well, we know why now, don't we? It was because Savage had taken her.'

'If only it were that simple, love.'

'I don't understand?' said Beth.

'It's the worst feeling in the world to know something so awful and not to have the guts to know what to do with it. I kept thinking... she's lost her mum, she can't lose her dad too, and what would happen to me and my family? I'd lied to the police. I waited all the time, hoping Suzy would turn up. Then the opportunity arose about six months later. Jean was out on a works do. I invited your dad around to mine. We had a few beers, and I told him I didn't believe Suzy had just upped and left. I quizzed him about the clothes and the fact she would never have left without you.'

Beth's throat tightened as tears pooled and snaked down her cheeks. She knew in her heart what was coming. She wanted to cover her ears… scream. Anything to block out what Ron was saying.

'He denied it at first, but I wouldn't let it go. I kept on at him… told him I'd go to the police until eventually he broke down and told me everything. How he'd come home and parked up in the back lane. I'd told him that's where Freda had seen the bloke. He was expecting him to be there, you see. I asked him how he knew, and he told me he worked it out from your mum's calendar.'

Beth thought of the dates ringed in red.

'Mad as it might seem, I think he wanted to catch them together. He was so riled up. I think he wanted to expose him with her there so he could see the affair disintegrate in front of him. Why else would he put himself through that kind of torture?'

'And did he… catch them together?' asked Beth, imagining the sordid showdown.

'No, he'd gone, but he had been there. Brian said the bed was still warm, the sheets crumpled and stinking of sex. Suzy's underwear was on the floor along with…' he trailed off.

'What?' asked Beth.

Ron looked embarrassed. 'Along with a used condom.'

It was too awful. 'Oh God,' choked Beth.

'Your mother was in the bath. She didn't deny a thing. She just sat there in the bath, rocking and hugging her knees and when he tried to touch her, she screamed and pushed him away. Can you imagine how that felt for him? Knowing your wife has just been with another man and it's you she can't bear to touch her. He told her the man was married, that he had children, and he'd never leave his wife. He said he forgave her, and they could work it out, but she was having none of it. She told him not to look at her, to get away from her. She said she had to leave and that she had to take you with her. Your dad lost it then when she said she was taking you. She said she was going to wake you there and then and leave. She was hysterical, screaming and carrying on. That's when he covered her mouth. He just wanted her to shut up.'

'Oh, Suzy…' groaned Jean, her head in her hands.

'Then you woke up and he panicked. He was certain you'd hear her. She was hysterical, fighting and flaying about in the water. That's when he pushed her under and held her there until she stopped.'

Jean let out a sob and ran from the room. Ron made no move to follow her. He stared straight ahead, his eyes glazed.

The words felt like pebbles in her mouth. 'Dad… killed her?'

'He held her like that, under the water, listening while you went downstairs. He said he didn't take his hand away until he heard you go back to bed. Then he left her to check on you. When he was sure you were asleep, he wrapped her body in a tarpaulin and buried her in the garden.'

A cold sweat covered every inch of Beth's skin as she envisaged her dad's strong hands pushing her mother beneath the water.

Go to sleep, Byrdie Willis.

'Mum is buried here. That's why you want this *house*.'

'You have to understand he wasn't himself. It was a moment of madness, but once it was done, there was no going back.'

Ron looked as if the weight of the world had been lifted from his shoulders. The trouble was it had been placed on hers.

'Didn't the police search the house and garden?'

'Why would they? Your dad had an iron-clad alibi, and we'd grown up with most of the lads from the local station. They knew him to be a good, honest man, and he was so cut up about Suzy. God almighty, he confessed it to my face, but I still had difficulty believing he could do such a thing.'

'That's why you were worried the other day when I was carrying the hoe. You thought I might be digging somewhere?'

Ron nodded.

'Why was Dad so obsessed with Savage when he knew all along it was him who had killed Mum? Was he the man he believed she was having the affair with?'

'I don't know, my 'andsome. Your dad never told me his name, but I think he must have been the man. I didn't know about the briefcase. Trust me, if I had, I would have got rid of the damn thing and saved you from all this. I don't know what went on between Savage and your mum before that night or on that night, for that matter. All I know is that he didn't kill Suzy. Christ knows why he's letting them think he did, but he didn't. Brian clearly tortured himself about Savage, keeping all those cuttings about his victims, but maybe it was to convince himself he'd saved your mum from a fate worse than death. Had he let her leave with you, not only her life would have been destroyed by that monster but yours as well. I can't deny it has haunted me that Brian got it wrong, and when he got home that night, he didn't find a wife who had just waved goodbye to her lover, but a woman who had been raped.'

Nothing felt real. Beth was struggling to imagine what

the real world looked like anymore. A world where people went about their business, not having to think about the police or deal with monsters or face the stark reality that your dad had killed your mum, and you had been in the house when he did it.

'How am I going to tell Grace her grandad was a murderer?'

'Only the three of us know the truth, and we don't need to tell anyone else. Neville Savage has confessed to raping and killing your mum, and as far as Freda and the rest of the world are concerned, there's no reason to doubt him. The truth won't bring your mum back, and your dad's dead. What purpose does the truth serve?'

'Am I meant to ignore the fact Mum is lying out there beyond that back door?'

'Would you rather she be on Bodmin Moor in a shallow grave dug by that monster because that's where the police and everyone else think she is? Your dad never forgave himself for what he did. Trust me, I know it, and so do you, Beth. He was a broken man. He could have moved Suzy's body any number of times over the years, but he didn't. I honestly believe her being there was his way of punishing himself. She was a constant reminder of what he'd done, what he'd taken from you.'

Ron rose to his feet, squeezing her shoulder as he passed, and walked through to the sitting room. Beth followed.

Jean was on her knees, placing the clippings one at a time on the fire Beth had envisaged lighting to do the very same thing.

'Let us buy the house from you,' said Ron, bending to help his wife to her feet. We will look after your mum, and when the time's right, we'll hand it back to you. We'll deal with it as a family the way your mum and dad would have wanted us to.'

Beth said nothing. She was too exhausted to speak.

She heard the front door shut behind them, and as the last of the flames flickered and died, she pulled herself up from the floor and, on leaden legs, made her way back to the kitchen and out into the garden. The rain had stopped, and the clouds had cleared, leaving a sky salted with stars. The air smelt of woodsmoke from the village chimneys. A solid, familiar smell in a world full of spectres. The fact her mum was here felt almost comforting. She'd had so little to remember her by, and until today, she had been as much a relic of childish imagination as a memory. Now, she was real. Her bones lay in the damp earth somewhere beneath her feet. She had loved her and would never have left her behind.

Her dad had wanted her to know about Savage, but had he wanted her to know the truth? Probably not. Then again, the truth was not all it was cracked up to be. It was painful and destructive. She imagined the scene. The village full of police cars. The tent in the garden; the men in white overalls collecting evidence as the gurney arrived for the body bag. Journalists hovering like vultures. Beth covered her mouth, desperate to smother the scream welling in the pit of her stomach.

She looked up to the heavens, longing for answers, Freda's words ringing in her ears. "Angels don't need tele-scopes. You'd do well to remember that, my girl."

Then, from nowhere, just as if her angel had chosen to counsel her across the years, his loving voice, gentle, caring and without judgement, whispered, "Go home, Byrdie Willis. Go home."

Tomorrow, she would ring Eden and tell her to call off

the sale, and when she had done that, she would drive home and hold Grace in her arms. She would tell her she loved her and would always love her, no matter what. They'd eat their takeaway, and afterwards, she would show her the faded photographs of her grandparents. She would tell her life was precious and had to be made the most of.

Hot tears streamed down her cheeks, dripping off her chin onto the ground. A belated requiem for the mother of a six-year-old child, a child finally free to grieve.

Epilogue

NEVILLE SAVAGE LAY on his bed, arms pillowing his head. He had accomplished all he had set out to and was content with the results... no, more than content, he was safe, and his mailbag was full again. He would never be returned to a mainstream prison, not now he was a poster boy for the therapy junkies, and for the first time in forty years, he was at peace.

Like a wily old spider, he had spun a yarn. It had not all been a lie. He had learnt the most convincing deceptions carried a good deal of truth, and this knowledge had served him well over the years. This and the exploitation of weakness. Something for nothing in the case of the mothers he raped, and kudos in the case of the police and Mason.

The irony this time was that the truth had been harder for his listeners to swallow than the lie. They could imagine he could rape and kill but could not countenance a man like him could be capable of love. He supposed they could just about admit to the possibility he might care for his kids... but romance, devotion? That was a bridge too far. The beast must stay a beast in their version. He had obliged and given them their victim.

He'd had no difficulty describing the murder. After all, he had plenty of material to draw upon both from his own experience and from fellow prisoners over the years. Strangulation with his bare hands, Othello style. Strength over weakness, man's weapon of choice against the fairer sex since time began. He had topped it off with a dramatic setting and given them a new Beast of Bodmin. One less likely to be dispelled than the sheep-slaughtering wildcat claiming the title before him. Suzanne would no doubt have a starring role in the tragedy, trapped in the mortal world. Destined to walk the moor for eternity. He could visualise the birth of the myth. He ought to demand commission from the tourist board.

The police had hardly scrutinised his lie at all. He supposed it was the story they wanted to hear, in the way small children wanted to be read the same fairytale every bedtime. Familiarity bred comfort as well as contempt.

The lie had been easy to spin, whereas the truth had hollowed him. He had never told anyone how he felt about her before, not even Lindsay the day she found out about them and quizzed him mercilessly. "Where? When? How often?" And the humiliating and agonising, "Do you love her?" The desperate and predictable interrogations of the wronged wife. The answers, no matter how cleverly couched, delivering nothing but heartache and betrayal.

He had told Lindsay that Suzanne was a one-night stand who meant nothing to him. That, of course, he hadn't planned to abandon her and the girls to set up home with a married woman he hardly knew.

It had been a shock that evening to arrive home and find Lindsay in tears. He had never intended to face her in person. His idea had been to phone and tell her he'd been delayed for a few days and, if everything had gone to plan with Suzanne, instruct a lawyer to do the dirty work. He had intended to take the blame and let her have the house and most of the money. He'd agree to see the girls on her terms.

Lindsay's ambush came on the back of a night etched on his mind forever. The night he had made love to Suzanne, and they had made silent promises he thought, up until now, only one of them had kept. He closed his eyes and thought of Suzanne's sweet lips, her soft, warm skin touching his. Those sad losers in the group had called it rape. What did they know about it? They weren't there. He knew all about rape, and he knew what he felt that night. His desire for her was burning, almost rabid in its intensity, but the release was joyous, not sordid and empty like the others. They had become one in a way he and Lindsay had never done when they had sex. He had run Suzanne a bath and gently washed her, committing every contour of her beautiful body to memory. He put her reticence down to fear of the unknown and resistance down to guilt. He had told her not to worry. That it would take time, but as long as they were together, everything would be fine. Lindsay and Brian were young. They'd get over it in time. They'd find someone new, and she needn't worry because they'd have Byrdie with them. He'd love her like she was his own. He'd said he'd rent a place and break the news to Lindsay.

Suzanne had been silent, stunned a man could worship her enough to give up everything, but he'd known she felt the same. He could see it in her eyes.; in that faraway look and the quiver of her lip.

He had left her that night, his heart bursting with love for her.

The next day, he had waited on the quay, and when she hadn't turned up for work, he had driven to Flushing and kept vigil outside her house, hoping she'd spot him and come out. She hadn't, and he had not dared to bang on the door or telephone, knowing Brian was sleeping inside.

He'd assumed she hadn't been able to get away for some reason and, in the absence of knowing what to do for the best, had finished his business in Cornwall and driven home to Taunton, planning to phone Suzanne that evening when Brian was at work.

When he got home, he found Lindsay distraught. She had been trying to get hold of him all day. She told him a man had telephoned and told her to tell her husband to leave his wife alone. He wouldn't give his name but warned if her husband tried to contact his wife again, he would call his employer to let them know what kind of man he really was, and his wife would report him to the police for harassing her.

He had been overwhelmed with anger and disbelief that Suzanne could betray him. That she thought she had the right to preserve her marriage whilst destroying his.

As the weeks passed, confusion turned to hatred, and the memories of their love affair became a thorn in his side. He was tormented by the thought she had been stringing him along the whole time, laughing at him. Playing him for a fool. She had probably had other men before him, like the other sluts at the hotel. She had never intended to leave her husband. Never cared for him... never felt the way he had.

Lindsay had understandably insisted he change his pitch and confine himself to the Bristol and Taunton area so he'd be closer to home and not have to stay away overnight as often. She had no idea that not seeing Suzanne didn't mean he didn't think of her day and night.

Every time he passed a dark-haired young woman who looked even remotely like her, his gut twisted. The feeling wouldn't go away no matter how much he tried to forget her. In the end, he had given in to it. Instead of looking away, he had followed the women who reminded him of her and eventually, anger and resentment turned to obsession, then to lust and something much darker he could neither control nor fully understand.

The rest, as they say, was history, set out in the indictment and then in the tabloids, available to anyone who cared to read it.

He had stalked his victims, hoping to replace Suzanne, reliving their night again and again, longing for the same sensation. He had even used the same soap when he'd bathed them. Each one had provided a release of sorts, a brief respite from the pain and the knowledge the love of his life had not loved him. He knew now he had punished every one of them for not being her.

It was only now, all these years later, that he could see it all, feel the shame of it and breathe again. All because he knew he had been wrong. Suzanne had not turned her back on him. He had no idea what had happened to her that night after he had left, but he could imagine it. He had met enough violent husbands to know what the worst scenario could mean.

He had come to the realisation Willis had killed her while trudging across that god-forsaken moor pretending to look for Suzanne's remains. The charade had suddenly seemed real to the point he actually began to imagine her there in the earth, waiting for him to find her. It had shaken him to his core: the terrible loss of her presence in the world.

Brian Willis had sought to keep Suzanne from him in

the only way he could but had ultimately failed. He, through his confession, had rewritten Suzanne's story to make certain of it.

Her name would forevermore be linked with his. He had reclaimed his soulmate, and they would never be apart again.

A Letter To My Readers

I have always been fascinated by the schizophrenic character of the windswept Cornish peninsula my family has been lucky enough to call home for generations. Occupied by a cast of reluctant bedfellows; city-slick escapees and us locals who carry the remnants of our myth-ridden history etched on our backs like tattoos, it teeters between the bucket and spade domesticity of modern-day tourism and a superstitious past, riddled with Pagan traditions. The resultant clash of cultures and sensibilities causes friction, resentment and drama. My aim, through my writing is to explore what happens when these divergent worlds collide to expose a darker reality at odds with the picture-perfect landscape. Whilst I was lucky to enjoy a fantastically satisfying career as a lawyer I cannot now imagine anything more joyous than being able to sit at my desk and write knowing others might read and connect with my words. Cornwall has captured the hearts and imagination of countless wonderful writers through the decades; their vivid images now woven into its rich tapestry. If I can add one colourful stitch I will be happy.

More by Julie Evans

vinci-books.com/cornishcrimeseries

Follow the link to stay up to date with Julie Evans' new releases

About the Author

After training as a lawyer, Julie returned to her native Cornwall to establish her own law firm and to raise her three children. After years of building a successful legal practice, it was time for a new adventure, and she decided to write the stories she had formulated in her head over the years about her community and the lives of those who find themselves on the wrong side of the law.

www.ingramcontent.com/pod-product-compliance
Lightning Source LLC
Chambersburg PA
CBHW011419010726
47494CB00011B/2410